TRICK OR TREAT!

Lloyd stared at the line of trees at least another full minute, waiting for…something. At last, he let out a breath and chuckled nervously, telling himself out loud to stop being so stupid and paranoid. He was about to begin loading pumpkins into the truck again when a dark figure emerged from the line of trees and began to cross the road.

All Hallow's Dead

Bryan Smith

All Hallow's Dead
First Paperback Edition
Copyright © 2015 by Bryan Smith
Cover Art Copyright © 2015

ISBN: 1517547245
ISBN-13: 978-1517547240

This one is for Ryan Harding, the slasher authority.
ALL HALLOW'S EVE is also dedicated to 80's slasher cinema in
general.

1

Seven days until Halloween
Willow Springs, TN

The wind kicked up again and sent scores of yellow and brown dead leaves skittering across the quiet two-lane road. It was a few minutes past six in the evening and most of the light had faded from the sky, with only a shading of light gray lingering at the horizon. Lloyd McAfee sat shivering in the creaky chair behind the pumpkin stand and watched what remained of the day fade away. He'd set out this morning attired only in jeans and a flannel shirt. The day had started out bright and sunny, with the temperature in the mid 70's, but it'd turned out chillier than he'd expected.

The sharp shift wasn't entirely out of the ordinary for this time of the year. This was the season of transition, a period when the weather vacillated wildly between a warmth more typical of early summer and chilly harbingers of the colder months ahead. He'd grown up in this area and was well acquainted with how conditions could suddenly change. He had no one to blame for failing to take that into account but himself. Tomorrow he'd make a point of bringing a light jacket along to wear later in the day, regardless of how warm it was at daybreak.

Lloyd's family had been operating the pumpkin stand at this same roadside location for generations. In his opinion, it was no longer a good spot, despite being conveniently located just a few miles from the family farm. Times had changed. People had changed. More folks lived and worked in town these days, causing the rural population to decline precipitously. As a result, the traffic along this stretch of state road was significantly lighter than it had once been. It was lighter every year, or so it seemed to Lloyd.

Today, in fact, had been one of the worst days he could remember in his fifteen years of operating the pumpkin stand. The traffic had been worse than light much of the day. It was simply nonexistent for long stretches of time. Most of the few vehicles that did come along zipped by so fast he doubted the people driving them even noticed him. He could only assume the people in them were on their way to somewhere far more interesting than here. Only a handful of people had stopped to take a look at the pumpkins. Of those, maybe half actually bought one. The entire haul for the day was just over twenty bucks. It hardly seemed worthwhile.

Just as he was thinking this, headlights appeared around the bend in the road about a quarter mile away. Lloyd cursed his laziness, hoping the car wouldn't stop here. He should have closed up shop an hour ago, but he'd procrastinated, knowing his return home to the farm would likely be marred by unpleasantness before long. He and his father didn't see eye to eye about much of anything anymore, the pumpkin stand being the least of it. Still, he'd been anticipating the pleasure of cracking open that first cold beer of the night for hours, and now it'd have to wait a little longer.

The car slowed down and pulled off the road. Muttering a curse, Lloyd reminded himself to smile and try to seem friendly when the potential customer approached. The silver minivan parked alongside his truck. A moment later, its doors opened, disgorging a family of six. A youngish, presumably married couple and their brood of four squalling brats. Lloyd guessed the youngest kid was maybe five and the oldest probably no more than twelve. The father was lean and handsome. The mother was a pretty, slender blonde. Both were attired in a manner that marked them as corporate types. What they were doing out here in the middle of nowhere, Lloyd had no idea.

But that mystery was solved when the mother approached the stand and engaged him in conversation. Turned out they'd learned of the McAfee pumpkin stand from an elderly acquaintance and had decided they could do with a bit of rustic flavor this Halloween season. Lloyd clenched his teeth at her use of the word "rustic", but he managed to maintain his fake smile while launching into a brief but extra-folksy account of the pumpkin stand's history. He embellished the tale with an anecdote about a giant pumpkin he'd grown years back that had gotten almost as big as his truck. This was pure bullshit, but Mr. and Mrs. Corporate America ate it right up. Meanwhile, the kids swarmed over the pumpkins arrayed around the stand, squealing and arguing at ear-piercing volume about which pumpkin was the perfect one for their porch.

Recognizing an obvious impasse when he saw one, the father snatched one up at random and paid for it. Lloyd commended him on his choice, saying he had a good eye. More bullshit. Soon they were on their way and Lloyd had a few more dollars to show for his day's work. It wasn't much, but what the hell, it was better than nothing. And now it was high time to secure the stand, load up his truck, and head back to the farm until it was time to do it all over again tomorrow.

He rose from his chair and yawned as he stretched his limbs. Another long day of sitting on his ass had left him feeling stiff-legged and tired. He couldn't wait to get back to the farm and start drinking. Knocking back a few cold ones always improved his mood. There might be a few of the usual mutters of disapproval from his kin, but he didn't care. He deserved to get a little drunk after so many pointless hours of sitting out here all on his lonesome.

Lloyd let down his truck's tailgate and began loading pumpkins into the blanket-lined bed. The tedious process would take the better part of an hour. He again cursed his procrastination and vowed to close up shop earlier tomorrow. He was only a little ways into the job when a sense of being observed made him stop cold and turn toward the dense stand of trees bordering the other side of the road. At first he saw only dark woods and chalked the feeling up to an attack of inexplicable paranoia. Unless another car came along, there was no one else out here. It was just him and the pumpkins.

But he kept staring at the trees and that feeling of being watched stayed with him. There was still nothing to see, but his other senses told another story. There was another presence here.

Something malign and predatory. He didn't know why he should feel this way. It made no sense. He'd never had the gift of precognition. Nevertheless, he was gripped by a powerful urge to get in his truck and head for home at high speed. The only reason he didn't was knowing how enraged his father would be upon learning he'd left the stand unsecured and all that merchandise unattended.

He stared at the line of trees at least another full minute, waiting for…something. At last, he let out a breath and chuckled nervously, telling himself out loud to stop being so stupid and paranoid. He was about to begin loading pumpkins into the truck again when a dark figure emerged from the line of trees and began to cross the road.

Lloyd's heart pounded. Whoever this was couldn't be up to any good. The son of a bitch had been lurking and watching. That was creepy behavior no matter how you looked at it. Where had he come from? And where was his car? The whole situation was too weird to be anything but bad news, yet Lloyd remained rooted to the spot, held there by a combination of helpless curiosity and the enduring prospect of his father's rage.

The stranger reached his side of the street and kept coming closer, his dark eyes and pallid, expressionless face fixed on Lloyd. His hands were shoved deep inside the pockets of a black trench coat. The stiff wind whipped his longish black hair about, leaving it in disarray. He had a slim build and was maybe a couple inches above six feet tall. There was something almost familiar in the lean, angular planes of his pale, hollow-cheeked face. But if he'd ever known the man, Lloyd couldn't quite place him.

Lloyd forced another smile as the stranger came closer still. "Can I help you?"

The stranger nodded. "I need thirty-one of your best pumpkins. Only the very best, mind you. Nothing less will suffice."

Lloyd's first reaction upon hearing this was a tenuous excitement. Thirty-one pumpkins all in one go? That would redeem the hell out of this otherwise miserable day. And it would make a heck of an interesting story to tell at the dinner table when he got home. But the excitement faded almost instantly. He took a slow, pointed look around at the vicinity before focusing his gaze

4

on the stranger again. "Listen, mister, I'd be happy to sell you thirty-one pumpkins. Hell, I'd be thrilled. But where's your car?"

The stranger smiled for the first time. One of his hands began to emerge from a pocket of his trench coat. "Good question, Lloyd. Glad you asked. I came out here in a stolen car. Ditched that back up the road a piece and made my way up here through the woods in order to retain the all-important element of surprise. I'll be taking your truck, by the way."

Lloyd frowned. "The hell you will. Hold on a minute. How do you know my name?"

The stranger's hand fully emerged from his pocket. Moonlight glinted off a long and shiny blade. He came at Lloyd fast and slammed the big blade into his abdomen up to the hilt. The pain was instant and searing. Lloyd screamed. The stranger yanked the blade out and slammed it in again. Lloyd dropped to his knees when the knife was again removed from his gut. Blood spilled from the holes in his belly and pattered on the dusty ground.

The stranger moved away from him and examined the selection of pumpkins. He picked one and knelt on the ground near Lloyd, who watched with a mixture of terror and incomprehension as the man plunged the knife into the top of the pumpkin and began to cut it open.

The man glanced Lloyd's way and caught his gaze. "It's too bad you don't remember me. If you did, you might have some idea why this is happening to you."

Lloyd looked at his truck. His keys were in his pocket. The part of him still desperate to survive urged him to dig them out, somehow find the strength to get to his feet, and lurch his way over to the truck. It might not be too late. If he could get to a doctor, maybe he could be saved. But what was left of his strength was draining away too fast.

Lloyd fell over on his side and stared blearily at his murderer. "Who...are you?"

The stranger scooped out pumpkin guts. "I'm the Ghost of Halloween Past. I've come to visit vengeance upon this town and those who hurt me long ago. Starting with you, Lloyd. Thirty-one will die by my hand this week. You have the honor of being the first."

Lloyd peered intently at the man's face a moment longer as his life drained away.

And then, at last, a spark of recognition. He spoke his last word as his eyes fluttered. "Oh."

He died knowing who his killer was.

The man in the trench coat dragged the body out of sight, stashing it behind the pumpkin stand. While crouched down behind the stand, he took a meat cleaver from another pocket of his trench coat and performed a necessary bit of surgery on Lloyd's corpse. With that out of the way, he loaded the pumpkins he needed into the truck and drove away.

Before departing, however, he left a gift for the investigators. Something they could search the area for, like the Halloween equivalent of an Easter egg hunt.

2

Twenty-five years ago
Willow Springs, TN

After deviating from his usual route home for over a week, Elliot Parker decided to chance going that way again when school let out the day before Halloween. It was Friday and he had a whole weekend ahead of him away from the many classmates who liked to taunt and tease him. Elliot loved Halloween and he looked forward to spending the next couple nights watching horror movies with his sick brother, Robert, who had spent most of the last year confined to his bed. His alcoholic parents refused to talk honestly with him about his brother's condition, but Elliot suspected this would be their last Halloween together. It made him sad, but he was determined to do whatever he could to make Robert's remaining time as happy as possible.

Someone had to try, at least. His parents certainly weren't up to the job. They spent most nights fighting and drinking themselves into a sloppy stupor. These fights were mostly conducted behind closed doors, but the drunken histrionics rendered any attempt at discretion ludicrous. Elliot's thirteenth birthday was still a month away. The ways of adults and the workaday world they inhabited largely remained a mystery to him. But he knew enough to understand that Linda and Mark Parker were not like most parents. The deep rift between them had started long before the onset of

Robert's illness. Both boys had been accustomed to hearing their mom and dad scream at each other for years. It wasn't right. Their eldest child was dying and all he was to them at this point was an inconvenience. In his darkest moments, Elliot was sure they wished Robert would hurry up and die so they could get on with their lives. When this thought occurred, Elliot found himself hating them with a scary intensity. Sometimes he fantasized about killing them and making it look like an intruder had done the deed. That way he and his brother might wind up in the care of their grandparents in Georgia, who at least weren't hateful drunks.

A car honked as he walked down the sidewalk. Elliot glanced to his left and saw Mr. Spurlock, a science teacher at his school, seated behind the wheel of his Hyundai. Clinton Spurlock was a kindly, bespectacled older man. Elliot thought he was probably about fifty. The teacher had taken a special interest in Elliot a while back, often intervening when other kids bullied him. Elliot was grateful at times, especially when Mr. Spurlock's interference headed off a certain beating. The problem was it only led to a deeper level of resentment among those who harassed him. The taunts always became more aggressive afterward, the threats against his personal safety scarier. He was called a "teacher's pet", a "sissy", and worse. Sometimes the other kids insinuated Mr. Spurlock was a pedophile and was "diddling" him on a regular basis. It was bullshit. The teacher was just kind and had taken pity on him. But this distinction meant nothing to his antagonists.

Elliot knew why they picked on him. He was a lonely, awkward child. Socializing with anyone outside his family circle had always been difficult for him. Often it was virtually impossible. He was skinny and kind of weird-looking and just plain different. And in the middle school he'd just started attending this semester, there was no greater sin than being different.

Mr. Spurlock hit a button, lowering his passenger side window. "Hey there, Elliot. On your way home?"

Elliot continued down the sidewalk at a slower pace, with the Hyundai gliding along next to him. "Yes, sir."

"Need a ride?"

Elliot's brow furrowed as he considered. A ride home with the teacher would eliminate the possibility of being jumped by

8

Lloyd McAfee and his asshole friends again. However, despite his fear of the bigger, meaner boys, there was a part of him that hated feeling like such a coward. He imagined going through life always being afraid of people like McAfee and his cronies. The prospect simultaneously filled him with self-loathing and ignited a level of fury that frightened him. When he got that mad, he entertained more murderous fantasies. He pictured Lloyd and the others tied to chairs and at his mercy, crying and quivering with fear as he did things to them with a knife. Sometimes the fantasies were so vivid he could almost feel the blade sliding into their tender bellies.

Elliot shook his head. "Thank you, Mr. Spurlock, but I'd rather walk."

Mr. Spurlock pursed his lips a moment before saying, "You sure about that? It's only a couple miles. I'll have you home in a jiffy."

Elliot smiled at the teacher's use of the word "jiffy". It was such a dorky old man thing to say. There was something strangely endearing about it. Not for the first time, he wished his father was more like this man. Better yet, he wished Mr. Spurlock *was* his father. But like Mark Parker always said, *Wish in one hand, shit in the other, see which one fills up first*.

Elliot nodded. "I'm sure. I like the weather this time of year. It's nice. And I like the scenery."

Mr. Spurlock glanced around at the tall trees lining the sidewalks on either side of the street. The leaves on all had turned varying shades of yellow, orange, and brown. There were drifts of leaves everywhere. "I guess it is pretty." He sighed. "Well, you just be careful, Elliot. You know I worry about you. Remember, you can always let me know if you're having any trouble."

Elliot smiled. "I know, Mr. Spurlock. Thanks."

Mr. Spurlock nodded, said goodbye, and drove off with a wave.

Elliot felt only a mild pang of regret as he watched the teacher's taillights diminish in the distance. He would have been safe inside that car. No doubt about it. But he thought the odds were in his favor. A week and a half had passed since the last time he got jumped by Lloyd and his cronies. They obviously didn't know about the longer, alternate route home he'd been taking. After this long, they wouldn't be lying in wait for him at the usual spot. It would be pointless.

But about that, Elliot was very wrong.

He was still another mile away from home. There were no houses along this stretch of the route back, just an unbroken expanse of trees lining both sides of the road. The patch of woods off to his right was deeper than one would think, given its proximity to a sprawling residential area. He knew this from traipsing through them with his brother back in better days, when they would pretend to be soldiers in war-torn Europe a half century ago, slinking around from tree to tree with modified fallen branches they pretended were machine guns. The branches were stripped of all tiny offshoot limbs and broken down to manageable size. Because their parents never spent money on the really cool toys, the Parker boys always had to improvise. The austerity fostered a vivid imagination in each of them and for a time both showed signs of becoming gifted storytellers. Elliot still had notebooks full of handwritten tales about aliens and lost worlds populated by dinosaurs and cavemen stashed away in the back of his closet. But, as with so many other things, the habit had fallen away with the onset of Robert's illness, though Elliot occasionally attempted to cheer his brother up by spinning a yarn while sitting with him at his bedside.

He was mulling over new ideas for stories to tell the dying boy when he heard a rustle of leaves somewhere behind him. This was followed by a crunch of feet on bramble. Someone was coming out of the woods. Elliot's heart started racing. He tried telling himself it was just some random kid who'd been out there playing, but his instincts told him otherwise. The smart thing here would be to take off running at full speed without even glancing back. It might even be a good idea to shrug off his backpack so he could run faster. He could come back for it later. If someone stole it, all he'd be losing were some textbooks and notepads. They could be replaced. At worst, he'd lose his class notes, but that was a small thing to sacrifice in the name of safety.

Another impulse intruded, though, forestalling an immediate transition into flight mode. This was the part of him that was weary of running like a little bitch—as his father would put it—at the first hint of trouble. He needed to be a man and stand up for himself, maybe even fight back for once. As usual when this notion came to him, he temporarily overlooked the fact that his adversaries were so much bigger and stronger. The anger burned away enough of the fear to keep him strolling along at the same unhurried pace, even though he heard footsteps on the sidewalk behind him now. He was being followed. That much was undeniable. But there wasn't necessarily anything sinister about that. The hypothetical random kid could be making his way home, too.

But Elliot had to know for sure.

He let out a breath and risked a glance over his shoulder. His eyes widened at the sight of Jimmy Martin's leering face. Jimmy was one of Lloyd's gang. The much bigger boy was only a few feet away. He had the large frame and beefy build of a future offensive lineman. His wrists were at least twice as thick around as Elliot's wrists and he was much taller. All at once, it became clear how ludicrous it was to even fleetingly consider standing up to this behemoth.

Jimmy chuckled. "Been waiting for you, pencil dick. About time you started coming back this way. You ready to take your medicine?"

The time to run was at hand.

Elliot shrugged off the backpack and got moving. He'd only managed to get a few feet down the sidewalk when the toe of a shoe stumbled over a slightly upraised section of concrete. He went sprawling painfully on the sidewalk, skinning his arms and knees on the rough surface. Before he could even try to regain his feet and resume the botched flight home, a pair of strong hands grabbed him by the back of his shirt and hauled him up. He heard a snickering that indicated Jimmy had company. The big boy spun him about and Elliot saw Lloyd McAfee and Chuck Everly standing on the sidewalk. Both had mean, pitiless smirks on their faces.

Chuck was holding what looked like a freshly carved jack-o'-lantern. Thin strands of pumpkin guts were visible at the corners of its sharply flaring eyes. Odds were the pumpkin was from the farm Lloyd's family owned. A very large percentage of all pumpkins sold in this town each Halloween season came from there, but of course Lloyd always had his pick of the best of the best. This particular pumpkin struck Elliot as the ripest, roundest one he'd ever seen. It looked fresh from the patch and probably was.

Lloyd picked up the backpack and tossed it into the street.

Elliot jerked his head around and saw it in the middle of the two-lane road. It'd landed squarely on the double yellow lines. He craned his head around some more and then back in the other direction, desperately hoping for signs of approaching vehicles. No such luck. The road was clear in both directions. Elliot cursed his complacency. He should have been moving with urgency his first day back on this route, but he'd had his head in the clouds.

Lloyd's mean smirk deepened. "I see you're still a fucking pussy, Elliot. You look like you're about to cry."

To his shame, it was true. Elliot's eyes were brimming with moisture. "Puh-please...don't..."

Lloyd laughed. "No use begging, you little snot. You're about to get your shit fucked up."

The other boys cackled at this witticism.

Lloyd stepped off the sidewalk, jerking his head toward the line of trees. "Come on, guys. Into the woods."

In a last fit of desperation, Elliot tried twisting his way out of Jimmy's grasp. The sudden, violent movement caught the bigger boy by surprise and for a brief moment one of his hands did get dislodged. Unfortunately, the other hand remained locked firmly around Elliot's upper arm and he was unable to get free. Jimmy gave him a hard swat upside the head before again securing his hold on him.

There was more of that mean laughter.

And then they went into the woods, from which Elliot would not reemerge for many hours.

3

Six days until Halloween
Willow Springs, TN

On the way back home from a family dinner at Logan's Roadhouse, Chuck Everly turned the Honda Odyssey down Hodder Street, his brow furrowing as he felt a stab of pain go straight through the center of his forehead. His three kids were in the back of the minivan. They were locked in a loud and increasingly bitter argument about the latest boy band sensation. The two girls were of the opinion that the group was possibly the best in the history of pop music. In particular, they vehemently maintained the act was certainly better than stodgy old crap like the Beatles.

Blake Everly, Chuck's eldest child and only son, disagreed with equal vehemence and more than a little snooty indignation. The boy was going through a big classic rock phase. He'd spent the last several months obsessively listening to and learning about all the biggest and most well-regarded bands from earlier music eras. Before that he'd been into hip hop and all the other pop stuff most kids his age liked. He was undoubtedly correct in his critical evisceration of the boy band's songs, but it was hard for Chuck not to smirk a little while listening to him hold forth on the subject. Only a short while ago he'd been every bit as taste-challenged as the girls.

Ah, well, it was just the way of things. The things kids liked changed as they got older. Someday soon the girls would disavow ever having liked the boy band and not just because pop acts tended to have short shelf lives. As they aged into their late teens, they would become embarrassed about the childish things that had once meant so much to them. A similar process had occurred with Chuck and his siblings growing up. For Chuck, it was an endlessly fascinating thing to observe. He never grew tired of watching them grow and evolve. His only regret was that it was happening too fast. Despite the excruciating volume of the current disagreement, he genuinely loved all his babies. They were good, well-adjusted, fun-loving kids. All too soon, though, they'd be grown and moving out, leaving for college or jobs, building their own lives out in the world.

Thinking about it made Chuck feel wistful. He glanced at his wife in the passenger seat and saw her smiling at him. As Chuck turned the minivan down another street, the sun shone upon Karen's blonde hair in a way that made it look particularly radiant. The sight of it made his heart skip a beat. She was still as beautiful as she'd been the day he met her nineteen years ago, back in their senior year of high school. A recent transfer from another town, she'd caught Chuck's eye immediately the first day of that fall semester. He'd had eyes only for her ever since.

Well...*mostly* only for her.

Like many young men who marry early and spend their entire adult lives locked into a single relationship, he'd occasionally harbored lustful thoughts regarding other women. But Chuck accepted this as normal. On one occasion years back, however, there'd been an oral indiscretion. Because vaginal penetration had not occurred, he was able to rationalize the incident as not really constituting cheating. He otherwise never acted on his lustful impulses. Until recently, that is. After enduring a torturous level of temptation, he'd committed a few much more serious indiscretions, all with the same person. But he felt terrible about them and had absolutely no intention of wrecking his perfect life with his gorgeous wife and wonderful kids.

The indiscretions would stop.

Soon.

Chuck slowed the Odyssey as he neared the Trenton Street

14

entrance to the sparkling new subdivision the Everly clan had called home for the last two years. As he steered his way through Brighton Estates and eyed all the perfect-looking new houses and the generally attractive people who inhabited them, Chuck again had occasion to reflect on what a lucky guy he was.

He had a good job that allowed his family to live in comfortable, safe surroundings. As a boy, he hadn't had it anywhere near as good. The financial struggles of his parents had been never-ending. They hadn't been bad people. Chuck and his brothers had never been beaten or emotionally abused. But the prevailing negativity caused by money issues had cast a pall over the Everly household through much of his youth. It'd led to some stupid acting out on his part when he was young. He did dumb things and got into trouble a bit. Thankfully, however, he'd gotten his act together before meeting Karen. He was so glad that had happened. His life could easily have gone in a much darker direction.

The argument about the boy band died down as they neared their house on Broadbent Lane, passions cooling rapidly as the kids anticipated retreating to their rooms to do their own thing a while before coming down to the den for movie night. Tonight's flick was the new Blu-ray release of the latest Marvel superhero blockbuster. It would look amazing on the 80-inch 4K screen, while the high-end sound system would shake the room in that deeply immersive way they all enjoyed. Movie night was a much-loved family tradition that had only become more firmly entrenched with Chuck's frequent tech upgrades. It was like having a little movie theater in their own house. This, of course, made it a popular hangout spot for other kids in the neighborhood. Chuck sometimes feigned grumpiness about this. In reality, it only added to his happiness. He liked that his house was known as a cool place to be, as well as a safe place.

The kids instantly piled out of the Odyssey as Chuck parked in the driveway outside their house and cut off the engine. Karen also wasted no time getting out, moving quickly with the kids to the front door. Chuck heard her mumble something about being in dire need of getting to the bathroom. He had a hunch she was regretting her spicy meal choice.

Her distracted urgency as she dug her keys out of her purse

allowed him a few moments to stand in the driveway and stare at the house across the street, a big multi-level country style house with a long porch and latticed railing. Fawn Hightower sat in a rocking chair reading a book at an end of the porch. Her shoulder-length hair was a bright shade of blonde similar to his wife's, but Fawn wore it in a different, more modern style. It was straighter and shorter, with the ends hanging about an inch above her shoulders, whereas Karen was all about the volume, sporting a big mane that reached the halfway point of her back whenever she took it out of the usual ponytail. Fawn was also smaller than his wife, shorter by a good five inches and slimmer. She had a deceptively delicate-looking frame. When he'd first spotted her at a distance upon moving into the new place two years ago, he'd assumed she was his neighbor's teenaged daughter. She was younger than him by several years. They'd spent an hour or so together in a hotel room just a few days later. Fawn had been especially energetic in bed that first time, twisting her little body around in astonishingly athletic ways while he did his damnedest to fuck the living daylights out of her.

At the end of their latest tryst, Fawn had told him she was in love with him. She went on to say she wanted to leave her husband and children so she could be with him. Chuck pointed out that he had his own family and had no interest in breaking it up. Things took a frosty turn after that. She hurriedly dressed and left without saying another word. He'd spent a fair amount of time since then fearing what she might do. He worried her obvious anger might prompt her to do something rash, like telling Karen about the affair. Since then, she'd refused to respond to his texts and calls.

Seeming to sense the scrutiny, she looked up from her book, turned her head in his direction, smiled, and raised her hand in a wave. She then put a hand to the side of her head in a "call me" gesture. Apparently she was ready to talk again. But the smile worried Chuck. The only reason he'd tried so hard to contact her was to seek reassurance that she wouldn't do anything stupid. But she might be under the impression he wanted a return to the status quo. Several days had passed. She'd probably gotten over her anger. Now Chuck feared how she might react when he told her he wanted to end the affair permanently. Based on prior experience, she probably wouldn't take it too well.

He'd just have to do his best to make her see reason. They'd had their fun and now it was time to move on and return to normal life. That was how he planned to put it to her, anyway. Chuck's actual feelings on the subject weren't so nonchalant. He was torn up with guilt at having put his perfect family life at risk. The shame of betrayal weighed on him heavily. Somehow he had to make sure Karen and the kids never found out.

Chuck went on into his house. As he closed and locked the front door, he heard a babble of excited voices emanating from the direction of the kitchen. His kids had a tendency to get unduly excited about all kinds of things, but something about what he was hearing now marked it as different from the usual teenaged burst of unwarranted enthusiasm.

The reason why soon became apparent. The faces of his wife and kids turned toward him as he entered the kitchen. Each bore a nearly identical expression conveying a mixture of confusion and disbelief. And, beneath that, an unspoken expectation that he could explain the inexplicable appearance of five pumpkins arranged in the center of the dining table.

Chuck shook his head. "Don't look at me. I had nothing to do with this."

A hesitant smile had begun to curve the corners of Karen's mouth. Now it withered as her brow furrowed in deepening confusion. "You mean it's not some kind of weird Halloween surprise?"

Chuck shook his head again as he stared at the pumpkins, which were arranged in a neat, tight circle, each with a precisely carved jack-o'-lantern face facing outward. A name had been written in red marker above the flaring eyes of each pumpkin. There was one for every member of the family.

"Did someone break into our house?"

The question was from Eva, his eldest daughter.

She sounded scared.

Chuck couldn't blame her. Once the initial moment of shock and puzzlement passed, he understood exactly how creepy this was. He knew for a fact the house had been locked up tight prior to their departure for Logan's Roadhouse.

Chuck's heart started beating hard and fast. "Everyone back

outside." He raised his voice when they all just stared at him in open-mouthed stupefaction. "*Now, goddammit!*"

They flinched at the edgy tone and uncharacteristically loud volume. But what really got them moving, probably, was his use of profanity. Chuck used adult language around other adults, but he never cursed in front of his kids. It told them more clearly than anything else that this was a very serious situation and they had better obey without delay.

The Everly clan headed back the way they had come and in moments Chuck's wife and kids were standing outside on the front lawn, while Chuck lingered on the porch, a hand grasping the edge of the open door. A glance across the street showed Fawn standing on her porch, leaning against the railing as she observed the unexpected development with obvious fascination. A paranoid part of him wondered if this might be her doing. As far as he knew, though, she didn't have a key to his house. And he had difficulty picturing her patiently carving all those pumpkins and arranging them like that. The true culprit was almost certainly someone else, yet the idea lingered and rendered her scrutiny unnerving.

Karen looked exasperated now. "Why did you herd us out here, Chuck? I don't appreciate being yelled at like that, by the way."

"I know, honey, and I'm sorry. I'm going back inside for a minute." Chuck nodded at the purse still dangling from her arm. "Your phone in there?"

She nodded slowly. "Yes. Why?"

"Call 911."

He started to edge back into the house.

Karen's exasperated expression gave way to a look of alarm. "You don't think someone's still inside, do you?"

Chuck shook his head and tried out a smile he hoped looked reassuring. "Of course not. I just need to check on something."

His kids called out to him in alarmed unison as he stepped back into the doorway.

But Chuck was already back inside the house. He closed the door and locked it. Then he went off in the direction of his office, where he kept a .44 Magnum locked in the bottom drawer of his desk.

18

4

Six days until Halloween
Willow Springs, TN

There wasn't much room for Sheriff Bob Lee to park his cruiser by the time he arrived on the scene that afternoon. Hours had passed since the discovery of Lloyd McAfee's body and most of the available roadside parking space was now taken up by an array of department cruisers, a white crime scene van, and some civilian vehicles. At a glance, he recognized Harlan McAfee's ancient powder blue Buick convertible. The sight of it made him wince. Few things were less conducive to a proper murder investigation than having family of the deceased hovering around a homicide scene. You needed to interview the relations, of course, but he preferred to conduct that kind of business either in his office downtown or at the family's home.

In general, he was seeing too many people who weren't here in an official capacity. The crowd included not just McAfee family members, but several of their friends and acquaintances. In scanning their faces, he spotted one in particular that made his stomach knot. Ricky Bennet, a frequent town hall agitator and former juvenile delinquent, stood away from the family, hovering around the edge of the taped-off area. Ricky and Lloyd used to cause a lot of trouble together in their younger days. Lee had been a deputy back then and had busted them and their pals for petty bullshit multiple times. But Harlan had been buddies with the old sheriff, which meant his boy and his shiftless friends had gotten off with a slap on the wrist nearly every time.

After finally finding a space for his cruiser, Lee heaved his considerable bulk out of the vehicle and carefully threaded his way through the crowd of onlookers, pausing only briefly to offer Lloyd's folks his condolences. He moved on after assuring them he'd be talking with them at length shortly. As he neared the pumpkin stand, he ducked beneath the yellow crime scene tape and stood up with a grunt, grimacing at his misfortune as he happened to make direct eye contact with Bennet, who was sneering at him.

"About time you got here, sheriff."

Lee's grimace became a glare. "Don't give me any grief, son. I ain't in a mood for it."

He moved away from the son of a bitch before he could say anything else.

Two of his best deputies, Pete Acker and Vic Bailey, were standing over the body as Lee came around the pumpkin stand. Both men had been with the department for over a decade. He was surprised these two had done such a subpar job of managing the scene. They were better than that.

The men glanced up at his arrival.

Acker had a pained look on his face as he said, "Sorry about the clusterfuck, sheriff. Lucas got the call on this one. We only just got here."

Lee nodded.

That explained it. Jason Lucas was the department's youngest deputy. He'd been on the job only a few months and wasn't very good at it. This wasn't the first time he'd handled a scene in a less than ideal way.

"Please tell me the techs were able to do their thing before the gawkers got here."

Bailey shrugged. "That jackass Bennet found the body. I guess he and McAfee knew each other."

Lee nodded. "That I can confirm. Partners in crime, more like. Used to be, anyway."

Bailey arched an eyebrow at this before continuing. "First thing he did was ring up Lloyd's folks. They came out here straight away. By the time they called it in, there'd been a fair amount of contamination. I'd have to call the scene degraded, at best."

Lee muttered a curse and shook his head. "All right, then. What's done is done." He looked at the corpse and was silent a moment before shifting his gaze back to his deputies. "I guess the pertinent question is obvious—what happened to the man's head?"

Acker and Bailey glanced at each other, eyebrows raised.

The pained look on Acker's face became more pronounced. "It's gone."

Lee snorted. "I can see that. No sign of it in the vicinity?"

Acker shook his head. "Not so far."

Lee took off his Stetson and ran plump fingers through his sweaty, close-cropped hair. "Well, ain't this shit just what we needed the week before Halloween? A goddamn psycho killer on the loose. I don't reckon you boys have identified a suspect yet."

Acker and Bailey shook their heads and uttered the same words in near unison: "No, sir."

Lee put the Stetson back on his head and straightened it. "Well, of course not. Why should this shit be easy?" He glanced in the direction of Lloyd's grieving parents, who were standing some twenty yards away. A sobbing, red-faced Carol McAfee was clinging to her husband, who was watching the lawmen gathered behind the pumpkin stand with a stony expression. Lee lowered his voice before addressing his men again. "If I were a betting man, I'd have to say this wasn't a random thing. Somebody out there had it in for Lloyd, which ain't too surprising. He didn't exactly have a winning personality. We should--"

His next words were drowned out as a commotion arose from somewhere nearby. There was a lot of loud, excited babble punctuated by a single piercing, feminine scream. Lee turned away from his men and craned his thick neck around, searching for the source of the disturbance. This didn't take long. Jason Lucas, the young deputy who'd mismanaged the initial handling of the scene so badly, emerged from a cluster of civilians gathered along the tree line on the opposite of the road and came running toward the pumpkin stand. Even at a distance, Lee read a mixture of horror and adrenaline-fueled excitement in his wide-eyed expression.

21

Clutched in his hands was a pumpkin with a carved jack-o'-lantern face.

Lee frowned, his stomach knotting in anticipation of a nasty surprise.

Lucas arrived at the pumpkin stand sweating and out of breath. He tried talking but his obviously jittery nerves rendered his words indecipherable. While he struggled to talk, a static-filled squawk emanated from Acker's shoulder mic. The deputy stuck a finger in his ear and moved away from the pumpkin stand to better hear the dispatcher.

An exasperated Lee reached over the stand and ripped the jack-o'-lantern from Lucas's trembling hands. He backed away from the stand and peered down through the pumpkin's open top. Deputy Bailey moved in for a look and gasped at what was inside.

"So that's where his head went."

Lee nodded slowly, unlocking his tightly set jaw with a conscious effort. His nails dug deep into the skin of the pumpkin. "We've got a sick bastard on our hands. Call the tech boys over here."

Bailey yelled for the techs.

Acker came back over to the pumpkin stand. Lee glanced his way and saw a promise of more headaches on the horizon in the man's gaunt expression. "What now?"

"Kind of a weird call, sheriff. May be related to this mess."

Lee suppressed a groan and said, "Spill it."

"Some lady out in Brighton Estates reported a break-in. Family went out to eat and found a bunch of carved pumpkins on their dinner table when they got home. Husband's still in the house looking for an intruder, apparently."

"For fuck's sake." Lee handed the pumpkin containing Lloyd McAfee's head off to a gloved tech in a white hazmat suit. "Bailey, you're in charge here. Acker, with me."

Acker nodded and they headed off to their cruisers.

5

Being forcefully marched through the woods was bad. The looming prospect of the humiliation awaiting him was even worse. Elliot didn't know precisely what the other boys had in mind for him, but he was sure it wouldn't be pleasant. They'd done mean things to him many times in the past. Once in elementary school he'd been held down at the edge of the playground and forced to eat dirt. Another time they cornered him in the restroom at school, pressed his face into a urinal, and told him to lick the pink cake at the bottom of the porcelain receptacle. That time he got lucky. His tormentors heard a murmur of adult voices from somewhere out in the hallway and bolted.

And then there were the beatings. He'd been knocked around too many times to count. But there was almost always a hit and run aspect to those incidents. The boys would catch him unaware outside of school or on the way home, move in fast to deliver a flurry of punches and kicks, and then head off before an authority figure could intervene. As much as he hated those encounters, at least they were over fast.

Elliot doubted that would be the case here. They had him in an isolated location, out of sight of anyone who might be able to help him. He feared Lloyd and his cronies would make the most of the rare opportunity and take their time meting out their sadistic impulses.

Lloyd and Chuck were walking ahead of him. Chuck was still lugging that freshly carved jack-o'-lantern. For the moment, they seemed to have forgotten all about him, their conversation focused on how nice Susan Rochon's tits were. Susan was the most popular "bad" girl in school. She had choppy black hair like Joan Jett and did indeed have nice tits. Elliot had lusted for her from afar since sixth grade, but he knew he'd never have the courage to talk to her. These idiots lusted after her, too, but they were too concerned with seeming cool to admit they liked her. Instead they hurled rude insults at her, "slut" being the go-to choice, and spread nasty rumors, like that she'd fucked the whole football team at their middle school.

On one level, it infuriated Elliot to hear these guys talk so crudely about his dream girl. But there was another part of him that wished he could join in the conversation. This was something they all had in common. It was a conundrum. He hated these boys. But he also longed to feel like an ordinary kid sometimes. Just one of the guys. But it was a stupid thing to want, even a little bit, because it was so obviously not in the cards for him.

Jimmy Martin's grip on his arms was tighter than necessary. Elliot could tell the boy was bearing down as hard as he could to maximize his misery. Making matters even worse was Jimmy's rancid breath, which reeked of horseradish. The odor was so strong it made Elliot's eyes water. He felt queasy. But at least the olfactory offence distracted him somewhat from the ordeal to come.

That lasted until they passed through a particularly dense grouping of trees and tramped through underbrush until they arrived in a small clearing. Another boy was waiting for them. Ricky Bennet sat cross-legged in the center of the clearing. He was wearing a Guns N' Roses t-shirt and dirty jeans with holes in the knees. Elliot's heart sank. In many ways, Ricky was the worst of the lot. Lloyd was the unquestioned leader of the asshole quartet, but Ricky was the evil mastermind behind their foulest deeds. Among other things, the aborted urinal cake incident had been his idea. Elliot knew this because Ricky had told him multiple times, always with a promise of worse things to come.

And now, apparently, the time for those things had arrived.

Ricky had a metal lockbox open on the ground in front of him. "So the stupid little shit finally showed up again. Awesome."

Lloyd chuckled and took the jack-o'-lantern from Chuck Everly. "You and Jimmy get fuckface tied up while I take a load off and have a smoke."

The leader of the gang plopped down on the ground next to Ricky Bennet, who passed him a crumpled pack of Camel cigarettes. Lloyd tapped one out, lit up, and smoked with the jack-o'-lantern in his lap as he watched Chuck and Jimmy steer Elliot over to a tree of moderate girth at the edge of the clearing. Elliot saw right away that preparations had already been made. There were multiple lengths of frayed-looking old rope on the ground next to the tree.

His wrists were jerked roughly backward and his hands tied behind the tree. Jimmy worked on the wrists some more after the initial binding was in place, drawing the rope so tight Elliot feared it would cut off his circulation. It hurt a lot and he finally started crying. The boys snickered at his tears and called him all the usual names. Chuck wound another length of rope multiple times around his ankles and then pulled the ends back behind the tree to tie off. Yet another piece of rope went around his waist and then behind the tree, anchoring his body more firmly to it.

Once the job was finished, Lloyd flicked his half-smoked cigarette away and got to his feet. He approached Elliot with a leering, eager expression. In that moment, Elliot hated him more than ever. He saw clearly that for Lloyd this went beyond the usual kicks guys like him derived from picking on the weak. He was reveling in it in a way that bordered on sexual, which made it even more disturbing.

He turned the pumpkin in his hands, showing Elliot its open bottom. "This is your Halloween mask, faggot."

The other boys laughed.

Lloyd came closer, lifting the pumpkin.

Elliot shook his head rapidly back and forth, the tears streaming down his pale face faster than ever now. "No," he said. "No, no, no. Please...please..."

His begging provoked yet another round of laughter. This time it seemed invested with a level of darkness and evil that bordered on the inhuman. The faces of the boys crowding around him now took on a monstrous aspect. They became twisted in Elliot's tear-bleared vision and looked to him like creatures from his worst nightmares.

A strong hand, probably Jimmy's, slid behind his neck and pushed his head forward.

Lloyd slid the pumpkin down over Elliot's head.

6

Sally Ann Wilson and Brad Oliver returned from their matinee movie late that afternoon. Brad parked his Chevelle in the row of spaces outside his apartment building. He reached for the door handle on his side, but Sally Ann gripped him by an arm and pulled him close. Smiling at the look of surprise on his face, she moved in fast to kiss him. Surprise gave way to eagerness as she pushed her tongue between his slightly parted lips. His hand came away from the door handle as he returned the kiss with fervency. As he twisted in his seat, his elbow bumped the horn pad on the steering wheel, yielding a loud squawk that made them laugh.

The clinch resumed after that momentary break, their passion intensifying as they pawed at each other. Sally Ann moaned as Brad slipped a hand between the buttons of her blouse and squeezed the swollen nipple of her right breast through the bra cup. She reacted by getting a firm grip on the bulge straining the crotch of his jeans, giving it a hard squeeze that made him squeal and shudder. This made her laugh and she did it again, eliciting a louder version of the same reaction.

Brad was panting heavily as his mouth came away from hers. "You're driving me crazy. Let's get upstairs so I can fuck the shit out of you."

27

Sally Ann's smile took on a wicked aspect. "Move your seat back. I want to go down on you right here."

Brad's brow furrowed as he stopped groping her breast. "You're kidding, right?"

Sally Ann shook her head and gripped his bulge again. "Not kidding. I feel naughty. Come on, let's do it."

She tugged at his zipper tab, pulling it down about an inch.

Brad grabbed her hand, stopping her. "We can't do that. Some of my neighbors have kids. They might get pissed and call the cops. We could get busted for indecent exposure or something."

"So?"

Brad's frown deepened. "Come on, Sally Ann. I'm the one who lives here. I don't want to upset anybody. Car sex is always awkward and un-fun anyway. We'll enjoy ourselves a lot more up in--"

Sally Ann took her hand away from his crotch and turned away from him, folding her arms beneath her ample breasts and setting her mouth in a pout. "Fine."

Brad sighed, shaking his head. "Oh, great. 'Fine', she says. The one word no guy ever wants to hear his girl say, because it actually means the exact opposite of the word's dictionary definition."

Sally Ann's head slowly swiveled back toward him. "Sarcasm at my expense. Awesome. Guess what, Brad? Things are even more 'fine' now."

Brad turned away from her and leaned his head back against the headrest.

They sat there and said nothing for a few long, uncomfortable minutes. At last, Sally Ann shifted in her seat and looked at the hot guy she'd been dating for a month. This wasn't the first time they'd shifted abruptly from hot and bothered to sullen and awkward. It didn't bode well for the future of the relationship. Sally Ann made a decision as she stared at Brad's handsome profile. She would make nice and have sex with him one more time. And then tomorrow she'd break it off with him.

She mustered a smile and leaned in a little closer again. "I'm sorry. You're right. It was a silly idea. Let's not let it ruin the day."

Brad stared stonily forward a moment longer.

Sally Ann grabbed his crotch again. His erection had not yet fully wilted. Good. Still being turned on despite his frustration with her meant he wanted her pretty badly. Brad responded with the expected moan. Sally Ann derived a simple satisfaction at hearing it. Sure, she liked fucking Brad. He was a big, good-looking guy with the solid build typical of a devoted weightlifter. He was also quite well-endowed. But she knew he was way more into her than she was into him. She liked that, too. There was a power in it. The power to wound deeply on an emotional level. She didn't always choose to crush the ones she left behind, but knowing she was capable of it always gave her a naughty little thrill.

They kissed again.

Brad apologized for his part in the spat.

Sally Ann said it was okay, even though it wasn't. Despite her callousness toward the simple guys she often dated, she did possess a romantic spirit. She still hoped to one day meet that one special man, a rich risk-taker like herself who would sweep her off her feet and take her away on many adventures before planting a baby in her and buying her a big house in suburbia. Until that day came, though, she would just have to make do with ordinary dudes like Brad, who was basically just a life support system for a big dick.

They got out of the car and climbed a flight of steps leading up to Brad's second floor apartment. She pressed herself against him and groped him as he laughed nervously and fumbled with his keys. He glanced around as this happened, obviously embarrassed at the possibility of his neighbors witnessing her wanton display.

Silly boy, she thought. *You should be proud to be seen with someone like me all over you.*

Brad finally got hold of the right key and opened the door. Before he could step inside, she reached around him and slid a hand down his pants, making him gasp as she gripped his thick cock in her soft, slender hand.

Sally Ann laughed and pushed him inside. She kicked the door shut behind her and gave her future ex a harder shove, causing him to stagger into the center of the little living room. As he turned around, Brad looked like he was about to admonish her for this, but the words went unsaid as she came at him fast and dropped to her knees in front of him. She smiled up at him as she tugged down his zipper and pulled out his cock. It had wilted slightly, but it stiffened instantly again as she took him into her mouth and began to work on him. The look of annoyance on his face went away as he began to moan. He pushed a hand into her hair, his fingers sliding around to the back of her neck.

He let out a shuddery breath and said, 'Oh, yeah. Oh, baby, that's so good."

Sally Ann pushed his hand away, removed her mouth from his wet dick, and bounced to her feet. She laughed at his look of dismay and turned away from him, strutting over to the other side of the living room, where he kept his stereo.

"Let's put on some music."

Brad made an exasperated sound. "First you come on like you're in heat. Next thing I know you're giving me blue balls. What the hell?"

Sally Ann glanced over her shoulder at him, smiling mischievously. "Some guys like a girl who's a challenge. I guess you're not one of those guys."

He stared at her in open-mouthed disbelief a moment before tucking his junk away and joining her at the stereo system. "What do you want to hear?"

"Nicki Minaj. You know which one."

Brad groaned. "Again? I was thinking something more classic. More romantic. Like maybe Etta James."

"Fuck that old shit. Put my song on, Brad."

She moved away from the stereo and waited for him to do as she wanted, which of course he *would* do. The boy's resistance to her demands had its limits. He did want to get laid, after all. Brad fiddled with the Bluetooth-enabled receiver a bit. Then he took out his phone and fiddled with that, too, connecting the receiver to Spotify.

"Anaconda" by Nicki Minaj started pumping from the speakers moments later.

Sally Ann started shaking her beautiful ass suggestively all over the living room. Despite his protest of her song request, Brad watched every highly sexualized movement of her body closely. She saw the mounting lust and frustration in his eyes and reveled in it. Fuck him for resisting her out in the car. No one did that to Sally Ann Wilson without getting some payback. But she could only take teasing him so long. She was at least as horny as he was and needed to get off. She ceased dancing and dropped to her knees again. Brad was about a dozen feet away. Her intent was to come toward him on her hands and knees. It would drive him wild.

But she forgot all about that an instant later, because her new vantage point allowed her a glimpse around the kitchen partition into the little dining room. A puzzled frown replaced her formerly lustful expression. Brad's look of anticipation also vanished as he turned and followed her gaze. Now they both saw the pumpkins sitting in the center of the dining table.

There were two of them.

Carved jack-o'-lanterns.

The pumpkins hadn't been there before they'd gone out to the movie. Sally Ann thought back a few hours. She'd sat at that table and drank a beer. The empty bottle was still there. She'd neglected to toss it in the trash. It'd been the only thing on the table prior to their departure, she was sure of it.

Brad's features twisted in confusion as he raised his voice to be heard above the thumping music. *"Were those there when we left?"*

Sally Ann rolled her eyes.

Of course not, she thought. *Someone broke in.*

Or a maintenance man had come in and left the pumpkins there, though that didn't seem at all likely. So that meant someone skilled at lock-picking. Sally Ann thought of how the lights had already been on as they'd come into the apartment. Now she remembered hitting the switch by the door on the way out, leaving the place in darkness.

She was about to suggest they leave the apartment when she caught a glimpse of rapid movement in her peripheral vision. Turning her head, she saw a tall, lean man dressed all in black step out of the dark hallway that led to the bedrooms. A black ski mask covered his features. Clutched in his gloved right hand was a large machete. He raised it above his head as he came striding rapidly into the living room.

Sally Ann screamed.

31

Brad began to turn, again following her alarmed gaze, but it was too late to matter. He had a split-second to understand what was happening and raised up a hand in a meager self-defense gesture. The machete's sharp blade sliced off three of his fingers as it descended. Sally Ann screamed again as the machete chopped into Brad's neck, halfway severing his head in one blow. Blood erupted from the wound in a spectacular spray as the assailant ripped the blade away from the wounded flesh. Brad fell to his knees and slapped a hand over the deep slice in his neck. Blood continued to pump from the wound, spurting between his trembling fingers and rapidly staining his white shirt crimson.

The man in the ski mask repositioned himself in front of his victim, raising the blood-soaked machete high over his head a second time.

This time when it came down it split open the top of Brad's head.

Sally Ann had felt paralyzed throughout the attack. It had been so thoroughly unexpected and brutal. And so bloody, like something out of the horror movies her little brother loved. As a result, it was initially hard to believe the reality of what she was seeing.

But now the paralysis broke.

She surged to her feet and made a break for the door. Unfortunately, in her haste, she stumbled and hit her head on the end table and slumped unconscious to the floor.

7

Six days until Halloween
Willow Springs, TN

By the time he made it back across the interior of the house to the short hallway outside his office, Chuck's fear level had soared. He knew he'd been rash in deciding to conduct a search of the house on his own. The smart thing would be to hurry back the way he'd come and wait outside with his family until the law arrived.

His affair with Fawn Hightower aside, Chuck was a man guided by reason in most things. However, while the smart move here was obvious, this situation caused him to set rationality aside. The illusion of home as a sanctuary had been shattered and it made him furious. Though his fear level was high, it was exceeded by an intense desire to get his hands on the intruder. His hands tensed at his sides as he imagined wrapping them around the scumbag's throat and squeezing hard until the man's face (he assumed it was a man, of course) turned purple.

Chuck edged up to the doorframe and peeked into his office.

It was empty.

Chuck entered the office and went immediately to his desk. He already had the key to the locked bottom drawer pinched between his thumb and forefinger. Kneeling behind the desk, he slid the key into the lock, turned it, and pulled the drawer open. The deep drawer was empty save for a metal lockbox at the bottom. Inside it were his gun and box of shells. He flipped through his keys until he found the one for the lockbox and opened it.

The gun was there, as expected, though until that moment, the paranoid part of him feared it'd been stolen. But the weapon was empty. He needed to take it out and load shells into the cylinder. His hand closed around the gun's molded grip.

Chuck flinched when his phone buzzed loudly in his pocket. He took it out and frowned as he glanced at the screen. Fawn was calling. An image of her in black lingerie filled the screen. Seeing the picture made Chuck feel stupid. He'd added it to her contact listing after a few beers one night a few weeks ago and had neglected to remove it. Having the picture on his phone at all was a very risky thing. Associating it with Fawn's number bordered on self-destructive, which was not like him at all. Lately he'd started turning the phone off when he was at home to reduce the likelihood of Karen spotting the image when his mistress called or texted, but that made it no less stupid. He made a mental note to delete the picture as soon as this hopefully very brief conversation was over.

He tapped the "accept" button and put the phone to his ear.

"Fawn, now's not the time. I've got a situation here."

"I can see that. That bitch you're married to is having a fucking hysterical meltdown. The boy's holding on to her to keep her from going in after you. What the hell's happening in there?"

Chuck grimaced. "Please don't talk about Karen like that."

Fawn grunted. "Why shouldn't I? She has what I want. I hate her. Now tell me what's happening before I march across the street and go in after you myself."

Chuck sighed. He told her the situation.

"Jesus Christ. And you went back in? How stupid are you?"

Chuck was about to reply, but he hesitated. Was that a creak he'd heard out in the hallway? Fawn's loud voice in his ear made him unsure. He might have imagined the noise. Even if he hadn't, houses creaked and settled sometimes. It didn't mean anyone was out there.

It didn't mean someone *wasn't* out there, either.

Chuck rose from his squatting position and moved out from behind the desk. "Look, Fawn, I don't have time for this. We'll talk later. I'm coming back outside. And please keep your voice down. Karen might figure out who you're talking to."

"Maybe I should just tell her."

Chuck ended the call and turned off the phone. He put it in his pocket and crept over to the door. Cutting Fawn off like that was a big gamble, but he really didn't think she'd follow through on the threat, not in the midst of such a tense situation. He could be wrong, of course. Fawn might be angry enough to allow emotion to overwhelm her common sense. And if that happened, well, the consequences would be terrible, but he'd ultimately only have himself to blame.

Right now, though, he needed to concentrate on what was right in front of him.

He reached the open doorway, took a big breath, and peeked around the edge of the frame. Though not precisely empty, the short stretch of hallway was devoid of stealthily creeping intruders. Moonbeam, the family's three-year-old black cat, peered up at Chuck from the center of the hallway, meowing once in a plaintive way when it saw him.

Chuck let out the breath he'd been holding and stepped out into the hallway. As he slowly traversed its length, the cat arched its back and attempted to rub up against his ankles. Not needing the distraction, Chuck gently nudged the animal away with the toe of a shoe. It meowed again in response. This time the sound had an annoyed quality.

Sorry, buddy, Chuck thought, and continued down the hallway.

But the encounter with the animal unsettled him and in another few moments he realized he'd given no thought to Thor, their big German Shepherd. The dog had stayed out in the back yard during the family outing to the restaurant. Belatedly, it occurred to Chuck he hadn't heard Thor bark even once since their return, which was highly unusual. His eyes widening at the sudden certainty that the intruder had harmed his dog, he abruptly abandoned caution and raced through the house to the den. One look through the French doors that opened onto the concrete patio was enough to soothe his worst fears.

Thor was alive, lying on the ground about a dozen feet from the edge of the patio. He was gnawing on a very large bone. It looked like the kind of butcher's shop leftover sometimes sold as a treat for dogs. Chuck opened the door and stepped outside. Thor let out a low growl as Chuck carefully approached the animal. The growl grew louder as he knelt before him and gently began to pry the bone from his slobbery maw.

"Sorry, buddy," Chuck said in his most placating tone. "But I can't let you have this."

What had happened seemed obvious. The intruder had entered through the back, but not before first bribing Thor with the giant bone. That the man had gotten around the ostensibly fearsome animal so easily was disturbing. The dog always unleashed a furious cacophony of noise any time it detected the scent of unfamiliar humans entering his territory. Chuck was at a loss to explain it, except that maybe the person who'd come onto his property was one of those people with a natural, easy rapport with animals. There were people like that in the world, he knew. Animals instinctively trusted them. The notion that this person had been someone like that seemed counterintuitive, but Chuck could think of no other way to explain it.

Chuck doubted the bone had been salted with poison. In that case, Thor would be sick or dying already. But he thought he should show it to the cops when they arrived, anyway. Taking the bone with him, he went back into the house, leaving a suddenly morose-looking Thor shut out in the yard for the time being.

Making a mental note to give the dog a rawhide treat later, Chuck set the bone on the kitchen counter, went back to his office to retrieve the gun, and resumed his search of the house. He looked everywhere—in every room, every closet, and under every bed—and found nothing. As he'd suspected, the house was empty, but it made him feel better to verify it. And with the search concluded, he felt a sense of accomplishment. He could have waited for the law to arrive, but he'd taken matters into his own hands, protecting his family and property the way any real man should.

After returning the gun to the lockbox, he went outside and joined his family on the front lawn, wincing when he saw Fawn Hightower standing with them. The woman had an arm around Karen's waist. His weeping wife's head was on her shoulder. A mischievous smile touched the corners of Fawn's mouth when

Chuck met her gaze.

The smile broadened when Karen's head lifted from her shoulder. "There he is. See, Karen, I told you he'd be fine."

Karen shrugged free of Fawn's embrace and came running toward Chuck, throwing her arms around him as she slammed into him, nearly staggering him. Chuck put his arms around her and gently patted her back, whispering words of reassurance into her ear as he stared over her shoulder at Fawn.

He kept staring at her as the kids crowded around their parents, babbling excitedly and peppering him with questions he didn't yet know how to answer. Fawn's smile faded, her expression taking on a nastier tinge now that no one else was looking at her.

Then she turned away and went back across the street to her house. Rather than returning to the chair on the porch, she went inside and slammed the door behind her. A deep frown etched itself into Chuck's features as the sound of sirens began to rise in the distance.

8

The creak of the leather swivel chair was embarrassingly loud as Sheriff Bob Lee settled his bulk into it. He grimaced as he stared across his desk at Pete Acker, who kept his expression neutral. Lee was grateful for the lack of visible reaction. The deputy was a friend. He knew how self-conscious Lee was about the perpetually mushrooming weight problem he couldn't seem to solve.

An apple sat at the edge of Lee's desk. It was the one thing he would allow himself to eat until his chicken salad dinner later tonight. He picked it up and took a bite from it. The crunching sound it made as he chewed was another awkward noise. It seemed to fill the closed office. Lee put the apple down after just the one bite. He leaned back in the chair and folded meaty hands over his big belly.

Acker glanced at the notepad in his lap as Lee's chair made that horrendously loud creaking sound again. He looked up when it stopped. "Chuck Everly seemed a little squirrely to me."

Lee nodded. "That he did. You think he knows more than he's letting on?"

Acker shrugged and flipped his notepad shut. "I've been at this long enough to know when someone's holding back on me. That look he got on his face when I asked him if he could think of anyone who would break into his house and do anything as plain fucking weird as that thing with the pumpkins…"

Lee knew the look Acker was talking about well. Anyone who'd been in law enforcement any significant amount of time would know it. It was that subtle tightening of the features that occurred when one was asked an uncomfortable question. Lee had been otherwise occupied during the time Acker was taking Everly's statement, but he could picture the look on the man's face well enough.

After trailing off a moment, Acker coughed and continued. "And it wasn't just the look. When I asked him the question, his eyes flicked to the house across the street. It was just a split-second, but it happened. May not mean anything, but…"

"But it might," Lee said, nodding again. "We know who lives in the house across the street?"

"Man named Hightower owns the place. Russ Hightower. His wife's name is Fawn. They have two young children, Scott and Abby. The wife's a real looker."

Lee cocked an eyebrow at this description of Fawn Hightower. Acker was possibly the most intuitive investigator he had. And he wasn't a man to waste words. "Something going on between Everly and the neighbor lady, you think?"

Acker spread his hands in a gesture of half-hearted uncertainty. "Hard to say. Got nothing but a hunch there." He smiled. "But it's a strong hunch."

"This woman or any other neighbors happen to notice any suspicious activity happening around the Everly place while the family was out?"

"No."

Lee frowned. "Strange."

Acker's smile abruptly disappeared. "Very strange. Lot of wide open space in that neighborhood and not many places for a bad guy to conceal himself or skulk around, which makes it even stranger. And even if Everly and the Hightower woman are carrying on in secret, it might not mean anything, though we'll definitely want to follow up on it. Right now, though, I'm thinking the connection between Everly and Lloyd McAfee might be more meaningful."

Lee was already acquainted with this part of the story, having been present for the early part of the scene investigation at the Everly residence. Turned out Everly and McAfee had been childhood friends, a revelation any lawman worthy of wearing the badge would immediately recognize as the potential key to unlocking the mystery behind all the bizarre events of the day. Upon sensing their interest in the connection, Everly had turned evasive and anxious, insisting his former friendship with McAfee was irrelevant. According to Everly, he hadn't talked to Lloyd in almost twenty years. There'd been a palpable note of disdain in his tone when speaking of the dead man. When pressed on that point, Everly dismissed the notion as nonsense, saying he and McAfee had merely grown apart.

It seemed obvious to Lee there was a lot more to it than that.

"We need to talk to him again."

He turned in the chair and glanced out the window at the gray-tinged sky. The sun was still visible above the horizon, but night was definitely beginning to fall in Willow Springs. Not for the first time, he was regretting his early departure from the second crime scene, if "crime scene" was even the correct terminology in this instance. There had been no obvious signs of forced entry, nor had the Everlys reported anything stolen. Lee wasn't fooling himself on that count, though. There was no mistaking the sinister intent in the placement of those pumpkins, nor was there any point in ignoring the likely connection to Lloyd McAfee's murder.

But his irritable bowels had started acting up partway through the interview with Chuck Everly and he'd been forced to excuse himself and hightail it back to the department building. Times like that, the occasionally entertained notion of early retirement became a more tempting prospect than usual. Though it pained him to admit it, he was on the verge of no longer being fit for the job.

One thing he would absolutely not do, however, was bail on the department and his town before apprehending the madman behind McAfee's murder. Capturing that sick fuck would at least be a decent capper to his legacy.

"Fuck it. I'll swing by there on the way home." Lee smiled. "Maybe I'll even check in on that looker across the street, see what I can shake loose there."

Acker shook his head. "They're not gonna be there. The Everlys, I mean."

Lee frowned. "Well, shit, where will they be?"

"Hotel in town. They're all too spooked to spend the night in their own house. Can't blame them, really."

Lee sat forward in the chair, making it creak again as he

leaned his bulk against the edge of the desk. "He tell you which hotel?"

"He did not, but I've got his cell number right here."

Acker flipped open his notepad again.

Lee took his phone out of his shirt pocket. "Let me have it."

Acker read off the number.

Lee punched it in and put the phone to his ear.

9

When Sally Ann Wilson regained consciousness, she was tied to a chair in Brad Oliver's living room and had a strip of duct tape stretched across her mouth. At first she was deeply confused about her situation. The last thing she remembered was sitting in a darkened movie theater with Brad, the two of them groping each other and making out in their seats at the back of the theater while intermittently laughing at the vapid movie playing on the screen. If not for Brad's prudish attitude about sex in public places, she would have gone down on him right there in the mostly empty auditorium.

The thought triggered an associated memory, one from after the movie. Recalling her failure to goad Brad into having sex with her in his car, she experienced a fresh flicker of the anger she'd felt then, but it faded rapidly, overwhelmed by the severe ache in her head. A side of her head felt wet with something sticky. It kind of felt like a clump of slowly coagulating blood in her hair.

But why—

The thought cut off as her vision began to sharpen. As her surroundings came into focus, she was gripped by a sudden burst of panic, which in short order blossomed into full-blown terror. The transition began when her brain belatedly registered the sight

43

of a man sitting in a straight-backed chair directly across from her. It was the same kind of chair in which she was sitting. Both had been taken from the dining table. The man was wearing the clothes Brad had worn for their movie date, but now the front of the white shirt was stained a dark crimson. She couldn't see the man's face because a jack-o'-lantern had been wedged down atop it. The man wasn't moving. His head was slumped forward. He looked like he might slide off the chair at any moment.

More memories cut through what remained of Sally Ann's post-concussion fog. Her eyes widened and she screamed behind the strip of duct tape as those moments of sudden violence and terror replayed in her head. She tried to rise from the chair, but she was unable to do so. She could scarcely budge a muscle. But maybe she could topple the chair over by rocking side to side. The wood frame might splinter on impact. This seemed unlikely, but if it happened, she might be able to kick her way free of the debris and her bonds and try to escape.

She was on the verge of attempting to do just that when a tall, slender man clad all in black entered her field of vision from her right and moved into the space between the chairs. He had something in his hands. It was dark and glossy. At first this only deepened her confusion. She thought some kind of small animal was cradled in his palms. The idea of a murderous maniac bringing a pet with him to the scene of a crime made no sense to her. Not that any of what was happening made sense. She couldn't think of anyone who hated her—or Brad—enough to do something like this. The only explanation was that they were random targets, which only made it worse. This wasn't fair. She hadn't done anything to warrant this. Nor had Brad, despite his general lameness.

The killer had taken off his ski mask. He had dark, haunted eyes, pale skin, and sharp-angled features, with a long, narrow nose that looked like it had been broken once and set badly. He had a wavy shock of black hair styled in a sort of neo-pompadour.

He smiled thinly as she met his gaze. "Hello, Susan. It's been a while, hasn't it?"

Sally Ann just stared at him.

Either this guy was even crazier than she'd imagined or she was the victim of the worst case of mistaken identity in recorded

44

history. In the event of the latter, however, it really didn't matter at this point. Even if she could convince this lunatic he had the wrong girl, he couldn't let her live after what she'd seen him do to Brad.

This thought sparked a moment of sickening awareness.

Oh, shit. This is it. I'm about to die. This is the last day of my life. Oh, shit.

Tears rimmed her eyes and she began to plead with the man from behind the gag. A part of her knew begging would do no good, but not trying it wasn't an option. Still smiling, the man shook his head and made shushing noises. He stepped closer and spread his hands slightly. A piece of the glossy object he was holding drooped downward. Finally, she saw it for what it was. The thing in his hands was a jet-black woman's wig, Bettie Paige style with short bangs in front.

Once again, confusion briefly cut through her terror, distracting her.

A wig? What the actual fuck?

The man came closer still and began to lift the wig above her head. Sally Ann held her breath as he leaned over her, settled the wig atop her head, and wedged it awkwardly into place. It didn't seem to fit her head well, but the rapturous look on the killer's face when he stepped back to appraise his work strongly suggested he didn't care. The effect was good enough to suit his purposes, whatever those actually were. Sally Ann experienced a passing desire to check herself out in a mirror and see how she looked. She had occasionally toyed with the idea of dyeing her blonde hair black. A guy had once told her she'd be a dead ringer for Megan Fox if she did it. But then the crazy man started talking again and the ridiculous notion went away.

"I've missed you, Susan. You have no idea. You're still all I can think about sometimes, even after what you did to me. You're still the prettiest girl I ever saw, you know. And I'll always love you, no matter what. I just want you to know that."

Sally Ann had no doubt this sad sack psycho's love for the true object of his desires had been of the unrequited variety. She had no idea who this Susan person was, but right now she kind of hated her. If the bitch had ever at least thrown the guy a mercy fuck, this psychotic breakdown he was having might not be happening. The thought was perhaps slightly hypocritical of her. After all, she'd spurned the affections of numerous creepy losers in her time. One particularly pathetic guy had even stalked her for a while, but he'd been too much of a cowering little shit to ever present a real threat.

Or so she'd believed.

Maybe this scary asshole was what ultimately became of that kind of guy after a lot of years of disappointment and things generally not working out. Sally Ann studied the killer's face a little more closely and decided he was probably somewhere in his late thirties. Not really old yet, but entering middle age. His bent nose and sharp-angled features were too severe to qualify as anything close to traditionally handsome. Putting herself outside the context of the current murder and weirdness scenario, Sally Ann knew she never would have given him the time of day, not even if they'd been closer in age. But she thought there were probably girls out there who might have been receptive to overtures from this guy, at least in his younger days. It was possible, though, that he'd spent his undoubtedly wretched life shooting for something out of his league.

So maybe he was still a virgin.

Sure, it seemed unlikely at his age, but it wasn't entirely out of the question, especially if he'd never lowered his expectations and settled for a homelier girl than this Susan he was so fixated on. Sally Ann tried to imagine going her whole life without ever getting laid. Not just at her current age, but deep into a hypothetical future when she was pushing forty. The idea chilled her, an austere, joyless life of never knowing the pleasures of the flesh. Something like that might well fuck up a person enough to do crazy things. She figured there were probably other factors that had pushed this man beyond the breaking point, but she had a strong feeling intimacy deprivation was a big part of the equation.

As she continued to study his face for clues as to his mental state, she abruptly realized he was doing much the same with her. He was watching her very closely, perhaps searching for something in her that reminded him of Susan, something that might imbue the fantasy playing out in his head with a deeper sense of reality.

The man smiled. There was a tinge of sadness in the

expression. "I know what you're thinking. Some of it, anyway. And I know you're not Susan. I'll see her for real before the end of the week, though. The thing with the wig is pretty weird, I admit, but there's a reason behind it. I'm practicing for the real thing. I want to feel steady in heart and mind when I talk to her again and I thought a bit of roleplaying might help. My former therapist was a big fan of the technique. If I remove the duct tape from your mouth, will you promise not to scream?"

Sally Ann nodded.

The man smiled again as he stepped closer. "Good. This will hurt a little, but I'll try to be gentle."

He was true to his word as he slowly, carefully peeled the strip of tape from her mouth. When he was done, he let it flutter to the blood-spattered floor.

Sally Ann coughed and cleared her throat. "I can pretend to be Susan if you want. What's your name? I need to know what to call you. It'll make the roleplaying better. More realistic."

The man shook his head. "You don't need to know my name."

Sally Ann felt a small flicker of hope at this statement. Maybe he didn't want to tell her his name because he planned to let her live. It seemed unlikely. She could easily identify him, after all, thanks to his distinctive features. But it was something to hold on to, at least.

She made herself smile, investing it with a hint of sultry playfulness. "You know, if you cut me loose from this chair, we could have some fun together."

"Are you saying you'd have sex with me?"

Sally Ann nodded. "That's exactly what I'm saying. And I'll make it good, the best you've ever had."

He swept a hand in the direction of Brad's slumped-over body, which looked even closer to sliding out of the chair now. "And you'd really do that, even after what I did to your friend?"

Sally Ann's fear returned as she stared at the limp form in the chair. She had felt contempt for Brad in some ways while he was alive, but she'd had sex with him often during their brief time together. She'd enjoyed *that* aspect of their relationship very much. His prudishness aside, he'd been a decent if sometimes boring guy. A *normal* guy, more importantly.

47

Pretty much the exact opposite of this freak, in other words.

Sally Ann started crying again.

The man nodded. "That's what I thought. No, we won't be having sex. Besides, I'm saving myself for Susan." He glanced again at Brad before directing another smile at Sally Ann. "Do you like his mask, by the way? I bet you're wondering why I put that on him."

Sally Ann sobbed. She was momentarily unable to speak.

"I've got one for you, too. I'm sure you noticed before I killed your lover."

Sally Ann struggled to find her voice again and at last succeeded. She stared up at him, her vision rendered blurry with tears. "Why are you doing this? Are you crazy?"

The man laughed softly. "I'm glad you asked. As it happens, I *am* a little crazy. I've been diagnosed with multiple mental disorders over the years. I won't bore you with the details. Suffice to say I'm a bit of a broken person. But it's not entirely my fault. Something bad happened to me a long time ago. Right around this time of year, actually. I've never gotten over it, as you've probably guessed. I *hate* Halloween." The first hint of real anger came into his voice with that last sentence. "To show how much I hate it, I've decided to kill thirty-one people this week. I've got a lot of work yet to do, work I'm spreading over a wide area to hopefully reduce the risk of premature apprehension. I don't want to be caught before reaching my goal, after all. Your boyfriend was just my second victim. And you, you filthy little whore, you're number three."

Sally Ann unleashed an agonized moan at this pronouncement. "No. Please. Please. Don't. You don't have to hurt me."

"I'm afraid I do."

The killer moved out of her field of vision.

Sally Ann sucked in a big breath and unleashed a piercing scream. The killer clamped a gloved hand over her mouth seconds later, stifling the sound. She moaned in misery again as she felt a press of cold, hard steel against her throat.

Then a low voice was speaking in her ear, warm breath tickling her flesh. "Be quiet and maybe I'll change my mind."

Sally Ann struggled to swallow a painful lump in her throat. Finally, she managed a nod.

The low voice whispered, "Good. Good girl."

The killer moved back into her field of vision.

Clutched in his right hand was a big carving knife.

Sally Ann heaved a big breath. "You don't have to hurt me. I'll do anything. I'll help you kill all those people."

The killer stared at her a long moment, his face blank.

Then he said, "You know how I said I might change my mind if you stopped screaming?"

Sally Ann nodded. "Yes."

He pressed the tip of the big blade against her throat. "Well, I lied."

More tears spilled down Sally Ann's already wet face. "No, please. Don't. Don't. I'll do anything."

The killer began to push the blade forward. The point of it pierced her flesh, drawing a trickle of blood. "You'll die. That's what you'll do. You're number three."

Sally Ann tilted her head back and the tip of the blade came away from her flesh briefly. "Don't. Don't. This can't happen. God, don't let this happen. Please. You don't have to do this."

The killer shook his head. "Yes, I do."

He rammed the blade into her flesh and Sally Ann choked on the steel in her throat.

10

Twenty-five years ago
Willow Springs, TN

Lloyd and his gang of miscreants taunted and tortured Elliot for hours, from late afternoon into the early evening. The extended exercise in sadism and humiliation featured the use of many items from, Ricky Bennet's lockbox, including a pair of pliers, a carton of earthworms purchased from a bait shop that very day, a large plastic zipper bag filled with fresh dog feces, a spray bottle filled with a mixture of water and vinegar, and a cat-o'-nine-tails whip Ricky had stolen from his parents' bedroom closet.

The first thing they did after tying him to the tree was cut away his shirt. This left him shivering in the late October chill. Each of the boys took turns torturing him with the pliers, twisting his nipples and crushing each of his fingers between the metal jaws to a point just shy of pulverizing bone. Elliot's resolve to remain stoic throughout the ordeal dissolved after enduring the first few minutes of searing pain. He sobbed and cried out inside the suffocating jack-o'-lantern that encased his head. When Lloyd threatened to use the pliers on his penis, Elliot pissed his pants. The boys evidently thought this was the funniest thing that had ever happened. They fell down in the clearing and rolled around on the ground, gasping for air as they laughed hysterically and pointed at him.

It got worse from there.

When they recovered from their collective laughing fit, the boys decided it was time to take a break from physical torture and focus on humiliation. A paint brush was used to smear the dog shit all over Elliot's torso. It was wet and runny and, even with the pumpkin covering his face, smelled awful. He was then forced to eat some of the earthworms. Initially he wouldn't cooperate, resolutely keeping his mouth shut when the first worms were pushed through the jagged teeth of the jack-o'-lantern. Again, however, his resistance came to nothing in short order, this time ending when Lloyd McAfee sprayed a bit of the water and vinegar solution through an eye of the pumpkin. He screamed when the mix hit his eyes and the worms were pushed into his mouth. When he attempted to spit them out, he got another squirt of the vinegar spray and was told this would continue to happen until he gulped down each and every earthworm fed to him.

His eyes stinging and dripping with constant tears, Elliot surrendered and ate the earthworms. He was fed about a third of the carton, the boys giggling at the gagging sounds he made and his pleas for mercy. The rest of the earthworms were dumped down the front of his pants. He felt them slithering around inside his underwear and crawling around his genitals.

The last thing they did was flog him with the whip. He screamed again each time the whip's multiple braids lashed his bare, shit-smeared skin. This was the worst physical pain they inflicted on him. It was also the shortest phase of the long ordeal, ending when Lloyd expressed concern about the marks the braids were leaving on Elliot's flesh. So far most of what they had done to him could be scrubbed away and denied, but this was possibly crossing a line into a place where they might wind up in real trouble. As much fun as it was to hear the geek scream and beg for mercy, they couldn't flay him alive.

Elliot never forgot Ricky Bennet's sinister chuckle that followed this pronouncement. "Nobody ever has to know. We could just kill him."

The startled silence that followed this suggestion struck Elliot as hypocritical even as it filled him with a bone-deep level of knee-shaking terror that made him piss his pants a second time. But no one laughed this time. For a long stretch of moments, Elliot was sure the rest of the boys would start nodding their heads and making increasingly enthusiastic noises of agreement.

But then Lloyd piped up and shot the idea down. "We're not gonna kill him. No fucking way. Maybe we wouldn't get caught, but we might. And I don't want to spend the rest of my life in jail."

Ricky Bennet snorted. "You wouldn't. You're too young. You'd just be sent to juvie until you turn eighteen. No big deal."

"Bullshit it's no big deal," Lloyd said, his tone sterner and more emphatic now. "Don't know about the rest of you, but I don't want to spend the next five years getting my asshole plowed by a bunch of fags. No way. We're done."

Another awkward silence followed this declaration. No one seemed much inclined to argue with it, including Ricky Bennet. Chuck Everly was the first to express a desire to be done with the whole thing, even venturing the idea that they'd gone too far already. "Seriously, guys. I think we shouldn't have done this. Jesus, look at him. We need to clean him up and get him some different clothes. He can't go home looking like that. His parents will lose their shit."

This earned barks of derisive laughter from Lloyd and Ricky.

Lloyd said, "And where are we supposed to get him new clothes? You see a fucking TJ Maxx around anywhere?"

No response.

Lloyd grunted. "No, you don't, because we're in the middle of the fucking woods, you idiot. Anyway, his parents won't freak. They're losers, just like him. Fuck it. I'm tired of messing with him anyway. I need to get back over to Jimmy's house so I can call my mom to come pick me up. Let's get out of here."

The other boys hesitated as Lloyd turned to walk away.

Jimmy Martin said, "But what if his parents *do* freak? What if they call the cops?"

Ricky Bennet chuckled. "Chill. We've got nothing to worry about."

Lloyd turned back toward his friend, eyeing him curiously. "Why do you sound so sure?"

Another chuckle. "Because I'm gonna take care of it. The rest of you head on back. I'm gonna have a little talk with shit-stain here and make him understand why he should never tell anyone about this."

There was yet another brief silence.

Then Chuck Everly nervously cleared his throat and said, "But you're not gonna kill him, right? We agreed not to do that."

Ricky Bennet shook his head. "Don't worry about it. I won't kill him. Just gonna have a little talk, like I said. Now hurry on out of here. It's getting late."

It was indeed getting late, well past time for all the boys to be home for supper with their families. There was a bit more hemming and hawing, particularly from Chuck Everly, but in the end they all walked on out of the woods, leaving a still sobbing Elliot alone with Ricky Bennet.

Ricky stepped up close to Elliot and stood there breathing heavily for several silent minutes. Elliot saw him only as a blurry blob at first. His eyes were still running from the numerous spritzes they'd taken from the vinegar solution. When his vision at last began to clear, he frowned, peering through the jack-o'-lantern's slanted eyeholes at Ricky's odd, slack-jawed expression. The boy's shoulder was moving up and down in a rapid motion. It took Elliot a few more moments to realize the other boy was beating off. Contempt cut through Elliot's otherwise all-consuming terror. Ricky had obviously had more than one reason for wanting to get rid of his friends.

When he finished, he zipped himself up and put his sweaty face even closer to the jack-o'-lantern. "You ain't ever gonna tell anyone about me and my friends doing this. If you do, I'm gonna sneak into your house some night and slit your throat while you sleep. And then I'm gonna do the same to your sick little feeb of a brother. Your parents, too, but I'll leave your mother for last. I'll play with her titties some before I cut her up. Your mom has nice titties. Even better than Susan Rochon's titties, because she's all grown up." Ricky thumped a fist against Elliot's scrawny chest, making him gasp. Then he did it two more times, each blow harder than the last. "Don't you agree, faggot? Doesn't your mom have nice titties?"

Elliot wanted nothing more in that moment than to kill Ricky Bennet, but he was powerless and could take no more abuse.

So he told Ricky he agreed about his mother's titties.

Ricky dispensed with the sick jokes at that point and warned him one more time. He told Elliot that even if they were arrested, he and his friends would get out on bail. And then they would come after him and finish the job. Whether this was true or not, Elliot had no idea. For reasons of his own, though, he'd already resolved to never tell a soul about this incident, at least not until he was older and could exact a proper revenge.

Satisfied at last that Elliot had gotten the message, Ricky packed up what remained of his torture kit and walked out of the woods, leaving Elliot alone in the clearing.

All the things they did to him through those long hours were bad. Really, really bad. He would be a long time getting over them, if he ever did. But the very worst thing they did was leaving him tied to that tree, where he remained for many more hours to come, deep into the night. During that time, he felt a deepening despair that alternated with fresh bursts of terror at the slithering and rustling sounds of various forest creatures stirring after nightfall. At one point, he felt a snake slide over his feet and nearly bit through his tongue as he tried very hard to remain still until it slithered away.

He fell in and out of consciousness. No one ever came looking for him. His alcoholic parents probably hadn't even noticed when he'd failed to return home from school. With their nightly habit of drinking to the point of passing out, this didn't surprise him. They didn't give a shit about him. *Nobody* gave a shit about him, except for his brother and Mr. Spurlock. He began to fear he would die out here in the woods, his body slowly turning into a rotten husk as it sagged within the tightly knotted ropes. His despair seeped into his dreams, torturing him with visions of all his worst fears.

The worst dream of all was the one about Robert joining him in the clearing. It was different from the others in how vivid and real it seemed. His brother was wearing the threadbare blue pajamas he'd had on for days. Their parents often neglected to change Robert into fresh clothes. Part of this was sheer laziness, of course, but the bigger reason was the pain the physical effort of changing caused him. The boy couldn't do it on his own anymore and usually required a significant level of assistance from one or both of his parents. This frequently elicited shrill squeals of agony, increasingly so of late. Elliot would sit in his room and cry as he listened to the sounds of his brother's suffering. Those sounds told him all he needed to know regarding the relentless, inevitable course of Robert's illness. He always felt at his most powerless in those moments.

But when Robert entered the clearing in the dream, he walked with a renewed vigor, standing straight and proud rather than stooped over. He had a smile on his face. For the first time in seemingly forever, it didn't seem false, lacking the usual telltale signs of strain at the corners of the mouth and eyes. In the bright glow of the moonlight, even his pallor looked better. But Robert's smile faded as he came closer and absorbed the details of his younger brother's humiliation. There was a flicker of something that might have been anger in his eyes, but it quickly faded, giving way to sadness.

"I wish I could help you, Elliot."

His voice sounded distorted and faraway, as if it were a faint, crackly signal emerging from the speaker of a shortwave radio.

Elliot didn't understand. His brother was standing mere inches away, looking stronger and healthier than ever. "Untie me. Please." He twisted his wrists against the uncomfortably tight length of rope that bound them, his sweaty face contorting in pain beneath the pumpkin. "It hurts. Please."

Robert shook his head. "I can't. I'm sorry."

Elliot squealed in frustration. "Why not?"

"You're going to be sad for a while," Robert told him in that same crackly, faraway voice, ignoring the question. "I'm sorry for that, too. But you're strong. The people who did this to you will pay someday. You'll--"

But the strangely invigorated dream version of Robert disappeared before he could finish saying whatever it was he'd meant to tell Elliot. This infuriated and frustrated Elliot as his eyes fluttered open and he emerged from the dream world back into the real one. Only the strange thing was he wasn't sure he'd been asleep at all. The vision of Robert had felt too real for that. He'd remained aware of the chill night air on his bare skin and the rustlings of the forest creatures the whole time. And there'd been that awful sensation of the rope burning his skin when he twisted his wrists. No other dream in his experience had ever felt like such a perfect approximation of actual, waking life, which made him wonder if it hadn't really been a dream.

But that made no sense.

How could Robert have found him out here in the woods? Why did he seem like he was no longer sick? And, most importantly, why wouldn't he help his brother out of this awful situation?

Before he could spend any significant time pondering these questions, Elliot became aware of another presence in the clearing. At first this new presence was just a slender form cloaked in shadows and standing at the far opposite edge of the open space. Elliot sensed a hesitation and skittishness in this new arrival. He had the feeling whoever it was might turn away and bolt from the scene at any moment, perhaps too terrified by the scene of degradation and horror he or she had chanced across to do anything else.

But then he heard a deep exhalation of breath and the figure stepped away from the far tree line and came striding across the clearing toward him. When the moonlight fell across the person's face, Elliot's heart started pounding with renewed fear.

The person coming rapidly toward him was Chuck Everly.

Elliot's burst of instinctive terror was diluted in the next instant when he took note of the things Chuck had with him. Clutched in his hands were some clothes, some old-looking wash rags, and a plastic gallon jug of water. He set these things on the ground and took a folding knife out of a pocket of his jeans. Elliot experienced another little flutter of fear at the sight of the blade as Chuck opened it, but his fear again faded as the boy stepped behind the tree and began sawing away at the ropes. The knife was sharp and the rope yielded to it with surprising ease. Despite his righteous hatred of this boy who'd tormented him for so long, Elliot felt an instinctive, shameful gratitude. That didn't stop him from fantasizing about taking the knife away from Chuck and shoving it through one of his eyes.

Once Chuck had finished cutting away the ropes, Elliot removed the pumpkin from his head and tossed it aside.

The two boys stood there eyeing each other warily for a few moments.

Then Chuck coughed and nervously cleared his throat. "Those clothes should fit. You should probably throw away what you're wearing. I know that's what I'd want to do."

Another silence descended.

Elliot stared at Chuck. He made no move to remove his clothes or avail himself of the things Chuck had brought him.

Finally, Chuck made another of those nervous throat-clearing sounds and said, "The water and rags are so you can clean yourself off, but you probably could have figured that out."

Elliot let out a breath. "Why are you helping me?"

Chuck grimaced. "Because I felt bad about what we did, okay? And I heard from Lloyd that Ricky left you tied up out here. I couldn't get to sleep thinking about it. So I woke up my older brother and told him what happened. He drove me out here." Chuck threw a glance over his shoulder and started backing away across the clearing. "I have to go. He's driving by again to pick me up in a few minutes. Listen, man. I'm sorry for what we did. I really am. I'm not really as bad as them. I just get carried away when I'm with those guys sometimes. But I'm not gonna hang out with them ever again, I swear." He heaved a shuddery breath as he reached the other side of the clearing. "Please don't tell anyone about this, Elliot."

Elliot said nothing, just stared at him.

Chuck disappeared through the tree line.

Once he was gone, Elliot took off his shoes and removed his soiled jeans and underwear. He pulled off the rest of the earthworms still clinging to his genitals and flung them away. After that, he used the jug of water and the wash rags to clean the shit from his torso. When he was finished and had dried off, he put on the new clothes and put his shoes back on. Chuck had been right about the fit, though the garments were slightly looser than what he usually wore.

He hurried through the woods and emerged onto the sidewalk at a spot near where he'd been abducted earlier in the day. A scan of the dark street revealed no sign of the backpack, not that he'd really expected to see it after all this time. After resigning himself to its loss, he took off running in the direction of home, a new fear gripping him all the way back.

That "dream" really hadn't seemed like a dream at all.

He had tears in his eyes as he turned down the street to his house, where he saw the lights of an ambulance parked at curbside flashing from blocks away.

11

Six days until Halloween
Willow Springs, TN

After getting his family checked in at the Embassy Suites hotel in downtown Willow Springs, Chuck left them there, saying he had to run back to the house to fetch a few more necessities. This was a lie. He had another agenda he couldn't tell them about. On his way out, he ran into Bob Lee. The sheriff gave Chuck a good fright just as he was getting into the Honda Odyssey. He had the door open and was about to step inside when he felt a hand land on his shoulder. Yelping in surprise, he shrugged the hand away and spun around, pressing his back against the frame of the open door. When he saw it was only the rotund lawman, he shuddered in relief and put a hand to his chest to feel the pounding of his heart.

The sheriff apologized for his abrupt departure from the scene earlier and said he wanted to follow up with him on some things. Chuck slid on in behind the wheel of the Odyssey while Lee continued to talk, rattling off several questions in rapid-fire fashion. Though Chuck did his best to maintain a calm exterior, some of the questions made him nervous and set his heart to racing again. The stuff about Lloyd McAfee and their childhood friendship was troublesome. His replies were non-illuminating. There were things from the past he needed to do some serious thinking about before sharing the information with the law.

But what really got to him was when the sheriff started talking about Fawn Hightower. This was so unexpected that it immediately shattered Chuck's outwardly calm exterior. His face flushed and a sweat rose on his brow. He stuttered an evasive reply, saying he didn't actually

59

know Fawn very well and didn't see how his neighbor could possibly be relevant to the investigation. The appraising look Lee gave him as he said this stirred a defensive indignation, causing him to snap at the sheriff for wasting his time with pointless bullshit. That there might be some cause to suspect Fawn's involvement in the break-in didn't matter. The law didn't need to know about his relationship with Fawn yet. Hopefully that would remain the case.

He wound up extricating himself from the uncomfortable situation with yet another made up story, this time about needing to fetch some prescription medicine from the pharmacy for one of his kids, who was ill and in dire need of relief. Sheriff Lee's expression was dubious, and it wasn't hard to understand why. The man had been at his house earlier and had seen his kids, who had been the picture of health at the time. Chuck began to regret his lie almost immediately. Lee's disbelieving expression made his gut twist with worry.

There was nothing he could do about it, though. The lie was already out there. After insisting one more time that he needed to get to the pharmacy and fetch that medicine as soon as possible, he closed the door on the sheriff, started the Odyssey and backed hurriedly out of the parking space. There was a squeal of tires on pavement as another motorist slammed on the brakes to avoid hitting the minivan. Not for the first time that day, Chuck cursed his stupidity, this time for forgetting to check for oncoming traffic. But the damage was done. The look on the sheriff's face as he continued to watch Chuck told him all he needed to know. The lawman couldn't know exactly what was going on with him, but he did know that something wasn't quite right.

Chuck tried to put it out of his mind as he finished backing out of the parking spot, changed gears, and sped away. Once he was on the road and the hotel was just a receding speck in his rearview mirror, he dug his phone out of his pocket and turned it on.

It rang immediately.

He glanced at the screen and saw the picture of Fawn in her lingerie. He answered the call and put the phone to his ear. "We need to talk."

Fawn laughed in that sultry, alluring way she usually saved for when they were in bed together. "We need to do a lot more than just talk, baby. I'm dripping wet for you."

She laughed again, but this time it was more of a schoolgirl giggle.

Chuck sighed. "I don't have time for games, Fawn. I need to know if you had anything to do with the break-in at my house today."

A brief, stunned silence ensued.

This was followed by a heavy exhalation of breath. "Have you lost your mind, Chuck? Why would I do that? And why would I do that thing with the pumpkins? How psycho do you think I am?"

She sounded believably indignant. Chuck sighed in surrender. "All right, all right, I believe you. Never really thought that was your style, anyway." Chuck slowed to a stop at a traffic light. "Look, I'm gonna have to let you go. I just left Karen and the kids at the Embassy Suites downtown. I've got some stuff I need to look into before I head back."

That sultry, alluring laugh returned. "I've got something you could look into. I wasn't lying before, you know. I really am dripping wet for you. I just got out of the shower and I'm sitting naked on the edge of my bed." She paused. "Can you picture that in your head, Chuck?"

Unfortunately for Chuck, he could, as the stirring at his groin proved.

He swallowed thickly and said, "Yeah, I can picture it."

"Russ is out of town again. As usual. We could get together."

Chuck said nothing.

Fawn laughed, the sound somehow softer, silkier, and more seductive than ever. "Or better yet, I'll do the thinking for us. I'm hanging up now. I'll call the usual place and reserve the room. I'll get back in touch with you in about an hour."

Again, Chuck said nothing.

Which said everything.

Fawn ended the call.

After driving around aimlessly for a few more minutes, Chuck pulled into the parking lot of a convenience store, parked in a corner near the road, and used the Internet browser on his phone to look up the name of someone he'd tried hard never to think about. He expected the search to turn up little to no information, but the first result brought up a listing for an Elliot Parker, who apparently was still residing in Willow Springs. Premium access was required for his street address. Chuck paid the nominal fee, saw that the address was in an area generally considered the bad part of town, and programmed it into the Odyssey's GPS.

Some twenty minutes later he pulled into the lot outside a blocky-looking two-story building tucked away behind a strip mall that had fallen on hard times. Many of the shops that had formerly occupied space in the strip mall appeared to have permanently closed, judging by the proliferation of realtor signs in their windows. Chuck felt no small amount of incredulity upon first glimpsing the building behind it, which the reverse lookup service had provided as Elliot Parker's legal residence of record. The gray cinderblock building had a large rollup metal door in front that was currently shut. A short set of steps next to it led to a windowless steel door. The place had a utilitarian, industrial feel to it. It did not seem like the kind of place where anyone would actually live. On the other hand, there were no signs anywhere announcing it as a place of business.

Chuck got out of the Odyssey and did a slow stroll around the building. All the windows on the first floor were blacked out, which was more than a little creepy. The second floor windows did not appear to be blacked out, but it was impossible to see anything through them from the ground, nor was there any way to ascend to the second floor from the outside.

There was another windowless steel door at the back of the building. Chuck took a look around the surrounding area. An old, rust-flecked pickup truck was parked by a Dumpster at the back of the rear lot. Something about it struck a distant note of familiarity, but when he couldn't identify where he'd seen it before—or even if he actually had—he shrugged the feeling off, figuring he'd seen numerous similar trucks before. Its presence here suggested there might be someone he could talk to on the premises, another resident, perhaps, if not Elliot himself.

He circled back to the front of the building and, after a brief hesitation, climbed the steps to the windowless door there and raised a hand to knock. Again, though, he hesitated and turned away from the door to take another look around. The rear of the strip mall was close, separated from this property by a narrow strip of sickly-looking grass. He saw no vehicles parked behind the mall, nor were there any people milling about. Though he could hear traffic from the main road, he had no view of it from this vantage point. All at once, he felt isolated and vulnerable. He wished he'd gone home to get his gun before attempting anything like this.

Chuck lowered his hand, stared at the steel door a moment longer, and then descended the steps back to the parking lot. He got back behind the wheel of the Odyssey and stared through the windshield at the squat little building, drumming his thumbs on the rim of the steering wheel as a burgeoning sense of anxiety continued to build inside him.

He wanted to believe Elliot Parker had nothing to do with Lloyd McAfee's murder or the weirdness with the pumpkins. On the surface, it seemed absurd. Many years had passed since that shameful day in the woods. Almost a lifetime ago, really. Too long, Chuck wanted to believe, for even the bitterest person to harbor a desire for bloody vengeance. So much time had passed, in fact, that the obvious correlations between that long ago incident and today's events didn't occur to him until well after the law had departed the scene at his house. At the time, he'd been too focused on paranoid thoughts about Fawn.

Later, however, a memory of Elliot tied to that tree in the woods with a pumpkin shoved down over his head came to him like a punch to the gut.

Like back then, it was Halloween season. Lloyd McAfee had been the instigator of the whole thing and now he was dead. His severed head had been shoved into a hollowed-out pumpkin. The arrangement of pumpkins on the kitchen table at Chuck's house could easily be seen as a symbolic connection to his involvement in what had been done to Elliot all those years ago.

It all added up, as crazy as it seemed.

Elliot had suffered miserably at the hands of Chuck and his former friends in the distant past, enduring what had undeniably been a severe level of psychological trauma and humiliation. Chuck felt disgust as more details came back to him. The truth about that day was stark and brutal. It hadn't been the usual sort of bullying they'd indulged in so often back then, which had been bad enough. They had tortured that poor kid for hours, had even briefly flirted with the idea of killing him to keep him from blabbing about what they'd done.

Bile rose into Chuck's throat.

He opened the Odyssey's door to lean out and puke on the pavement. When his stomach was done voiding its contents, he wiped his mouth with a shaking hand and leaned back in, settling behind the wheel again. He thought about Elliot. From what he could remember, the kid's parents had been pretty worthless. Elliot had been a smart kid, well above average, really, but life had stacked the deck against him in so many ways. And then there was the matter of his brother, who'd died that same night. As he stared at the sad little building, Chuck found he could imagine someone like Elliot winding up there. It was a fittingly dead-end destination for someone who'd likely lived a sad, dead-end kind of life. He pictured Elliot sitting up there behind those grim, gray walls night after night for years, always alone, stewing in his bitterness until it turned toxic.

Until he finally snapped.

Chuck slapped a palm against the steering wheel. "Fuck!"

The smart thing now would be to ring up that obnoxious hillbilly sheriff and tell him everything he knew about Elliot Parker. He picked up his phone and removed a card from his shirt pocket. It was the sheriff's business card. The man had passed it off to him immediately prior to his abrupt departure from the scene earlier in the day. The number printed on the front was his personal cell number. Chuck got as far as inputting the first three digits before he deleted them.

He cursed again and kicked at the floorboard.

The thing about telling the sheriff what he knew was that it would include talking about what he and his friends had done to Elliot twenty-five years ago. He dreaded doing that for many reasons, not the least of which was picturing the look of disgust on his wife's face when she inevitably heard all about it. And what of his kids? He'd tried so hard to be a good man since those wayward early years, had tried so hard to be a good father and good example to his children. What would they think of him now? It pained him to imagine it. On top of the situation with Fawn, it felt like too much. The beautiful life he'd built was already tottering on the brink of ruin. This might be just the last nudge necessary to blow it all apart forever.

His phone's text alert sounded.

He looked at the screen and saw the picture of Fawn in her lingerie. He tapped it and read the message. As promised, she'd reserved a room at the usual place.

She was already in route.

Chuck stared at the message a full minute before typing his response: *Be there soon.*

He needed a break, that's all. A quick romp with Fawn could be just what he needed to clear his head and figure out how to handle the situation. Part of him knew he was just rationalizing what he was about to do. By seeing Fawn he was surrendering to his baser instincts in a moment of high stress, an act that exhibited weakness rather than strength. And he was yet again betraying everything that really mattered in his life. But he simply couldn't help it. Fawn would make him feel good. And, at least for a short while, he could forget all about the things troubling him. Tomorrow would be different. He would be a man and deal with the Elliot situation head-on by telling the sheriff an edited version of the truth, one calculated to cast him in a somewhat less damning light.

But that could wait.

It could *all* wait just a little bit longer.

Chuck started up the Odyssey and drove away from Elliot Parker's home.

12

Five days until Halloween
Near Nashville, TN

Gabriella Nofzinger was just under fifteen miles outside Nashville when her late 90's Chevrolet Caprice died on her. A high school graduation gift from her parents a few years back, the dark green Caprice was still the only car she'd ever owned. In all that time, she'd had only the most minor issues with it. Never once had she experienced engine trouble of this magnitude.

The first sign of something wrong came in the form of a slight sputter. She frowned when she felt it, surprised because until then the Caprice had been humming along smoothly, just like always. When several uneventful moments passed, she shrugged the sputter off as a meaningless anomaly and turned up the volume on the radio. Seconds later she heard a loud bang from somewhere beneath the hood. After that, the car started sputtering and jerking nonstop. She just managed to get the Caprice pulled over to the side of the road before the engine quit completely.

Gabriella was in shock. At first she was simply unable to believe what had happened, such was her faith in the invincibility of her car. A part of her had been sure it would run forever. But now, in the space of just a few moments, that illusion had been shattered. Never having been in this situation before, she had no idea how to handle it. She wished she had someone with her to tell her what to do.

Once that first moment of stunned disbelief passed, she turned the key in the ignition. The car did not start, nor did the engine sound like it was trying to turn over. There was only a flat, dead click when she turned the key. This was disheartening, but it was what she'd expected. That big bang she'd heard was something bad. She knew little about the inner workings of automobiles, but she knew that. The Caprice wouldn't run again until a mechanic had done some serious work on it.

Okay, so next step.

She grabbed her purse from the passenger seat and took out her cell phone. There were several people she could call. Her father would definitely know what to do, but she didn't want to talk to him. He would want to know why she was headed out to Nashville at half past midnight. The truth, that she was meeting up with her friends Jodi and Alysha to do some late night clubbing, would earn her a lecture. The old man didn't care for her partying ways, believing she needed to be more serious and focus on her studies at the university. Which was grief she didn't need right now.

She tried to call Jodi instead. Her friends weren't that far away. They could just come get her. But when she pulled up the number from her contacts and put the phone to her ear, the call didn't go through. Frowning, she looked at the screen and saw the words "no service" in the left-hand corner. That was just as unusual as the death of her car. She wasn't out in the fucking boonies. There should be a damn signal. Apparently, though, this was her night for all things mechanical to quit on her.

Before she could let out a scream of impotent rage, bright illumination filled the interior of her car. A glance at her rearview mirror showed headlights directly behind her. Someone had pulled off the road to check on her, apparently. The glare from the headlights was such that it made discerning anything other than the vaguest outline of the other car impossible. She hoped it was a police cruiser. This seemed the most likely possibility, but the lack of flashing blue lights made her unsure.

Squinting at the rearview mirror, she caught a glimpse of shadowy movement and realized someone was getting out of the other car. This was confirmed a moment later by the sound of a door closing with an emphatic thunk. She glanced at her side mirror and saw a tall, slender form approaching. The headlights of a passing vehicle briefly lit up the side of the road, giving her a better look. What she saw was a man in a black trench coat with pale skin and a wedge of thick, jet-black hair fashioned in a way that made him look like a rockabilly singer at the tail end of a long bender.

Whoever he was, the stranger definitely wasn't a cop. Upon realizing this, Gabriella felt a twinge of instinctive wariness. But she was optimistic by nature. She had a deep faith in the basic decency of most people. Of course, she knew there were bad people in the world, but she believed they constituted a tiny minority. This guy had stopped for a simple reason—he'd spotted a fellow motorist in distress and was merely doing his duty as a good citizen.

There was nothing to worry about.

He reached her driver's side door and rapped a knuckle against the window. Gabriella pressed the button to lower it. The only result was a faint click. She felt silly. With the engine dead, of course the power windows were non-functional. Shaking her head, she cracked the door open.

"Hi there! Boy, am I glad you came along."

The tall man nodded. "Having trouble?"

"My car died." She arched an eyebrow and made her smile extra flirty. "I don't guess there's any chance you're an ace mechanic, are you?"

"Afraid not. But I could give you a ride to wherever you're

going."

Gabriella's eyes widened in delight. "Oh, that would be awesome! Thank you so much. You're an angel...what's your name?"

"Steve."

"Pleased to meet you, Steve. I'm Gabriella."

"Hi."

Gabriella grabbed her purse and keys and stepped out of the Caprice. Steve sidestepped away from her as she emerged from the vehicle. She got the sense he was nervous around girls, particularly attractive ones. He looked like he was somewhere in early middle age, which made the skittishness a little strange. It made her feel sorry for him. She decided she would have to do something nice for him before they parted ways. A big kiss on the mouth would give him something sweet to remember her by. If he'd been better looking, she might have been up for even more than that.

She smiled again. "Thank you again. You really don't know how grateful I am."

He nodded. "Okay."

They walked over to his car and Steve opened the passenger side door for her, holding it open in a display of old-fashioned chivalry as she slid inside. She flashed him another high-wattage smile as he eased the door shut. "Such a gentleman."

Steve ignored this and circled around to the other side of the car. After settling in behind the wheel and checking his mirrors, he pulled out into traffic and rapidly accelerated.

He stared straight ahead as he said, "Where are we going?"

"I was on my way to see my friends Jodi and Alysha. They have a rental house in Hillsboro Village. Do you know where that is?"

"Nashville. Near Vanderbilt University, right?"

Gabriella nodded. "Right by Vanderbilt, actually. Have you been there before?"

"Once or twice." He nodded at a device mounted on the dash of his Honda Civic. "Put their address in the GPS. It'll make getting there easier."

"Good idea."

Gabriella turned the device on its swivel stand so that the screen was facing her. "You really are a godsend, Steve. You just have no idea." She entered the address, glancing at him when she was done. "It was the weirdest thing. First my car quit on me, then my phone had no service. I thought the universe was conspiring against me."

Steve made a soft sound that might have been a low chuckle.

He said nothing.

After a couple miles rolled by in absolute silence, Gabriella began to feel uncomfortable. She had a low tolerance for conversational lulls in general. Being in an enclosed space with a total stranger made the restlessness she felt in such moments worse than usual.

"So, Steve...tell me about yourself. Do you live in Nashville?"

He shook his head. "No."

Gabriella frowned when he failed to elaborate. "Well, where *are* you from?"

She saw his hands clench tighter around the steering wheel. Only then did she begin to sense the depth of the tension gripping him. It triggered her first real feelings of trepidation. Again, however, she chose to brush them aside, reminding herself that some people—especially obviously shy people, like Steve—were as uncomfortable with small talk as she was with conversational lulls.

In a few moments, though, he relaxed his grip and said, "Nowhere that matters."

Gabriella laughed. "That's a strange answer."

He glanced at her for the first time since pulling into traffic. "I'm a strange person."

Gabriella laughed again, but this time there was a nervous quality to it. "We're all a little strange, I guess."

He nodded. "Some more than others."

Another awkward silence ensued.

Gabriella decided she was done prodding him. She slumped down in her seat, getting comfortable as she stretched her legs out beneath the dash. When she did this, she glanced again at Steve. She had good legs and was wearing a very small party dress. Though she wasn't at all attracted to him, she nonetheless felt a mild pang of disappointment when he didn't sneak a look at them. She wondered if maybe he just didn't like girls, but quickly decided that probably wasn't the case. Otherwise that nervousness she'd sensed when she was close to him wouldn't have been there.

She was still stewing over this when she happened to look at the tray beneath the radio. A strange device with a blipping red dot in front was plugged into the cigarette lighter slot. "Hey, Steve?"

He sighed. "Yeah?"

She pointed at the device. "What's that thing? Some kind of radar detector?"

He didn't look at it, but somehow he knew what she was talking about. "That's a cell phone jammer."

She frowned at the matter-of-fact tone he used when telling her this. A full minute passed in silence as she stared at the device and thought about the strange revelation. She remembered seeing the words "no service" in the corner of her phone's screen. At the time, it hadn't struck her as sinister. Outages were a pain in the ass, but they happened. But here was this guy who, frankly, was a weirdo, and he was driving around with a cell phone jammer.

Who did that?

And why?

Gabriella shifted in her seat again, sitting up straighter. The Civic's headlights picked out a green exit sign just ahead. She glanced to her right and saw a cluster of lights nearby. There would probably be gas stations and fast food restaurants just off the exit. And people, even at this late hour. People and lights meant a greater likelihood of safety.

She looked at Steve. "Can we pull off here? I have to pee."

Steve hit the blinker switch.

Per usual, he didn't say anything.

But Gabriella didn't care this time. All that mattered now was getting out of this deeply strange man's car as soon as possible. She had no intention of ever getting back inside it. Wherever they stopped, she would beg the clerk to let her use the store phone. The only question was who would she call first—her friends or the police? The latter option seemed the wisest way to go. She no longer had any doubts about this guy being some kind of creep. She didn't know what he was up to, but it couldn't be anything good. As the realization hit her full force, she cursed her trusting nature. She tried hard not to tremble or otherwise let her deepening anxiety become obvious.

Steve pulled off the highway and guided the Civic down the curving exit ramp at a leisurely pace, showing no signs of having sensed the change in her mood. He remained silent as he came to a stop where the end of the ramp met a two-lane road. There were cars coming from either direction, two from the left and one from the right. The other vehicles were too close to risk pulling out onto the road. The cluster of lights Gabriella had glimpsed from the highway were off to the left. She glanced that way and saw the brightly-lit parking lots of two convenience stores and a Wendy's restaurant. To her right was a winding stretch of road that curved away into darkness. Under ordinary circumstances, a turn to the left would be the obvious choice, but she didn't trust Steve not to go the other way, carrying her off into the dark unknown.

The converging vehicles had almost reached the ramp. They would pass by within seconds and then Steve would be able to pull out onto the road. Acting on impulse, Gabriella grabbed the door handle on her side and yanked on it, popping the door open. Before she could shove it fully open and climb out of the car, though, Steve seized her by a wrist and twisted in his seat. She screamed as the three oncoming cars reached the interstate junction and zipped by the ramp. Something slammed into her jaw in the next instant, stunning her and rendering her instantly woozy. As Steve leaned over her to pull the door shut, she belatedly realized he'd punched her in the face as hard as he could. Her earlier impression of him as sweetly shy and chivalrous now seemed like a sick joke. He was actually some kind of psycho who'd been putting on an act.

With the door shut again, Steve hit the gas and turned right. The Civic's engine revved as he kept his foot down on the gas pedal for several seconds. The lights of the stores in the other direction fell away as the car disappeared down that dark stretch of road. After a few moments, some of the initial wooziness faded and Gabriella took a look around at the dark trees zipping by on either side.

Then she looked at Steve and said, "You hurt me."

He didn't say anything.

Stealing a glance at the speedometer, Gabriella weighed the advisability of opening the door again and rolling out of the speeding vehicle. They were currently going well in excess of 60 MPH, which she was pretty sure was way above the posted speed limit for this kind of secondary road. Then again, Steve didn't strike her as a guy with much respect for the rule of law.

She sniffled, her terror level suddenly spiking. "Let me out. Please. You don't need to hurt me."

There was a loud, ear-piercing squeal as Steve stomped down on the brake pedal and the Civic skidded to a stop at the side of the road. He turned his sharply angular profile in her direction. His face looked ghostly pale in the moonlight shining through the windshield. "Oh, you're getting out, don't you worry about that."

Before she could say anything or otherwise react, he threw his door open, got out of the car, and hurried around to the other side. He was almost to the passenger side door when she noticed the keys still dangling from the ignition. The engine was still running, too.

Again acting on impulse and fueled by a burst of panic-driven adrenaline, Gabriella surged out of her seat and into the driver's seat. She felt a short-lived thrill of triumph. In another second, she'd be on her way, leaving the strange creep standing bewildered in the middle of the road while his intended victim sped away in his car. In her haste, however, her knee bumped the gearshift lever. The car was already rolling before she could settle in behind the wheel. She shrieked in panic as the Civic left the shoulder of the road and slid into a deep ditch clogged with fallen autumn leaves, where it stalled out.

She wrenched the gearshift over to park and cranked the key in the ignition. Nothing happened, which made her think of her poor dead Caprice. She wondered if Steve had something to do with its demise. She'd stopped at a gas station to refuel several miles ahead of where she'd first started experiencing engine trouble. Maybe Steve had spotted her there and done something to the engine while she was in the store using the bathroom. She didn't remember seeing him or his Civic there, but that didn't mean anything. He had jammed her cell phone, hadn't he? And he'd shown he was a violent predator. It stood to reason he was behind everything else that had happened.

These thoughts flashed through her head within seconds. She kept cranking the key in the ignition the whole time. On the third try, the engine sputtered to life and she reached for the gearshift again. But before she could put the car in reverse, Steve pulled the door open and hauled her out of it, throwing her down into a pile of wet leaves.

She shrieked and spluttered as she twice tried to get to her feet and start running, but she fell each time. Before she could make a third attempt, Steve seized her by an arm, jerked her upright, and slugged her in the face again. Once again, everything turned fuzzy. She was dimly aware of being dragged away from the road and into the woods. By the time the world swam back into focus, they had emerged into a small open space, where Steve threw her down on the ground.

Gabriella cried out in pain as he planted a booted foot on her stomach and pinned her there. She stared up at his lean, tall form. He looked like a ghoul limned in the moonlight. As she began to beg for her life, Steve opened his trench coat, reached inside, and took a meat cleaver from an inner pocket. Its sharp blade was coated in dried blood.

She shook her head. "No. No, no, no."

Steve lowered himself to her, straddling her body and pinning her arms beneath his legs. He raised the meat cleaver high above his head.

"Steve, please, you don't have to do this. I'll do anything."

He nodded. "I know you would, Susan. That's why you deserve this."

His use of another girl's name momentarily distracted Gabriella from her terror. "What? Who's Susan? That's not my name. Please, you've mistaken me for somebody else."

He shook his head. "No, I haven't. I know exactly who you are. You're number four."

Gabriella opened her mouth to scream again as the cleaver began its merciless descent. The blade punched into her neck. The scream gave way to a low, desperate burble as her throat filled with blood. Her killer held the blade there a moment, watching the contortions of her face. Then he yanked it out and a spray of blood leaped from the wound, spattering his trench coat and the front of his shirt. Her consciousness started to fade as she watched him raise the cleaver again, adjust his aim, and bring it down again. This time the blade chopped deep into the center of her face.

The killer got up and walked away as Gabriella died.

In a few moments, he returned carrying a pumpkin.

13

Alysha Cummings peeled off her slinky black dress as she came out of the bathroom. She tossed the scrap of shimmery fabric on her bed and reached for her bra clasp. Before she could unhook it, she sucked in a breath as she felt someone press something hard against the back of her head. The person behind her had slipped into the room with impressive stealth, making nary a sound.

She trembled. "Please don't hurt me."

The hard object pressed a little more firmly against the back of her head. "Stop your sniveling, whore. Take off that bra."

Alysha's fingers were still on the clasp. They continued to tremble as she unhooked the bra and tossed it on the bed, where it landed atop the shimmery black dress.

"Good girl. Keep doing as you're told and maybe I won't have to hurt you." A cruel-sounding laugh followed this statement. "Now turn around and get down on your fucking knees."

Shaking harder now, Alysha crossed her arms over her bare breasts and turned around until she saw the black barrel pointing straight at her face.

"Drop your arms. I want to see those sweet titties."

Alysha did as instructed.

"Nice. I told you to get down on your knees. Don't make me

say it again, bitch."

Alysha dropped to her knees. "Why are you doing this?" she asked, a slight quaver coming into her voice. "I thought we were friends."

"That's what you get for thinking, whore. Open your mouth."

Alysha obeyed and the hard black cylinder slid between her lips, which were still painted with the cherry red lipstick she'd applied in anticipation of a night of clubbing. But things hadn't gone as planned and now this was happening. She felt weird about it, but only a little, not nearly as much as the first few times.

"Now close those pretty lips and suck that barrel like a cock."

Alysha closed her mouth and felt the plastic sight of the toy gun scrape the roof of her mouth while she mimed fellatio. She made some orgasmic noises that were only partly faked. The bizarre scenario was having the usual effect. Despite the underlying weirdness, she was getting turned on.

Jodi McIntyre took the toy gun from Alysha's mouth. They'd purchased the cheap children's toy during a recent excursion to a chintzy flea market. Its original color had been bright green, but Jodi had painted it black to heighten the realism factor in their roleplaying.

She pressed the plastic barrel against Alysha's forehead. "Up on the bed, bitch. And be quick about it or I'll blow your fucking brains out."

Alysha felt a smile tremble at the edges of her mouth, but she quickly suppressed it and tried hard to maintain her look of fake terror as she got to her feet and did as Jodi said. She pushed pillows out of the way and stretched out flat on her back, trembling and pleading for mercy. Her friend, currently playing the role of Psychotic Lesbian Home Invader, nodded in leering approval.

Jodi was wearing only a blue men's button-down shirt, unbuttoned. It was long on her, the shirttail hitting at mid-thigh. She shrugged it off and let it fall to the floor. Alysha's arousal increased at the sight of her friend's bare breasts, which were

76

larger than hers with wide pink areolas and thick, jutting nipples. Her excitement level continued to increase as Jodi climbed up on the bed and again aimed the toy gun at Alysha's face.

"You're gonna do whatever I want, you hear me? Nod if you understand."

Alysha nodded. "Please don't hurt me."

Jodi smirked. "I promise nothing."

She positioned herself over Alysha, planting her feet to either side of her head. The she lowered herself to her, pressing her clit against her mouth. She tossed her head back and started moaning as Alysha began to flick her tongue. Alysha gripped her friend's smooth thighs and lifted her head a little to probe at her pussy more effectively. She'd never performed oral sex on another woman until just over a month ago, when these twisted roleplaying sessions began after a long night of rolling on X and downing a massive amount of vodka. But she'd gotten good at it quickly and had come to enjoy it far more than going down on men.

Just as they were really getting into it, a loud crash from elsewhere in the room startled them. Jodi rolled away from Alysha, both of them screaming as the closet's accordion-style door exploded outward. A man clad all in black and wearing a ski mask came charging out of that dark space, trailing an array of colorful garments. He nearly tripped over the clothes multiple times before kicking free of them to stand panting in the middle of the room.

A long-handled axe was clutched in his gloved right hand. The girls screamed again as he brandished it at them. "Shut up. Just…shut up, you, uh…you fucking…"

The women stared at the masked man as he lapsed into awkward silence.

Jodi groaned in disgust. "The word you're looking for is 'whores'. How many times did we go over this?" She got up off the bed and snatched the foam prop axe from the man's hand. He cringed away from her as she swatted him upside the head with it several times, chasing him toward the open bedroom door, where she abruptly ceased the assault. "Jesus, you suck at this. You know that?"

The man pulled off the ski mask, revealing a handsome face and a mop of bushy brown hair. "I'm sorry. Jesus. This playacting stuff just isn't my thing. Can't we just have a good old uncomplicated threesome?"

Alysha giggled.

Jodi rolled her eyes. "Like there's any such thing as that, you unimaginative asshole. Go get us some beers, Tod. Hurry your ass or we won't let you play with us anymore."

Tod disappeared back down the hallway without another word.

Alysha laughed as Jodi rejoined her on the bed. "Did you see how fast he moved? You've sure got him trained well."

Jodi smirked. "It's easy when they're stupid."

Alysha glanced at the open door and saw that it was still empty. Tod was probably still out in the kitchen, well out of hearing range. "He really is stupid, isn't he?"

Jodi plucked at one of Alysha's nipples with her thumb and forefinger, eliciting a pained gasp. "They're all stupid. The only reason men run so many things is because we let them. They're our slaves without even realizing it."

Alysha winced as Jodi plucked at the same nipple again. "That hurts."

"Good."

Jodi did it again, pinching harder than before.

Alysha frowned. "Jodi, seriously. You're really hurting me."

Jodi smiled. "I *know* I'm hurting you, bitch. I'm taking you against your will, remember? I can do whatever I want to you."

Alysha gripped Jodi's wrist and pried her hand away from her breast. "When I tell you you're hurting me and I'm clearly not playing along, you need to stop."

Jodi smirked. "Oh, yeah?"

"Yeah."

"Drawing a line, are you?"

Alysha started to pull away from Jodi. "Fuck it. I'm not in the mood anymore."

Jodi grabbed her by a wrist, stopping her. "This is about Gabriella, isn't it? You're usually up for getting as wild as possible. But you're distracted."

Alysha sighed, speaking softly as she said, "Yeah. I'm really worried about her."

Jodi let go of her wrist. "Sorry for getting rough. I'm worried about her, too."

Much of the day had been spent in anticipation of their friend's arrival from out of town. Gabby lived about an hour out of the city and came out to visit only a couple times a month. The three had been friends for years, dating back to an initial fresh-out-of-high school stint at a local university, where they met while living in the same dormitory. The three remained close and still hung out whenever possible. Alysha and Jodi had been trying to talk Gabby into moving in with them for the longest time. Gabby had resisted because of family and money issues, but just lately it'd started to seem like she was coming around to the idea, probably because they had offered to cut her a deal on the rent. It would be worth it just to have their friend around all the time again.

Gabby hadn't said yes yet, but Alysha and Jodi were cautiously optimistic. They'd been prepared to seal the deal once and for all by showing her the time of her life tonight. In anticipation of being up until at least the break of dawn, they'd done some cocaine. Jodi had snorted up considerably more of it than Alysha, who liked coke but didn't want to get too carried away too early.

But the party mood wilted as hours passed with no sign of Gabby. She'd called ahead to let them know she was on her way more than three hours ago, but had been out of touch ever since. They called and texted her multiple times. Each time there was no response. During that first hour of no contact, they weren't really worried. Their friend was late, but they could easily imagine legitimate, non-scary reasons for the delay. Gabby was a bit flighty, to put it kindly, prone to wander and get distracted. Maybe she'd stopped off to see some other friends on the way.

Another hour later, they gave up waiting for her and dove back into the cocaine. And, again, Jodi indulged more than Alysha. Gabby's failure to show up negated their interest in a night of clubbing, but the girls decided they would have a different kind of fun instead. So they called up Tod, proposed a drug-fueled kinky threesome, and here they were.

Only now even this wasn't as much fun as usual.

The whole night felt tainted.

Jodi said, "She's probably okay. You know how she is."

Alysha grabbed one of the pillows she'd pushed aside and wedged it under her head. This made it easier to look Jodi in the eye while they were talking. "I know she flakes out sometimes, but this is different. You know it is. She always eventually lets us know what's going on, even if it's just a simple text saying she'll fill us in later. This whole completely off the radar thing bugs me, especially when we know for a fact she was in her car and headed our way three hours ago." She frowned. "I'm really kind of scared, actually."

Jodi's brow furrowed as she thought about it. "I guess I kind of am, too, but there's not much we can do."

"We could call 911."

"And say what exactly? That our friend has been out of contact for a few hours? They're not gonna take that seriously. I guess we could try calling her parents and see if they've heard anything."

Alysha grimaced. "In the dead of night? They probably wouldn't answer. Even if they did, we'd scare the hell out of them, maybe for no good reason."

"Right," Jodi said, nodding. "This is what I'm trying to tell you. The situation sucks, but like it or not, we're stuck for anything to do about it right now. Look, we'll wait until daylight and then if we still haven't heard from Gabby, we'll call her parents. They can take it from there. How's that sound?"

Alysha sighed. "I guess it really is all we can do."

Jodi smiled. She climbed atop Alysha, straddling her again. "Well, it's not *all* we can do. We can play some more. Come on, it'll take our minds off it."

A resumption of the roleplaying game no longer bothered Alysha. Taking a few moments to talk the situation out had eased her mind enough to focus on the moment at hand rather than on things out of her control. She was reaching for Jodi's breasts when she glimpsed a flicker of movement from the direction of the doorway. The movement occurred at the outer periphery of her partially blocked vision. She might not have noticed it at all if she hadn't wedged the pillow under her head.

She raised her head off the pillow now and craned it as far she could to the left in order to see around Jodi. The man standing just inside the bedroom doorway met her gaze. His dark brown eyes were all she could see of his face, the rest of which was obscured by a ski mask. Clutched in his gloved right hand was an axe. He held it by the handle at his waist, with the head of the axe touching the carpeted floor. Her first thought was that Tod had donned his mask again and was ready to get back in the spirit of things.

But Tod's eyes were a piercing, brilliant blue, not brown. Nor had he been wearing a trench coat. Also, this man was thinner than Tod and taller by about a head.

The man raised the axe off the floor and stepped toward the bed.

Alysha screamed.

Jodi twisted her head around and saw the stranger approaching. She chuckled when she saw him, not immediately discerning the differences between this man and their friend. "Oh, hi, Tod. Ready to play again, I see. You forgot our beers, asshole." Her head swiveled back toward Alysha, her face twisting in a smirk. "Boy has the attention span of a magpie. Good thing he has a big dick. Otherwise he'd be useless."

Alysha screamed again. She tried to push Jodi away from her, but the bigger woman once again failed to budge. The masked man had reached the bed. He raised the axe higher and in a moment swung it around in a lethally smooth, powerful arc. An oblivious Jodi was still smiling when the blade punched into the side of her neck and took her head right off her shoulders. The blow was delivered with enough force to send the severed head flying through the air until it smacked against a window blind and fell with a heavy thump to the floor. It left a bloody smear on the blind, but Alysha didn't see this because of the massive amount of blood erupting from Jodi's neck stump. The first geyser of gore leapt high enough to spatter the ceiling. Much more of it hit Alysha right in the face as Jodi's now headless torso toppled toward. She spluttered as blood filled her mouth and was temporarily blinded as more of it coated her eyes.

She coughed several times to clear her throat and mewled in terror as she felt the man haul Jodi's corpse away from her and fling it to the floor. Still blind from the gore in her eyes, she rolled to her right, narrowly escaping impalement as the heavy head of the axe slammed into the mattress. She rolled over the side of the bed and dropped painfully to the floor as the axe-wielding maniac shrieked in frustration and ripped his weapon from the perforated mattress.

Alysha swiped furiously at her eyes, partially restoring a level of blurry vision that allowed her to scuttle away from the bed on her hands and knees. Even in the grip of gut-twisting terror, she knew this wouldn't be an effective way out of her predicament. She needed to get to her feet and start running. When she got to the door, she reached up and grabbed the doorknob, intending to haul herself up and do just that. Once again, however, she was saved by primitive instinct. There was no conscious thought involved, just an overpowering sense of imminent death bearing down on her from behind. She ducked her head just in time to avoid decapitation. The blade of the axe slammed into the door, punching all the way through the wood.

Another scream of murderous frustration rang out as Alysha finally regained her feet and took off running down the hallway. The house wasn't a large one and she made it to the kitchen within seconds. Tod was on the floor near the open back door. He was flat on his back, his dead eyes open and staring blankly at the ceiling above. A big carving knife had been rammed into his open mouth up to the hilt. The tip of it had exited through the back of his neck and was embedded in the wood floor.

Alysha heard a crack of splintering wood as the madman tore the axe free of the door. Then his footsteps came thundering down the hallway.

Still naked, Alysha leapt over Tod's body and ran for the door. In another moment, she was outside and headed for the street. Hope bloomed inside her and she began to laugh in hysterical relief at her narrow escape. She would be okay now. This was the city. Even in the wee hours, there were people and cars around. Headlights, multiple sets of them, were headed this way. Tears spilled down her cheeks as she walked out into the middle of the street and awaited salvation.

I'm saved, she thought. *Saved. Thank you, Jesus. Thank you.*

She was still thinking this when the blade of the axe ripped into her spine, severing it as the force of the blow briefly lifted her off the ground. Alysha felt nothing from the waist down as the killer guided her body to the pavement, planted a booted foot on her ass, and wrenched the head of the axe out of her back.

The last thing Alysha heard before she died was the sound of the axe blade scraping across asphalt as the winded killer retreated from the scene, dragging his weapon with him.

14

Nine years ago
Willow Springs, TN

The season he dreaded had come around again. This time the anxiety it always triggered was worse than ever. He was tired all the time from sleepless nights and his job performance was suffering. Just the other day he'd received a reprimand for falling asleep at his desk. He was told a repeat of the incident would result in his immediate termination. This scared him badly. He had no savings and needed the weekly income just to keep a roof over his head, but these practical concerns were overshadowed by his mental health issues. And what little sleep he *was* getting was plagued by disconcertingly vivid bad dreams.

In most of the dreams, he was back in the woods on that long ago night, alone in the dark after the departure of the bullies. He was crying, a result of his extreme level of physical discomfort and the humiliation he'd endured. The knotted ropes binding him to the tree were too tight, cutting off his circulation. Stinky dog shit was smeared all over his torso. His eyes were still stinging from the many squirts of vinegar-laced water. Slimy earthworms were crawling around in his underwear. He could still taste the worms he'd been forced to eat. And then there was the pumpkin shoved down over his head. He felt like he was suffocating inside it. It all felt so real, like it was still happening. But there were some differences. In the dreams, Chuck Everly never returned to set him free.

In the dreams, he knew he would never leave those woods. He was in hell, a sinner condemned to spend all eternity tied to that tree, forever re-experiencing all the worst things about the most miserable night of his life.

Elliot decided he couldn't take much more of the nightly torture. A trip to his therapist became a necessity. He'd made the appointment the day of the work reprimand and now here he was, feeling awkward in a waiting room at the building where his shrink had her office. He sat slumped down in an uncomfortable chair in a corner of the room, lanky legs stretched out in front of him, hands shoved into the pockets of his trench coat. He kept his head down and refused to look at anyone else in the room. Interacting with strangers was something he avoided whenever possible.

His therapist shared a floor in this building with several partners. An unavoidable consequence of this was that the waiting room was always a crowded place. Several people waiting with him were kindred spirits of a sort, psychologically damaged misfits desperately seeking some kind of relief from the things that troubled them. He didn't have to look them in the eye to know that. Most arrived alone, kept to themselves, and didn't say anything. Just like him.

But then there were the others, a disparate assortment of people from all walks of life. Men in expensive-looking business suits and their blue collar counterparts, harried young mothers with obnoxious children in tow, elderly people with canes and walkers, and virtually every other type in between. They were black, white, brown, whatever. Mental health issues crossed all cultural borders, it seemed. The worst were the garrulous types, the perpetually grinning, overbearing assholes who couldn't resist chatting up strangers. Elliot Parker resolutely ignored them all, even on the rare occasions when they tried to engage him.

He got called rude a lot.

He didn't care. They didn't—and never could—understand.

But on this day, as he waited, he sensed someone staring at him intently. Against his better judgment, he looked up from the floor and saw a moderately attractive young woman seated directly across from him. She had long, curly blonde hair and blue eyes. She was dressed somewhat frumpily, in loose sweatpants and a black hoodie too big for her. Elliot guessed it belonged to a boyfriend. If she had a boyfriend, though, he was elsewhere today. She was alone.

When he met her gaze, she smiled.

The smile had an immediately damaging effect on him, melting a bit of the permafrost around his heart. He felt his cheeks flush and a rare smile trembled at the edges of his mouth.

Then she put the ball of a thumb against the tip of her nose and pushed it upward.

Elliot quickly looked away, his cheeks flushing redder.

I get it, he thought. *I'm a pig. You bitch. This is what I get for daring to believe someone might be nice to me.*

The woman made a barely audible oinking sound.

A nearly overpowering urge to flee the waiting room and skip his appointment came over Elliot. He was on the verge of getting to his feet to do just that when the door to the right of the receptionist's desk opened and a woman with a clipboard appeared in the doorway.

"Elliot Parker?"

There was another moment during which Elliot hovered on the brink of making a run for the exit, but in the end he got up and headed in for his appointment. What swayed him was a combination of the direness of his seasonal depression and a desire not to give the hateful young woman the satisfaction of seeing him run.

He heard her make another of those oinking sounds as he followed the woman with the clipboard through the open door. This time she raised her voice enough for everyone to hear.

Elliot's hands clenched into fists in the pockets of his trench coat as he trailed the assistant down the hallway. He imagined stabbing the bitch in the waiting room with a big knife, some kind of hunting knife or kitchen carving knife.

Moments later, he was seated in a chair opposite the desk in his therapist's small office, a place he'd visited so often over the last few years it was nearly as familiar to him as his own apartment. Nothing of significance in it had ever changed. The muted beige color of the walls, the diplomas and pictures mounted on the wall behind the desk, and the bland furnishings and art prints had all been the same since day one. Elliot figured this was to avoid upsetting her more fragile clients, the ones terrified or intimidated by change of any kind.

His therapist looked relaxed in the leather chair behind the desk, smiling and leaning back with her hands steepled above her bosom. Her name was Lillian Rosewater. She was a stylish and attractive woman in early middle age. As always, her hair, nails, and makeup looked perfect. He couldn't see her legs behind the desk, but he thought there was a good chance she was wearing the shiny high-heeled red boots he liked. She always wore them with this particular outfit.

Elliot always rushed home to masturbate after his sessions with Lillian. He often wondered if she was aware of the effect she had on her male clients.

Probably.

"What's troubling you, Elliot?"

He sighed and shifted in his seat. "The usual. Halloween's almost here and--"

"I don't mean that," she said, shaking her head as she cut him off. "There's something else bothering you. Am I right? Something more…immediate."

Elliot hesitated only a moment before telling her about the woman in the waiting room. He didn't want to talk about the incident. It was embarrassing. It made him feel small and worthless, the way things like that always did. But Lillian was the one person in the world with whom he'd always been completely honest.

Well...*almost* completely honest.

Lillian let out a sad-sounding sigh as he finished relating the story. "How did this make you feel?"

Elliot scowled. "How do you think? Bad. It made me feel really fucking bad."

Lillian nodded. "You understand that this young woman is not representative of all women, correct?"

Elliot shrugged. "I guess."

"You *do* understand that, I hope."

Elliot sighed. "Sure."

"What you experienced just now had nothing to do with you. Not really. I don't know the young lady in question. From your description, I don't believe she's a client of mine. But I'd hazard a guess that what she did is a manifestation of her own issues and insecurities. She's projecting, turning some of her own hurt outward. Again, it had nothing to do with you." She smiled. "Say it for me, Elliot."

"It had nothing to do with me."

Elliot thought it was just as likely the girl was simply a mean person who derived pleasure from hurting other people. He'd encountered more than his fair share of similar individuals throughout the course of his lonely and troubled existence. It was nothing more complicated than cruelty perpetrated for the sake of it. But Elliot had no interest in arguing the point with his therapist and thus had managed to fake a believable level of sincerity when parroting her assertion.

Lillian nodded, seemingly satisfied. "Excellent. Now then, back to the reason for your visit today. I believe you were saying the seasonal issues have recurred."

"Yeah."

She stared at him a long moment before replying. He knew

what she was doing. She was taking stock of him, assessing his mood based on the palpable despondency in his voice, his haggard expression, and even his posture. Lillian Rosewater wasn't his first therapist. He'd seen many in the years since his brother's death. Long experience had taught him much about their techniques, enough that he'd long ago become cynical about the whole process. But a good therapist—a really sensitive and intuitive one—could sometimes pull him out of the darkness. And Lillian was a good therapist, maybe the best he'd ever had. She might well be the only person capable of pulling him back from the brink this time.

"Are you having bad dreams?"

Elliot nodded. "Yes."

"How often?"

"Often. Whenever I sleep." He grunted. "Mostly I try *not* to sleep."

Lillian frowned. "That's not good. Tell me about the dreams. And about any other adverse effects the season is having on you."

Elliot sat up straighter in his chair, took a deep breath, and launched into a detailed description of the dreams, taking care to emphasize how achingly vivid they were. He told her he felt like a part of him was still trapped in those woods and would never get out. Tears came as he said this. He hated himself for it, feeling ashamed at the display of weakness, but he was incapable of holding them back. The feelings had been contained too long. Tears gave way to sobs and at times he lapsed into silence as he struggled to regain his composure. Lillian passed him tissues. Her features conveyed only sympathy and concern. Seeing it made him feel worse. There was no one else in his life to whom he could say these painful things. The only person who would listen to him he paid for the privilege. As usual, recognizing this made him feel even worse.

At last, he managed to finish telling her about the dreams and how they made him feel. He then told her about the incident at work and the terror he felt at possibly being out of a job soon.

"Would you say the season is having a worse effect on you this year than in recent years?"

Elliot grunted humorless laughter. "That's an understatement. This is the worst it's been since '97."

Lillian frowned. "That's the year you were arrested for assault, yes?"

"Yeah."

Elliot was almost twenty when Halloween time rolled around in 1997. He was living on his own for the first time, in a rundown apartment complex. The night before Halloween, he took a walk out to a nearby convenience store to buy cigarettes. There were some other young people in the store, his age or thereabouts. A couple of big jocks and their leggy girlfriends. Based on their costumes, he guessed they were on their way to a Halloween party.

One of the girls was dressed as a sexy devil, wearing a tiny red dress, red stockings, red heels, and horns on her head. He couldn't help staring at her as he walked into the store. She caught him looking and said something to her boyfriend, loudly calling him a "creeper". The belligerent jock walked right up to Elliot, making him cringe as he got in his face. The guy insulted him in a lot of the usual ways and made some threats. Elliot apologized in the most obsequious, pitiful way possible. The jock laughed at him. They all laughed at him, even the foreign clerk behind the counter. The jock walked away, considering him unworthy of further attention.

Elliot knew he should have considered himself lucky. He didn't often get out of those situations without getting beat up. Later on, when his case went to court, the jock would say he'd only been putting on a show for his girlfriend. He'd had no interest in hurting Elliot. So he said. By then it didn't matter. The damage had been done.

When the jock turned away, Elliot opened a beer cooler and took out a forty ounce bottle of malt liquor. There was no conscious decision to do what he did. Something inside him just snapped. He'd been pushed around and mocked one time too many. He walked up behind the jock and smashed the bottle across the back of his head, causing him to fall unconscious to the floor. The blow opened a big gash in the young man's head. A rapidly spreading pool of blood formed around his unmoving body. The girl in the devil costume screamed and screamed.

Elliot fled the store, but he was soon apprehended by police. Because it was a first offense, he was sentenced to just a year in jail. He got out after six months on good behavior. His record was the biggest reason he was terrified about possibly losing his job. As a convicted felon, acquiring gainful employment was difficult verging on impossible. He'd been incredibly lucky to land the position he had. Another one like it would be hard to come by.

Lillian's look of concern deepened. "Are you having violent thoughts again?"

Elliot sniffled and wiped moisture from his face. "Yes."

"Tell me about them."

Here Elliot departed from his usual policy of complete honesty with Lillian. He didn't know how she would react to the truth. Probably with horror. But what she might think of him wasn't what most worried him. No, his biggest concern was more practical. He didn't want her to know specifics about his murder fantasies in the event he decided to act on them.

Instead he told her about the increasing anxiety he'd felt throughout the month as the weather turned chillier and the trappings of the season began to appear. Seeing pumpkins piled up outside of stores made him feel sick to his stomach. He felt a deep bitterness when he saw the Halloween displays inside the stores, a revulsion at the knowledge that something so deeply tied to his suffering was a source of fun and commerce for nearly everyone else. He told her about how he sometimes wanted to hit costume-wearing young adults because they triggered his seasonal PTSD.

He *didn't* tell her about the plot he'd hatched to ruin

Halloween forever—at least on a local level—by turning it into a night of unrivaled carnage and horror. He said nothing about his fantasies of chopping off the heads of alpha male types or slashing the throats of attractive young women. Nor did he say anything about how he longed to watch the blood flow from the wounds of his victims and revel in their suffering, just as so many others had reveled in hurting him over the years.

Lillian Rosewater strongly urged Elliot to follow up with his psychiatrist and see about adjusting his various medications to better control his anxieties. Elliot agreed this was a good idea. At the time he still had hopes of turning away from his more dangerous urges. He made that follow up appointment and for several years the new meds helped.

And then he stopped taking them.

15

The brass headboard thumped repeatedly against the motel room wall as Chuck gave it to Fawn Hightower from behind. She was holding onto headboard slats for support, which caused it to hit the wall harder than it might have otherwise each time he thrust himself into her. Chuck had a firm grip on her slim waist and was pounding her for all he was worth, eliciting shrill screams of ecstasy tinged with more than a little pain. He knew he was hurting her, but she urged him not to stop, to keep giving it to her harder and harder.

Chuck was more than happy to oblige. Fawn had always turned him on intensely, but never more so than tonight. His dick felt like it was made of steel. He felt like he could rip her in half with it. As he continued to thrust into her and bring out more of those lovely screams, he drank in the stunningly erotic shape of her lithe little body. He loved it from any angle, but there was something especially pleasing about this view. And it wasn't just the quivering of her upthrust ass or the hypnotic jiggle of her dangling breasts. It was also about the contours and planes of her toned thighs, tapered back, and slender shoulders.

Her body was a work of art. This wasn't the first time he'd had thoughts along these lines. Even when he was feeling guilty about the affair, that sense of total lust he felt for her physical form never diminished. He loved Karen and still enjoyed sex with her, but it had never quite been like this between them. The sex he had with Fawn was the best he'd ever had, no contest.

He felt himself building toward orgasm as his hands came away from her waist and began to roam all over her body, sliding up and down the length of those smooth thighs before moving to her torso to grip her breasts. Feeling the head of his cock swelling within her, Fawn let go of a headboard slat and seized him by a wrist as she twisted her head around to look at him, flinging sweat-drenched blonde hair out of her face.

"Come inside me." She thrust her ass against him, bringing him closer still to release. "Come inside me, motherfucker."

A distant part of Chuck knew this wasn't a good idea. He wasn't wearing a condom and didn't know whether Fawn was still on the pill. But he was too lost in the throes of animal passion to pay much heed to common sense. When Fawn thrust herself back against him again, it was just too much. He exploded inside her. Fawn let go of his wrist and grabbed on to the headboard slat again as he continued to pump away at her until he was spent.

At last, after several gasping, sweaty moments, he removed his still-engorged organ from Fawn's pussy and fell away from her. He stretched out on his back and struggled to catch his breath as he stared up at the ceiling. In another moment, Fawn let go of the headboard, shifted around on the bed, and curled herself around him.

She walked her fingers over his hairy chest and made a low purring sound. "Mmm. That was the best ever."

She laughed.

Chuck squinted in bleary-eyed exhaustion at her. He was bone-tired and it wasn't just from the intense physical exertion of their coupling. He'd had a long, stressful day. Something possibly very sinister was happening on the periphery of his life, a thing that might be tied to a shameful episode from the distant past. He should be with his family right now, protecting them and doing whatever he could to make sure that possible threat from the past didn't become something more serious. It was his duty as a husband and father.

And yet here he was, in bed with his mistress in a cheap motel room on the other side of town.

"Something funny, Fawn?"

Smiling, she lifted one small shoulder in an amused little shrug. "Kind of, yeah."

A silent moment passed.

When she failed to elaborate, Chuck prompted her. "Care to tell me what it is you're finding so fucking amusing? Because I'm not seeing the humor in this situation."

Fawn's smile morphed into a smirk. "You wouldn't. You're too uptight." She laughed again. "I'm amused by how completely incapable you are of resisting me. Oh, you make a lot of noise about needing to do the right thing. You swear you're gonna break it off with me. But in the end, we always end up right back here. Over and over." Her smirk became more pronounced. "You're addicted to me. You *need* me. Admit it."

Chuck stared into her twinkling eyes and said nothing for a long moment, the smugness in her expression stirring anger. Fawn's cutting comments often got under his skin, but he knew this was because they frequently contained an element of uncomfortable truth. It hurt him to realize how truly powerless he was when it came to her. Sometimes, like now, he suspected his affair with her would come to light regardless of how desperately he tried to hide it. And then there would be plenty of emotional hurt to go around for everybody.

He felt like such a fool.

A wave of self-loathing came over him, causing him to abruptly extricate himself from Fawn's embrace and swing his legs over the side of the bed. He scooted to the edge of the mattress and bent over to grab his underwear and pants from the floor.

Fawn made a huffing sound of disappointment as he got to his feet and began to dress. "Oh, come on. You're not going already, are you? You're usually good for at least one more round."

Chuck grimaced. "Not tonight. I need to get back to my wife and kids. I made some lame excuses when I left. I should have been back hours ago."

Fawn glanced at his phone on the nightstand. There was a hint of that smugness in her expression again when her eyes shifted back in his direction. "Is that why you turned your phone off? So you could fuck me in peace without having to tell your family more lies?"

Chuck's face reddened.

Fawn laughed softly, knowing she'd struck a nerve.

Chuck pulled on his shirt, grabbed his shoes, and sat on the edge of the bed to pull them on. "This is the last time we're doing this."

Fawn laughed again. "There's an answer to all this, you know. A way you won't have to tell any more fucking lies. Leave your wife. Confess everything. Tell her you're in love with me. And that'll be the end of it, Chuck. Think of it. No more hiding. Being together whenever we want, having amazing sex whenever we feel like it. You can't honestly tell me you wouldn't love that."

Chuck sighed and put his face in his hands. "I can't abandon my kids."

The mattress shifted as Fawn got up and crawled over to him. She pressed her breasts against his back and wrapped her arms around his midsection. "You can do whatever you want," she said, putting her lips against his ear, letting him feel her warm breath. "This isn't the olden days. You don't go to jail for infidelity. And they say one of the biggest mistakes people in troubled marriages make is staying together for the kids."

Chuck took his hands away from his face. "My marriage isn't troubled."

Fawn kissed his neck, nipped at it slightly with her teeth.

"Isn't it? You fuck another woman, Chuck. You've admitted you like it better with me than with her. How is that not troubled?"

Chuck groaned.

He wished he'd never admitted that to her. It was true, but he should have known she would one day use it as psychological ammunition against him.

Chuck disengaged himself from her and stood up. "We'll have to leave this discussion for another day, Fawn. This isn't the time for it. I'm expected back. We'll talk later."

He headed for the back of the room.

"Hey, Chuck?"

He paused at the open door to the bathroom and glanced wearily back at her. "Yeah?"

She got up from the bed and crossed the room in her slinky, sexy way, putting on a little show for him as she went to the table and picked up the bottle of expensive bourbon she'd brought with her. "I get that you have to go. Or at least feel like you do. But you can have one last drink with me." She smiled again and this time it came across as sweet and almost demure, absent that usual tinge of smugness. "Can't you?"

Chuck sighed. "Sure. But just one."

He went into the bathroom and relieved himself. It was a good, long piss, the kind he always had to take after sex, this time exacerbated by the three glasses of bourbon he'd had prior to fucking Fawn. When he came out of the bathroom, she'd already refilled their glasses.

She handed him a glass as he reached the table. "To us."

She clinked glasses with him and tossed her drink back in one long pull.

Chuck grimaced. "I can't drink to that."

Fawn rolled her eyes. "Just drink."

She poured more bourbon into her empty glass.

Chuck sipped from his glass. "Don't get too drunk. You don't want to get a DUI on the way home."

Fawn smiled and moved closer to him, holding her glass with one hand and hooking the fingers of her other hand over the waist of his jeans. "Aw…you're worried about me. How sweet."

Chuck took a long pull from his glass and set the half-finished drink on the table. "I don't want you to get hurt, that's all." He gripped her wrist and tried to pull her hand away from his jeans, but she resisted, tightening her hold on him. "Fawn, what are you doing? Let go."

She arranged her features in a mock pout and shook her head. "No. Don't wanna."

She downed the last of her second drink and threw the glass across the room. It shattered when it hit a wall.

Chuck sighed. "Jesus. You're already too drunk to drive."

"I know. So stay here and keep me company."

Chuck shook his head. He was about to remind her yet again why he couldn't do that when he realized he was feeling woozy. "Shit. Let go. I've gotta sit down."

Fawn laughed and finally released her grip on his jeans. "So sit."

He reached for a chair at the table.

She pushed his hand away from the chair and steered him over to the bed. "No, silly. Here. You'll be more comfortable on the bed."

Chuck didn't resist. He couldn't resist. He was too dizzy. Within moments of sitting on the bed, he flopped backward and slipped into unconsciousness. When he came to an indeterminate time later, he felt groggy and bleary-eyed. He sat up and rubbed at his eyes to clear his vision. Looking around, he saw a fully-clothed Fawn sitting at the table and smoking a cigarette.

"Jesus. How long have I been out?"

Fawn tapped ash on the table. There was no ashtray in the supposedly non-smoking room. "About six hours."

"Fuck!"

He got to his feet and, still groggy, staggered over to the

nightstand, looking for his phone. It wasn't there. Confusion tinged his mounting sense of panic. "What the fuck?"

"Looking for this?"

Chuck turned in Fawn's direction. His phone was in her upraised left hand. He could see that it had been powered on. His confusion continued to deepen and he struggled to fight his way through the mental fog still gripping him. "What's happening, Fawn?"

She smiled and looked at the phone. "I like that you set this picture of me in your contacts. It proves what I've been saying all along. You need me. You can't resist me."

Chuck took an unsteady step in her direction. "What did you do? Did you drug me?"

Fawn nodded. "Yes. But that's not all I did."

Chuck groaned. "Why? Why would you do this? Karen probably thinks I've been in an accident. She's probably out of her mind with worry."

Fawn shook her head. "No. She isn't."

Something in the way she said that struck terror in Chuck's heart. "What do you mean? Why would you say that?"

Fawn puffed on her cigarette and blew smoke in his direction. "Because it's the truth. I had a little talk with Karen."

Chuck felt sick. "No."

Fawn smiled. "Yes."

"What did you tell her?"

"What do you think? Everything."

Finally reaching the table, Chuck pulled out the other chair and collapsed into it. He had tears in his eyes as he stared in dumbstruck disbelief at Fawn. "I can't believe you'd do something so underhanded. So dirty. So *low*. Why would you do this?"

Fawn's expression sharpened. She stubbed the cigarette out on the table and leaned toward him. "Because I've had enough. I'm sick of you stringing me along. So I decided it was time to force everyone's hand and bring everything out in the open." She reached for him, clasping hands with him. "I know you're mad, Chuck, but everything will be better now. You'll see."

Chuck pulled his hand away from her.

"I can't be around you right now. Not after this dirty fucking trick."

He pushed himself out of the chair and looked around until he found his wallet and keys. Once his wallet was tucked away in his pocket, he staggered over to the door.

Fawn hurried after him, grabbing at his arm. "Chuck, you can't leave. You're in no shape to drive."

Chuck laughed bitterly. "Yeah, no thanks to you. I'm going anyway. I have to make things right. Somehow."

He opened the door and lurched outside, shivering at the shock of the chilly early morning October air. His head wobbled as he scanned the parking lot outside the dumpy little motel for the Odyssey. Spotting it, he set off in that direction, struggling not to look like a drunk staggering home after last call.

He heard the slap of Fawn's feet on the pavement as she came running after him.

"Leave me alone, Fawn."

She caught up to him as he reached the Odyssey, grabbing at his arm as he fumbled with the driver's side door. Anger rose up inside him again as he turned to face her. Although the idea of hitting a woman had always repulsed him on a primal level, he felt an urge to strike her. He wasn't functioning at full capacity and just wanted her to get away from him. At the very least he wanted to scream at her and call her a cunt for wrecking his life.

Before he could lash out at her in either manner, he saw the tall masked man emerge from behind the rear of the Odyssey and step up behind Fawn. In his debilitated state, he was initially unable to comprehend what was happening when Fawn's eyes popped wide open and her body began to convulse. Understanding dawned belatedly when she dropped to the ground and the masked man stepped over her to approach Chuck.

That was when he saw the stun gun in the masked man's gloved right hand.

Then he felt the prongs of the device against his neck.

A button was pushed and then it was Chuck's turn to convulse.

16

Five days until Halloween
Willow Springs, TN

A lingering odor of chloroform was the first thing Chuck was aware of upon his return to groggy semi-consciousness. There was also a trace taste of the chemical in his mouth. Full cognizance of all that had happened did not immediately return, but he was dimly aware that this was the second time within a short period that someone had used artificial means to render him unconscious. Fragments of actual memory came back in the ensuing moments. Fawn had drugged him. She'd told Karen about the affair. An echo of the panic he'd felt at this revelation briefly gripped him, but it faded as another, far more troubling memory surfaced.

The man in the mask.

The stun gun.

Chuck's eyes snapped open. His heart pounded and his breathing came in ragged gasps. The terror surging within him was compounded by two additional revelations. Someone had tied him to a chair. The bindings were tight. There was no give at all. A tingling in his extremities suggested the thick lengths of rope were cutting off his circulation. This scared him, but in those early moments of being wide awake again he was more concerned about the total darkness engulfing him. His eyes perceived an absolute blackness and nothing else. At first he feared his attacker had somehow blinded him, but then he felt the itchy sensation of burlap against his face.

The masked man had put a bag over his head. Chuck started breathing heavily in and out, his deepening panic bringing him to the verge of hyperventilating. He felt scratchy burlap on his tongue with each sharp intake of air. The small measure of relief he felt at realizing his eyes hadn't been gouged out was overwhelmed by the certainty that he was about to die.

He had been taken by force and brought to an unknown location. Chuck had no prior personal experience with this kind of situation, but he'd seen enough true crime shows on TV to know they rarely ended in a happy way for the abductee. The prospect of his likely imminent demise brought tears to his eyes. It wasn't fair. He deserved a chance to make things right with Karen and the kids before he died.

Didn't he?

His breath caught in his throat when he heard a metallic clank from somewhere nearby. Not being able to see, he could only guess at the nature of the sound, but for some reason he pictured a heavy implement of some type being dropped on a table. Whatever it was had produced a slight echo, which gave him the sense of being in a large, wide-open space. As soon as this impression materialized, he thought of his visit to Elliot Parker's odd place of residence.

He grimaced behind the burlap bag.

Of course that's where he was. Where else? It was the only thing that made any sense. As with all the other disturbing insights that had come to him since waking up, it did nothing to make him feel any better. To the contrary, any slim hopes he might have harbored of bargaining his way out of this predicament now withered and died.

Elliot Parker had killed Lloyd McAfee. There could be no doubting it now. Clearly he was a man bent on taking belated revenge for the wrongs done to him so long ago. Not for the first time, Chuck felt like an absolute fool. He should have spilled his suspicions about Elliot to the sheriff when he had the chance. Instead he'd been a coward, concerned only with what other people might think of him when the story came out. Yes, he'd planned to fill the sheriff in later, but that didn't matter.

The delay had doomed him.

He heard another sound from somewhere nearby, again with that slight echoing quality. Footsteps. Someone—almost certainly Elliot—was moving around in the big, open space.

Chuck heaved a breath. "Elliot? Is that you?"

The footsteps came closer, unhurried. Soon he sensed a presence in front of him, someone looming over him. Whoever it was just stood there and stared at him for a long moment, saying nothing. Chuck sat there feeling powerless and vulnerable, like an insect caught in the sticky strands of a spider's web.

Then the bag was snatched away from his head and tossed aside.

A tall, lean figure stared down at him. The man was wearing a black trench coat. The ski mask was still in place, obscuring most of his face, but Chuck perceived a hint of distant familiarity in the eyes. It was Elliot. He was sure of it. The flaps of the trench coat hung open over a black shirt and jeans. The flaps sagged slightly, suggesting the presence of heavy things shoved deep inside the inner pockets.

Chuck expelled another heavy breath and tried to keep his voice steady as he said, "You don't have to do this, Elliot. Whatever it is you're planning, it's not too late to stop."

The man who was probably Elliot Parker maintained his silence. He stared at Chuck a moment longer before moving away again, disappearing from sight this time. A sound of receding footsteps from somewhere to his rear was followed by the sound of a heavy door opening and then closing again.

The surge of relief he felt at temporarily being out of Elliot's creepy presence came to an abrupt end when he spotted the wire dog cages set against the wall directly opposite where he was sitting, some twenty or more feet away inside the large room. Curled up on the floor inside one of the cages was a slender, nude woman. Her hands were tied behind her back. She had a bag over her head.

Chuck's heart sank.

He didn't need to see her face to know who this was. He'd recognize that beautiful body anywhere. The removal of her clothes was disturbing. It suggested some perverse sexual angle to whatever Elliot had in mind for her, a notion backed up by the fact that he hadn't removed a stitch of Chuck's clothing. The sick bastard had wanted to see her naked body. He'd probably had his hands all over her, groping and exploring her vulnerable flesh while she was unconscious. Chuck didn't know what Elliot looked like these days, but he hadn't exactly been popular with the girls back during their school days. Opportunities to fondle a nude woman probably didn't come along very often for him.

The son of a bitch had probably raped her.

Thinking about it, Chuck felt a weak stirring of impotent anger. He wished he could make Elliot pay for whatever transgressions he might have committed against Fawn, for what he was still doing to both of them. But there was nothing he could do.

He sniffled and craned his head around, taking in more of his surroundings. The lighting was dim, probably intentionally so, and most of what he could see was restricted to the center of the room. Off to his right, he discerned the shapes of large objects that were probably vehicles. He thought of the big metal rollup door he'd noted during his survey of the building's exterior earlier. The place might have been an auto body repair shop or something similar in a previous existence, though how Elliot had come into possession of such a property was a mystery. The longer he stared at the vehicles, the more he was able to make out about them. His eyes were still adjusting to the dim lighting, but he soon recognized the shape of the Odyssey. The vehicle next to it was undoubtedly Fawn's Lexus. At first Chuck was puzzled by the presence of the vehicles. Elliot was just one guy. Bringing the cars from the motel to this place must have been an insanely complicated process.

But then he noticed the other dark shapes sprawled on the floor near the vehicles. He sucked in a breath when he realized they were two bodies lying in pools of blood. There was a ripeness emanating from the corpses unrelated to death. They smelled…unclean. Fragrant. Chuck had a sudden insight. These were homeless men Elliot had talked into driving the cars here for him, perhaps with the promise of money or booze once the job was complete. Of course, there was a chance his theory was way off, but Chuck had a hunch it wasn't too far from the truth.

A soft feminine whimper came from the direction of the cages. Fawn was stirring.

Chuck looked at her. "Fawn? Are you awake? Can you hear me?"

Her only reply was another of those pitiful-sounding whimpers. She lifted her head a little and made a sound of confusion, not yet cognizant of the bag over her head. Observing this gave Chuck a chill-inducing sense of déjà vu.

"Fawn, please…listen to me. Are you okay? Did he hurt you?"

She lifted her head a little higher off the floor. "Chuck?"

She sounded weak, on the verge of lapsing back into unconsciousness.

Before Chuck could reply, the heavy door opened again behind him, its hinges squealing as Elliot came back into the building. He pushed it shut with a grunt of exertion, apparently having to force the metal door back into the frame. Then echoing footsteps came Chuck's way and in a moment Elliot, still wearing his mask, again appeared in front of him. Clutched in his hands was a carved jack-o'-lantern. If Chuck had possessed any lingering doubts as to who'd broken into his house, they were now dispelled.

Elliot set the jack-o'-lantern in Chuck's lap and disappeared behind him again. This time he was only gone for a moment. Before he reappeared, Chuck heard a clanking sound he identified as heavy chain links being wound around a fist. This was followed by a whirring sound that made him tilt his head back. Squinting against the light directly overhead, he saw several metal tracks attached to the ceiling. He saw the chain before he saw Elliot. It was attached to something inside one of the tracks, which allowed him to slide the length of chain from one end of the room to the other.

Chuck lowered his gaze as Elliot reentered his field of vision and approached Fawn's cage. As he'd suspected, the bottom end of the chain was wound around one of his fists. Upon reaching the cage, he unwound it and let it dangle. He then produced a key from somewhere inside the trench coat and slid it into the padlock on the cage door. It clicked open with a twist of the key. After removing the padlock from the clasp, he tossed it aside, then reached inside to grab Fawn and haul her out of the cage. She cried out and seemed closer to full consciousness as he dragged her away from the cage and forced her to her knees.

"What are you doing, Elliot?"

The masked man didn't respond. He'd turned Fawn so she was facing Chuck, and now he tore the burlap sack away from her head and tossed it aside.

Chuck gasped. "Jesus fucking Christ. Why did you do that? What the fuck is wrong with you?"

Again, Elliot didn't respond. He grabbed the dangling length of chain and attached it to a studded black dog collar on Fawn's neck. After giving it a yelp-inducing snap to ensure it was properly secured, he moved away from her, slipping into the shadows beyond the small pool of light. A few moments passed. Then there was a click, followed by the ratcheting sound of some kind of motor. The length of heavy chain jerked tight and began to

110

move along the track toward Chuck, dragging a gasping Fawn along with it. She grabbed at the chain and struggled to remain at least semi-upright rather than being dragged, but she was only intermittently successful.

There was another click and then the sound of the motor ceased. Fawn was now about five feet in front of Chuck, on her knees again, but sagging, her eyes blinking slowly as she gazed blearily at him. He grimaced and felt tears sting his eyes as he stared at her. Elliot had shaved off all her hair. He'd even shaved her eyebrows, which enhanced the wrongness of what he was seeing in a way her shorn scalp alone could not. Her face didn't look right without them, almost freakish. He hated himself for the thought, but he couldn't help it.

She wobbled a little closer to him on her knees. "Chuck…what's happening? Where are we?"

A tear tracked down Chuck's cheek. He said nothing. What could he tell her? There was nothing reassuring he could say. For him, there was no mystery. He knew exactly where they were and what was happening. Moreover, he knew *why* it was happening. And there was simply nothing comforting that could be derived from that knowledge. Besides, there was that shame that had made him hold his tongue during his talk with the sheriff. He couldn't bear the idea of Fawn knowing he was the reason for all of this.

Chuck heard footsteps.

Elliot reemerged from the shadows and approached them. He took the pumpkin from Chuck's lap, moved into position behind Fawn, and lowered it over her head. She squealed and began thrashing her head in an attempt to dislodge it. Elliot grabbed her by the neck and forced her to remain still while he curled his other hand into a fist and drilled it into her lower back several times. Chuck screamed at him to stop, but he was ignored. By the time Elliot finally did stop, Fawn had gotten the message. She remained very still on her knees, sobbing behind the pumpkin with her head drooping forward.

Chuck seethed as he strained uselessly against his bonds. "You sick piece of shit. You're not even really human anymore, are you? You know what? Ricky Bennet had the right idea all along. We should have killed you that night in the woods. You were a loser then and you're a loser now. We would have been doing the world a fucking favor."

Though emboldened by his rage at Elliot's brutal treatment of Fawn, Chuck was still terrified. He trembled as their abductor moved away from her and approached him. A whimper emerged from his constricted throat an instant before the back of a gloved hand snapped hard across his face.

Chuck screeched in pain.

Then more shameful whimpers as he started begging. "Please don't hurt me. Please."

Elliot backhanded him again.

After that, he moved out of sight behind him again. A whirring sound told Chuck he was dragging another of those heavy chains along one of those other ceiling tracks. The guess was confirmed a moment later when Elliot reappeared. A heavy tool of some type was connected to the second chain. After staring at it perplexedly for a moment, Chuck's eyes widened as he recognized it as an industrial grade pneumatic bolt gun.

Chuck shook his head, his heart pounding again. "No. Don't. Please don't."

Fawn raised her head slightly and looked at Chuck through the slanted eyes of the jack-o'-lantern. "Chuck...what's wrong? What's he doing?"

Yet again, Chuck found himself incapable of telling her the dismal truth.

The masked man let go of the chain connected to the bolt gun once he'd dragged it out of sight behind Fawn. He then prodded her forward with the toe of a booted foot until she was just a few feet directly in front of Chuck.

Chuck shook his head again. "Don't. Jesus Christ, don't. I'll give you money. I could come up with a hundred grand in cash, easy. You can have it. You can have whatever you want. I'll do anything."

Yet again, no response from Elliot. Once he was satisfied with how he'd positioned Fawn, he backtracked and grabbed hold of the dangling bolt gun. There was enough slack to this longer length of chain that he was able to get himself into position behind Fawn without straining.

He aimed the bolt gun at the back of her head and looked at Chuck.

"Kill me," Chuck said, at last tapping into a previously hidden vein of selflessness somewhere deep inside him. "Seriously, just kill me. She's doesn't know who you are. She knows jack shit about why this is happening. Your grudge is with me. Kill me and drug her again, then drop her off somewhere." A strangled sob emerged. More tears spilled down his cheeks. "I was wrong before. It's our fault you turned out this way. Me and my friends. We did this to you. Kill us, not her. She's innocent. There must still be some trace of goodness left inside you. You don't want to do this. Not really."

The masked man held Chuck's gaze a moment longer.

A muffled sniffle emerged from inside the pumpkin as Fawn raised her head a little higher. "You called him Elliot. I heard you."

There was a loud clack and a *whumph* of compressed air as the masked man squeezed the bolt gun's trigger. The bolt that emerged punched through the back of the pumpkin and went all the way through Fawn's head, the tip emerging coated in dripping blood between the slanted eyes of the jack-o'-lantern.

Chuck screamed.

Fawn's body fell forward, hanging lifelessly from the end of the chain as more blood pattered on the dirty concrete floor. Elliot let go of the bolt gun and stared at Chuck for several moments as he wailed and sobbed. Chuck was so lost in the depths of his despair and grief over the loss of his lover that he didn't notice when Elliot finally moved away again, not until he felt a gloved hand slap down over his forehead and pull his head backward. He spluttered when a hard rubber object was pushed into his mouth. When Elliot began fastening the straps, Chuck realized he'd been fitted with a ball-gag. The discomfort this caused was considerable, but it intensified when another object, this one with a clammy interior, was slid down over his head. After an instant of blindness while the object was wedged into place, he was able to see again through slanted, triangular holes.

Awareness dawned.

Like the corpse at his feet, he had a pumpkin on his head.

Once it was firmly in place, Elliot turned out the overhead light and left the building for a while, leaving Chuck alone in the dark with the dead.

17

Five days until Halloween
Willow Springs, TN

The Everly family, minus its patriarch, was preparing to flee the hotel when Sheriff Bob Lee pulled up in his cruiser. Karen Everly was loading some things into the open rear hatch area of a black Mercedes SUV, a vehicle Lee didn't recognize. It hadn't been among the cars on the premises at the Everlys' residence yesterday.

All the SUV's doors stood open. As Lee got out of his cruiser and began to waddle over, he caught a glimpse of a teenaged girl sitting in the front passenger seat with her bare feet propped on the dash. It was Eva, the eldest of the two daughters. She had nice legs, an observation Lee pushed aside, recognizing it as inappropriate. The girl had only just turned sixteen. Her sister, Kaelyn, younger by about a year, was standing several feet away from the SUV, with her attention glued to the screen of her phone. Lanky with prominent cheekbones, she looked like the type certain to turn into an absolute knockout in a couple years. The sole male among the Everly offspring was hovering near his mother as she worked at rearranging the travel bags stashed away in the back of the SUV. The boy's name eluded Lee for a moment, but it came to him as he consulted his memory of the reports filed by his deputies. Blake was the oldest of the Everly kids. The look of grim seriousness on his face as he conversed with his mother in a low voice didn't hide his handsomeness.

They were a good-looking bunch all around, there was no denying that. That definitely included the mother of these kids. Karen Everly had long blonde hair and a sexy body, with a pleasant amount of roundness in all the right places. That roundness was maybe a touch more pronounced than a lot of women liked to carry these days, but for Lee only enhanced her sexiness. He couldn't understand why any man would want to cheat on her with the likes of skinny little Fawn Hightower.

The whole clan, with the obvious exception of the missing father and husband, exuded a picture-perfect aura of all-American wholesomeness. Looking at them, Lee felt a new stirring of anger at Chuck Everly. He had everything. The man had been living the dream in every way. Nice house, good job, beautiful family, the works. What kind of man would risk throwing all that away?

A stupid man, seemingly. But Lee knew it wasn't as simple as that. Over the course of his decades in law enforcement, he'd seen similar scenarios play out countless times, but rarely under such odd or dramatic circumstances.

"Afternoon, Ms. Everly."

Karen Everly jumped at the sound of his voice. She had a hand to her chest when she turned away from the SUV's open hatch to face him. "Sheriff Lee. What are you doing here?"

Lee's smile was strained. "Sorry to startle you, Ms. Everly." He tilted his head and took a pointed look at the bags loaded into the SUV's rear compartment before meeting her gaze again. "Looks like you're going on a trip."

Karen grunted. "We're going home. We brought a lot with us because we'd planned on an extended stay."

Lee glanced at the boy, who was still standing nearby with that grim look on his face. "Not sure that's a good idea, Ms. Everly," he said, shifting his gaze back to Karen. "I understand you're upset over the situation with your husband, but don't forget that someone broke into your house yesterday and did a very strange thing there. Might not be safe to go back yet."

Karen rolled her eyes. "Oh, please. That was obviously Fawn's doing, her way of sending my husband a message. Some kind of messed-up ultimatum. She wanted him to make a choice and he did. He picked that bitch over his family. And now they've skipped town together. To hell with it all, sheriff, and the hell with them. I'm taking my kids home, where we belong."

Lee glanced again at Blake Everly, tugging at his sagging belt as he did it, an unconscious gesture of mounting nerves. "Could we talk in private a moment, Ms. Everly?"

"Whatever you have to say about Chuck, you can say in front of my son. He should know all about what kind of degenerate his father has become."

The boy groaned. "Dad's not a degenerate, mom. Something's not right about all this."

Karen cut a glare at him as she said, "No kidding something's not right. Your father's a degenerate scumbag." She looked at Lee. "What is it you need to tell me, sheriff?"

Lee sighed. "Look, Ms. Everly, you've got every right to be angry. There's no excuse for what your husband's been up to with the neighbor lady. But there's more to what's going on than that, and I'm sure it's tied somehow to Lloyd McAfee's murder. The two were friends when they were boys. Very tight, from what I hear. And the pumpkins left at your house suggest a connection. They almost had to have been stolen from Lloyd's stand and put in your house by the killer."

Karen frowned and chewed on her bottom lip a moment, staring at the sheriff as she digested this information. A lot of it she'd already known, of course, but it hadn't quite all been laid out for her this way. While she was mulling it all over, her daughters joined the little group clustered at the rear of the SUV, making Lee nervous as they crowded close.

At last, Karen let out a breath and said, "What are you trying to tell me, sheriff? That something has happened to Chuck and the Hightower woman?"

Lee shrugged. "I'm not saying that. Just that it's curious they've gone missing at this particular time. There's a killer on the loose and there's a chance he may have some kind of link to your husband. I tried talking about all this with him yesterday and I have to tell you I didn't like how he was acting."

Karen frowned again. "What do you mean?"

"He was being evasive. And he was nervous as hell." Lee tilted his Stetson back and wiped sweat from his brow. Though the nights were chilly now, the afternoons were still warm, especially for a fat man in full uniform. "Now maybe some of that had to do with Fawn Hightower, but he got especially jittery when I questioned him about Lloyd and their past together. There's something there that bothers the hell out of him, something he doesn't want to talk about."

Karen held his gaze a moment longer before sighing and shaking her head. "Sounds like nothing but speculation to me. You're only guessing at a link because you've got nothing else to go on."

Before Lee could refute that, a new voice intruded. "We about ready to head out, gang?"

A tall man with an athletic build joined the group at the back of the SUV. He was good-looking with blond hair. Lee knew he was related to Karen somehow at first glance. The resemblance was striking. Karen confirmed the guess when she said, "Sheriff, this is my brother, Kyle. He'll be staying with us for a while."

Kyle extended a hand and Lee accepted it with some reluctance, doing his best not to grimace at the man's firm grip as they shook. "Nice to meet you, Karl."

"Kyle."

"Right. Sorry."

Karen waved the others out of the way and closed the SUV's

hatch. Once it was shut, she faced the sheriff again and said, "I think you can see we'll be in good hands, sheriff. And I'm really not worried, anyway. Even if there is someone out there with a grudge against my worthless husband, well, he's gone now."

Kyle smirked. "And good riddance, too. Don't worry, sheriff. I'll take good care of Karen and the kids. Anyone who tries messing with them is gonna be in a world of hurt." He twirled a key ring around an index finger, making the keys jingle. "Pile in, guys. We'll swing by Sonic for some burgers and shakes on the way home."

The kids looked less than enthused by this attempt to pump up their moods, but they obeyed their uncle and got in the SUV.

Karen lingered at the rear of the vehicle a moment longer. "I learned all I need to know about what's going on with Chuck when that whore called me last night. Maybe I'll feel differently later when the anger fades, but right now I don't even care if anything else has happened to him. Please try to understand. We're going home and that's all there is to it."

She turned away from him and joined the rest of them in the SUV before Lee could respond. Not that there was anything left he could say. He still thought they were making a mistake by going home, but he couldn't blame Karen Everly for her current lack of concern regarding her husband's well-being. Just to be safe, though, he'd station a deputy outside the Everly home for at least a night or two.

After waddling back over to the cruiser, he got back in behind the wheel and reached for the gearshift. His hand came away from the knob when a squawk of static came over the radio. After taking the mic off the clip, he thumbed the button on the side and recited the usual jargon.

Deputy Acker told him to hurry on back to the department. There was some strange news out of Hooperville and he would definitely want to know all about it right away. Lee pressed for additional information, but Acker refused to be more forthcoming over the radio.

Sighing, Lee signed off and drove away from the hotel.

18

Five days until Halloween
Willow Springs, TN

The single wide trailer Jimmy Martin called home was located on an isolated patch of rural property about five miles down the road from the McAfee farm. Until about ten years ago, a decrepit, uninhabitable old house dating from the early twentieth century had occupied the same patch of land. The land and the old house had belonged to Jimmy's Uncle, Irwin, who passed it on to him when he died. Renovating the house would have been impossible. It was rotten throughout, from its frame down to its foundation, so he had it razed. Not having the funds necessary to rebuild, he bought a used trailer for a fraction of the cost, saving himself the bulk of the monetary portion of his inheritance.

A house would have been nice, of course, but all that really mattered was he had a place of his own to call home, one he owned free and clear, with no rent to pay a landlord or mortgage owed to a bank. The patch of land itself was a scraggly clearing in the middle of nowhere that no one but himself cared about, least of all the local government, which meant his property taxes were only a few hundred bucks a year.

It all added up to a pretty sweat deal for Jimmy, who'd managed to make the cash left to him by Uncle Irwin last for years.

He was a simple man with simple needs. Cable TV, Internet porn, and a large enough supply of Pabst Blue Ribbon to float him through each day without feeling anything other than the most surface, meaningless emotion was all he needed. His monthly disability check from the federal government for his morbid obesity was just icing on the cake. He'd only ever worked in construction and had managed to convince the powers-that-be that he was no longer physically capable of performing that kind of labor, thus they should pay him money.

Which they did, the gullible cocksuckers. Jimmy figured he was only about a hundred or so pounds overweight. Not that big a deal, really, and he could actually get around just fine on his supposedly bum knees, though they did get awful sore sometimes if he stood for too long, which, thank the lord, didn't happen too often.

As Jimmy drove his Ford pickup past the McAfee farm that day, he took his beefy right hand off the steering wheel and thrust an upraised middle finger in the direction of the property. The farm was too far off the road for anyone to take notice of this, but Jimmy got a nasty bit of visceral satisfaction from it, anyway. He'd heard about Lloyd's murder, of course. Even for a shut-in like him, the news was kind of hard to avoid. It was the talk of the town. The boys down at Coogan's General Store had been jawing about it when Jimmy stopped in to pick up his daily case of PBR. Recalling Jimmy's former association with Lloyd, old Bert Coogan had asked him what he thought about the news.

Jimmy mumbled something about it being a terrible tragedy and got the hell out of there. In truth, he wasn't at all unhappy to see Lloyd take his leave of this mortal realm. The guy was a mean son of a bitch who'd picked on him when they were younger and had cajoled him into doing some pretty shitty things he didn't like to think about now, like when they'd done that terrible thing to little Elliot Parker. He'd gone along with it, the way he always did back then, and he'd put on a pretty good act, making Lloyd and

Ricky think he was as into all that evil shit as they were. But he wasn't. Not one damn bit. He'd been sick about it for months afterward, plagued by insomnia and often physically ill from the memories. Not long afterward, he'd stopped hanging around with those assholes for good.

Once the McAfee property was in his rearview mirror, Jimmy lowered his hand and tore open the case of PBR, which was resting on the passenger seat. The truck swerved a bit on the narrow back road as he pried a can out of the big carton and popped the tab. A bit of foam rushed out of the opening and he blew it off his fingers as he straightened the wheel and got the pickup back on a relatively straight track. He'd finished off the first can and was reaching for another when he turned down the little dirt drive that led to the clearing where he had his trailer.

His hand came away from the carton, though, when he saw the sheriff's department cruiser parked alongside the trailer. An open pack of gum sat in the tray beneath the radio, just like always. Jimmy was a big believer in being prepared for situations like this. He rarely drove out anywhere without at least a mild buzz going, so having some means of covering up beer breath handy was an obvious necessity. Slowing the truck as he continued up the drive, he worked at keeping his torso as motionless as possible while furtively removing a stick of Big Red from the pack.

After working the wrapper free with a quick exercise in practiced one-handed dexterity, he popped the stick of gum into his mouth. The deputy stood leaning against his cruiser with his arms folded across his chest, but he was facing the trailer rather than the approaching vehicle. He'd spared the truck only a fleeting glance upon hearing its engine. Thankful for the man's nonchalance, Jimmy gave the wad of gum an energetic chewing, swishing around the flavorful juice this produced. He flattened the gum by pressing it against the roof of his mouth and then worked it across his tongue. Once he'd coaxed all the juice out of it he could, Jimmy took a moment to ensure the deputy still wasn't looking his way. Then he turned his head and spat the wad of gum out the window. Or he attempted to, anyway. It hit the doorframe instead and stuck there.

Jimmy grimaced.

For fuck's sake.

He left the thoroughly masticated wad of gum where it was as he slowed to a stop, parked behind the cruiser, and got out of the truck. The beer stayed where it was, too. No point in letting the deputy see that the carton was already open. After throwing the door shut—it closed with a squeal of unoiled hinges—he ambled over to where the deputy stood.

"Help you with something?"

When the deputy's head turned toward him, Jimmy saw that he was very young, probably somewhere in his early twenties. He was tall and fit, but one glance at the young man's face told Jimmy he lacked the self-assuredness of more experienced lawmen. Despite his lazy posture, there was something hesitant and uncertain in his demeanor.

He tipped back his Stetson and removed the mirrored sunglasses covering his eyes. "That beer on your breath?"

Jimmy snorted. "That peach fuzz on your cheeks? How old are you, boy?" He laughed. "Are you a real lawman or are you just playing dress-up for Halloween?"

The deputy tried for a tough scowl, but he couldn't quite pull it off and gave up the effort almost immediately. "You're Jimmy Martin, right?"

"That's right. What do you want with me, son?"

The deputy pushed away from the cruiser and stood up taller, again trying hard to seem more imposing than he actually was. It worked about as well as the aborted scowl. Jimmy almost felt sorry for him. "I'm Deputy Lucas with the sheriff's department. Just wanted to follow up with you on something I heard this morning. Some old gossip. Could be related to an investigation. You know about the pumpkin stand murder down the road, I take it."

Jimmy nodded. "You know I have. Whole town's talking about it."

"Right. Well, I heard you and the victim used to be tight."

"A long time ago. I ain't talked to Lloyd McAfee in almost twenty-five years."

The deputy's expression turned thoughtful as he scratched at his peach fuzz. "That may be, but I also heard you boys used to be real troublemakers, that you got up to no good all the time. You and the rest of your little group."

Jimmy just managed not to roll his eyes. The young deputy's source for all this was obvious. He'd been hanging out at Coogan's, listening to those old farts flap their gums. "That's the truth So what? It's got nothing to do with what happened to Lloyd."

"Why do you say that?"

Jimmy heard the eagerness in the man's voice. He was obviously out here on his own initiative, hoping to blow the case wide open all on his lonesome and accomplish something big early in his career. "Because it was so goddamned long ago. Did you not hear the part where I said I ain't talked to the son of a bitch in twenty-five years? I reckon we made some folks hate us back in those days, but nobody holds onto a grudge that long. Nobody in their right mind, leastwise."

The deputy looked like he was about to disagree, but whatever he'd been about to say went unsaid because in the next moment both men were distracted by the sound of another vehicle turning down the tree-shrouded drive to the clearing where Jimmy's trailer sat. A mud-splattered silver Honda Civic with tinted windows pulled to a stop next to Jimmy's truck.

Deputy Lucas frowned. "Friend of yours?"

Jimmy shook his head. "Don't think so. Nobody I know drives those Jap cars. I don't get too many visitors way out here, anyway. Place is starting to look like the parking lot outside a football stadium on Sunday compared to usual."

The Civic's driver's side door popped open, but the driver did not immediately emerge. Judging by what Jimmy could make out through the tinted glass, it looked like this new visitor was reaching for something on the floor. For the first time, he felt a tingling of alarm, which caused him to glance toward the closed door to his trailer. A strong urge to get inside the trailer and get his hands on his shotgun intensified with each passing second.

He'd just taken a tentative step in that direction when the Civic's door came all the way open and a tall, lanky man in a black trench coat stepped out of the car. The man's gloved left hand was empty, but his right hand was initially hidden from sight by the open door. There was a frozen moment during which Jimmy studied the man's face and tried to decide if he knew him. He'd discerned a very faint note of familiarity. Then, seemingly out of nowhere, the man's identify came to him, and in a flash he understood everything. He'd been wrong and the young deputy's intuition had been right on the money, after all.

"You better take out your gun, son."

The deputy glanced at Jimmy, confusion etched in his features. "What? Why?"

A breeze ruffled the slender man's tall shock of jet-black hair as he came away from the Civic and raised a crossbow. Jimmy's eyes widened when he saw the weapon and he immediately started backing away with his hands upraised. The deputy's head swiveled back toward the man with the crossbow. He gasped and reached for his sidearm, but it was too late.

Elliot Parker squeezed the crossbow's trigger, firing a bolt that struck the deputy in the side of his neck. The young man made a spluttering sound and staggered sideways, falling against the cruiser. He tugged at the bolt in his neck, which only caused more blood to jet from the wound. Elliot calmly removed another bolt from a mini-quiver attached to the underside of the weapon, fitted the bolt in the stock, and aimed again at the deputy. This second bolt went through the side of the deputy's head, killing him instantly.

By then Jimmy had already taken several backward steps. Now he turned and started running, seeking cover in the trees lining the clearing. He instinctively knew he wouldn't have time to dig out his keys, unlock his door, and get inside the trailer. This was his only chance. But it was no real chance at all. He was too big and too slow. The next bolt Elliot fired hit him in the back of the knee and he screamed in agony as he went crashing to the ground.

Jimmy clawed at the scraggly ground and mewled like a baby as he waited for the man he and his friends had wronged so badly long ago to reach him and administer the kill shot. As he would soon find out, however, Elliot had other things in mind for his former tormentors than a quick, merciful death.

19

After spending several intensely uncomfortable hours unable to move and alone in the dark, Chuck lapsed into a tenuous and troubled state of unconsciousness, from which he would periodically emerge for a few moments at a time. These brief periods of wakefulness were tinged with a groggy confusion about his situation, as well as an overriding desire to again retreat from reality. Even in the midst of that confusion, some part of him remained aware that the bad dreams he was having were preferable to what awaited him in the waking world.

He was finally stirred back to full consciousness when a loud, metallic ratcheting sound intruded on his sleep. His eyes fluttered open and he turned his head toward the sound. A large rectangular hole had appeared in the wall off to his right. Bright sunlight filled the space. Even behind the slanted eyes of the jack-o'-lantern, Chuck had to squint his eyes against it. A mud-splattered Honda Civic drove through the opening and into the large, open space. As the Civic moved past the other vehicles and subsequently slowed to a stop close to where Chuck sat, his eyes adjusted to the brightness.

He felt a fresh stab of guilt and grief when he saw Fawn's nude body on the floor at his feet, the blood-covered bolt still protruding between the eyes of the pumpkin over her head. Looking away, he saw again the other bodies he'd noted before, more clearly defined now in the sunlight. He saw enough to confirm within a reasonable degree of certainty his previous guess about the killer enlisting the help of homeless men to move the other vehicles. They certainly had the typical look of long-time vagrants, with their rumpled and threadbare clothing and scraggly beards. Both had died after having their throats cut. Their bodies rested in wide pools of coagulating blood. The sunlight also definitively confirmed the presence of his Honda Odyssey and Fawn's Lexus.

Chuck's gaze came back to the Civic when its engine stopped running and the driver's side door popped open. In a moment, the madman behind all this blood and death emerged. Though still clad in the black trench coat, he wasn't currently wearing the ski mask. One look at him was enough to finally and definitively confirm his identity for Chuck. He was taller now and his pale, hollow-cheeked face was more severe-looking than he remembered, but there was no question this was Elliot Parker.

Elliot ignored Chuck's muffled curse as he opened the Civic's back door, reached inside, and, with several loud grunts of exertion, hauled out the large form of someone else with a familiar face. At first Chuck thought Jimmy Martin was as dead as Fawn and the bums, but the soft gurgling sound he made when his large butt hit the concrete floor told him otherwise. He was alive, but apparently unconscious, probably subdued by chloroform or some sedative. This guess was based on the slender metal bolt sticking out of his leg. The man should have screamed in pain when that leg hit the floor, jostling the bolt, but he remained silent.

Taking hold of Jimmy's thick wrists, Elliot grunted in exertion again as he dragged the big man over to the wire cage formerly occupied by Fawn. Getting him inside the cage took an even more concentrated effort, causing the muscles in Elliot's long neck to stand out as he struggled to push Jimmy through the opening at the front of the cage. He almost didn't fit. Finally, though, he managed to get it done and again secured the cage with the padlock.

Once this was done, Elliot heaved a breath and stalked back over to the Civic, the heels of his boots clomping in the usual echoing way in the big room. He leaned through the still open driver's side door and a moment later the loud metallic ratcheting sound that had signaled his return recommenced. As the big rollup door began to descend, the trunk of the Civic popped open. Elliot then reemerged from the Civic and moved out of sight behind Chuck for a moment. The dim overhead light Chuck remembered from before reappeared as the rollup door finished closing.

Elliot's footsteps sounded again as he moved back into view and approached the rear of the Civic. After lifting the trunk lid and reaching inside, he hauled out another body. The effort required wasn't as strenuous because this other person was nowhere near as hefty as Jimmy. Unlike Jimmy, however, he was definitely dead. The bolts sticking out of his head confirmed this pretty much right away. This was bad enough, but even more shocking was the sight of the dead man's uniform.

Chuck didn't recognize the dead lawman, but he knew that uniform. Sheriff Bob Lee and the deputies he'd talked to yesterday had all worn one just like it. Seeing this sent the already profound despair gripping Chuck spiraling down to new depths. He'd already known he was dealing with a deeply disturbed individual, but this development represented a new, previously unimagined level of unhinged. Now that one of their own had gone missing, the law would turn up the heat in an unprecedented way. Elliot had to know that, yet he'd killed this man and taken his corpse anyway.

This told Chuck two things about whatever this psycho had in mind. One, it was something he knew would play out over a short period of time. Whatever he was hoping to accomplish would be over and done with by the time the law could track him down.

More chillingly, he had no concerns regarding his own mortality, thus why he was being so brazen. He'd probably planned this whole thing knowing full well he was unlikely to come out of it alive.

The implications regarding what this meant for Chuck made him sick with terror. He started shaking uncontrollably as Elliot dragged the dead deputy closer and deposited the body on the floor next to Fawn. Elliot then stood up straight and arched his back, twisting it to work out some kinks, sighing and groaning as he did it. He sounded tired. Chuck had to wonder how much sleep the man had gotten since starting all this madness with Lloyd's murder the other day. Probably not much. Running all over the place killing and abducting people didn't leave a lot of time for rest, after all.

After glancing Chuck's way, Elliot reached into his trench coat and took out a black folding knife with a long, thick handle. The blade that appeared when he opened it was a big one, a thick and nasty-looking length of steel with a serrated edge. Elliot nudged Fawn's body with the toe of his boot, evidently hoping to flop her over flat on her back. But rigor mortis had set in. She was too stiff.

Elliot glanced at Chuck. "You're not ready for her yet, anyway."

Chuck found this statement confusing on multiple levels, but terror again displaced confusion as Elliot approached him and raised the knife. He squealed behind the gag in his mouth and started shaking harder than ever, certain that Elliot had decided to finish him off now. Instead, he plucked at the front of Chuck's shirt, pulling the fabric away from his chest. He then pushed the blade through the fabric and began to saw away at it. After tossing aside the shredded remnants of the shirt, he removed the pumpkin from Chuck's head and set it on the floor.

He nodded, the faintest hint of a smile touching the corners of his thin lips. "Yes. Now you're ready for her."

Chuck squealed again as hot tears rushed from his eyes and spilled over the straps of the gag pressing into his face.

Elliot knelt next to Fawn and flipped her over. Grotesque cracking sounds ensued as he worked to break through the rigor mortis and straighten her limbs so that she was lying flat on the floor. Once that was done, he rammed the big blade into her belly. He braced one hand between her breasts to hold her body still while with the other he sawed away at the hole he'd made in her abdomen, continuing to work at it until he'd cut away a large enough flap of bloody flesh to expose the contents of her abdominal cavity. Slick with blood and other slowly congealing bodily fluids, the knife slipped from his fingers and hit the floor with a clatter. He made no attempt to retrieve it, not initially, instead pushing his hands through the big opening in Fawn's belly. His face twisted from exertion as he grabbed hold of something and began to pull it out of the body.

Bile surged into Chuck's throat as the first length of intestine emerged from the hole. He was overcome with horror and helpless to choke back the sickness rising up inside him. His stomach heaved and a forcefully ejected tide of vomit followed the surge of hot bile into his throat. But the obstruction in his mouth meant it had no means of egress. His face turned red as he began to gag. Terror intermingled with repulsion as he realized he was on the verge of choking to death.

Elliot's head swiveled his way as the gagging sounds intensified. Letting go of the drooping length of intestine, he got to his feet and hurried over to Chuck, disappearing behind him to undo the straps of the ball-gag, which were snapped shut at the back of his head. He got the snaps open within seconds and tore the gag away from Chuck's head, dropping it on the floor. This did not immediately solve Chuck's problem, because now the sodden, partially digested remains of his last meal were lodged in his throat, congested in the narrow passageway. A hand pressed against the back of his head, pushing it forward. The hand remained there as the base of a fist began to thump against his back. Some of the congested matter in his throat came loose and he gagged again as chunks of it spilled out of his mouth and dribbled down his chin before sliding down his bare torso. The fist continued to hammer away at his back and more chunks of vomit came loose, oozing out in the same way. Then his stomach heaved again and his mouth opened wide as he sprayed puke all over the floor in front of Fawn's corpse.

Apparently satisfied that his prisoner was no longer about to choke to death, Elliot moved away from him and dragged Fawn's body away from the pool of vomit. This struck Chuck as odd, given the grossness of what the man had been doing moments ago. You'd think a little puke wouldn't bother him at this point. Chuck's bottom lip trembled and drool laced with bile dribbled from the corners of his mouth as he watched Elliot drop to one knee next to Fawn and start rooting through her guts again. Loops of intestine coiled on the dusty floor as he continued to pull the viscera out through the hole.

Chuck spluttered and coughed to clear his throat. He spat on the floor and heaved a breath. "You sick fuck. Why are you doing that to her?"

Elliot glanced at him as he leaned over and reached with one of his long arms to retrieve the knife he'd dropped. "Don't talk."

Chuck grunted. "Fuck you."

Elliot started sawing through the section of intestine connecting the coiled loops at his feet to Fawn's body. "If you continue talking, I'll have to hurt you." He glanced at Chuck again. "I'm sure you believe there's nothing worse I could do to you than I've already done. You're very wrong about that. Keep your mouth shut or I'll show you *how* wrong you are."

Chuck ached to spew more insults at him. Verbal assault was the only weapon remaining to him, after all. But he'd seen enough to know a lot about the depths of depravity existing within Elliot Parker. He also clearly was not the type to make idle threats.

So Chuck kept his mouth shut, saying nothing even as Elliot gathered up the pile of droopy guts in his blood-soaked hands and got to his feet, turning to face him with a look of leering anticipation on his hollow-cheeked face, which looked cadaverous in the dim light. He already had a pretty good idea of what Elliot had in mind. His stomach roiled again at the thought of it and he again felt bile tickle the back of his throat. Fortunately, there was nothing solid left to eject as a dry heave forced his mouth open. Only more sour spittle emerged.

Elliot draped the loops of intestine around Chuck's neck. Chuck whimpered at the vile feel of the slick viscera against his bare torso. The urge to scream and spew venom at his tormentor returned, but he remained thoroughly intimidated by Elliot's threat.

Once he was satisfied with how he'd arranged the loops of intestine, Elliot returned to the violated corpse and knelt at its side again. He used the knife to widen the hole he'd created and then peeled back the big flap of flesh as far as he could, exposing more glistening organs. After groping around inside her for a few moments, he used his knife to cut something else loose.

He got to his feet and approached Chuck.

"Open your mouth."

Chuck glanced at the chunk of dark red meat in Elliot's left hand, then he looked him in the eye and said, "What?"

"What did I tell you about not talking? Open your mouth." Elliot grinned. "It's feeding time."

Chuck shook his head.

"Come now, Everly. You haven't eaten since last night. You must be famished." He glanced at the red chunk of something in his hand, arching an eyebrow. "I believe this is a bit of kidney. I've yet to resort to cannibalism, but I imagine it's very tasty in this raw, juicy form."

Chuck kept his mouth shut and shook his head again.

Elliot's mad grin faded, his eyes widening in anger as his thin lips peeled back from his crooked, yellow teeth. "Do as I say or

I'll cut off your balls and feed those to you instead."

Chuck sniffled, his eyes filling with tears as he arrived at yet another moment of utter defeat. His jaw trembled as he forced his teeth to unclench. Once his mouth was open wide enough, Elliot pushed the raw chunk of whatever it was through the opening, clamped a hand under Chuck's jaw to keep him from spitting it out, and ordered him to chew.

Chuck's jaw worked until the little piece of Fawn was sufficiently masticated to slide down his gullet. When Elliot was satisfied that it had indeed been ingested, he let go of Chuck's throat and moved away from him, again taking up a position over Fawn's mutilated body. He was sure the madman meant to kneel at the body's side again and cut loose another piece of meat, but it soon became clear he had something else in mind.

Elliot opened the fly of his jeans and took out his penis. In a moment, a strong stream of urine emerged as he began to piss all over the corpse. The stream was so strong Chuck suspected this was something Elliot had been planning all along. He'd been saving up for it, letting his bladder swell for hours beforehand like a guy preparing for a pre-employment pee test. Piss went into the opened abdominal cavity. More of it splashed against her breasts. Still more of it went through the holes carved in the face of the jack-o'-lantern. Chuck was shaking with rage long before Elliot finished emptying his bladder. All the things that had happened until now had been bad enough, but this extra level of insult was intolerable.

It was obvious the gesture was symbolic of his contempt for the life he had taken, a guess Elliot confirmed when he glanced Chuck's way and said, "Bumped into this cunt while spying on you last month. There's a GPS tracker on the underside of your Odyssey, by the way. I was lurking around outside that crappy motel where you and the whore always went to fuck. She came out of the room by herself that time. Usually you came out together, but not that time. Anyway, she looked around and saw me. There's a vending machine in an alcove near that room and I was pretending to study the snack choices." By now Elliot's stream had slowed to a trickle. He gave his dick a final shake and stuffed it back in his pants. "Anyway, I looked at her and smiled, trying to seem normal. Like usual, I failed. Big time. She got this look on her face, a sort of disgusted cringe, like she'd never seen anything so revolting. So many women look at me like that. Like I'm beneath them. I've been working out how to put this one in her place ever since that night. This works for me."

Chuck pushed out a breath and worked to keep his voice steady as he glared at Elliot and said, "I'm going to kill you for that."

Elliot was smirking as he turned away from Fawn's body. "Maybe you'll get your chance yet, tough guy. I've got plans for you, you know. Big plans. But before we get to that, I've got a lot more killing to do. Eleven are dead. Twenty still need to die."

Chuck shook his head at this insanity. "You're crazy."

But Elliot was no longer listening to him. His head was swiveling side to side, his features drawn into a look of deep concentration. "In the meantime, let's get you situated again. Now where did that ball-gag go? Ah, yes. There it is."

20

One year ago
The day before Halloween
Willow Springs, TN

Elliot sat slouched down behind the wheel of his Civic and watched the stream of first shift workers leaving by the factory's back entrance. Black clouds hung low over the horizon, threatening a downpour that so far hadn't occurred. After about ten minutes, he caught a glimpse of Susan Rochon's face as the glass door opened again and she finally emerged. She was smiling and talking to a female coworker. Both lit up cigarettes the moment they were outside.

All these years later, she still wore her hair in that choppy jet-black rocker style. Elliot supposed it marked her as old and resistant to change, but he thought the style still looked cool on her. Another thing that hadn't changed was her fashion sense. She still dressed in tight black everything most days, today being no exception. On her, it looked good. Unlike a lot of her female contemporaries, she hadn't packed on excess poundage after squeezing out a bunch of babies. The tits all the boys had drooled over back in school still looked amazing, straining the fabric of her long-sleeved black top. On an aesthetic level, the only way she'd changed since middle school was in the lines on her face. It seemed to Elliot they were deeper than usual for women her age.

They made her look slightly haggard and older than she really was. He figured this was related to all the smoking and drinking she did.

Susan continued conversing with the coworker until they reached the parking lot. After pausing there a moment to exchange a few final words, the two hugged and parted ways, Susan flicking away her half-smoked cigarette as she stalked off in the direction of her car. The clinch she'd shared with the coworker had been a little too intimate for Elliot's taste. From tracking Susan over the years, he knew she was bisexual in an indiscriminate way, having flings with men and women seemingly at random. This other woman could well be one of her many lovers, it was hard to tell.

The promiscuity bothered Elliot. He didn't like that so many people of both sexes had been intimate with the woman he considered the one true love of his life. It made her seem tainted, in a way. The upside was that she'd never married or settled down with anyone. In Elliot's mind, this technically meant he still had a chance with her. Of course, his paralyzing inability to interact with members of the opposite sex in anything other than a painfully awkward way meant the possibility was an extremely remote one. Not once in all the long years of stalking and admiring her from afar had he ever worked up the guts to approach her and attempt a conversation.

That had to change. Soon, hopefully. Maybe even tonight.

Susan's old Dodge Dart was parked in the row directly opposite from where Elliot sat behind the wheel of his Civic. He ducked his head down as she neared it, but the precaution was unnecessary. She didn't so much as glance his way as she got in her car, started the engine, and backed out of her space. He waited until she was gone to look at his phone and see by her route that she was heading toward the bar she frequently visited after work rather than home. Elliot then started the Civic and drove away from the factory, heading in the same direction.

He got there less than ten minutes later, parking several spaces over from the Dart, which was empty. She was already inside, probably already with a drink in her hands. Elliot's nerves jangled as he sat behind the wheel and stared at the bar's entrance. This was it, what he'd been waiting for ever since his last session with Lillian Rosewater. He'd been seeing the therapist again since the beginning of October. She'd recently suggested he attempt to take something that was a negative in his life and try to turn it into a positive. He needed to confront at least one of his fears. Once he'd done this, the thing he confronted would be robbed of its power over him.

Elliot decided he would make an attempt to approach Susan Rochon. A seemingly chance encounter at her favorite watering hole seemed like the best way to go about it. With booze in her system, she would be looser and friendlier, maybe more receptive to talking to an old schoolmate, even one who'd been an ostracized loser. Susan had been kind of a rebel back then herself. Obviously she remained one to some degree. Maybe she would even feel some kind of kinship with him. This seemed unlikely, but it was something to hope for at least.

Nonetheless, Elliot considered driving away from the bar and heading home. In general, he avoided places where people congregated for social reasons. Most of his free time was spent at the old auto body shop, a place he'd bought with money received in settlement for his part in a class action lawsuit against the makers of a psychotropic drug he'd taken for many years. He trembled at the thought of walking into this place and being overcome by all the loud noise and the spectacle of human beings laughing and reveling in each other's company. He couldn't go into something like this and not feel like a visitor from another planet. Everyone would look at him and know he didn't belong.

So tonight he'd tried to dress like a normal person. The old trench coat was at home. So were the black jeans and combat boots he usually wore. Instead he was wearing a beige sweater, blue jeans, and white sneakers. All were items he'd purchased at Target the previous day. He'd even done what he could to tame his hair. The tall black pompadour had been slicked back. He worried the amount of gel he'd used to accomplish this made it look too greasy, but he figured that was still better than looking like some kind of weird rockabilly ghoul.

The thought of all this effort going to waste was what finally made him get out of the car. He'd spent too much of his life shrinking away from the things that intimidated him. The accumulated mental weight of all that humiliation had reached a point of critical overload. Something had to give. This might be his long hoped-for chance to turn everything around and join the rest of the human race. He was done with inaction. Done with being a coward.

As he neared the entrance, the door opened and an attractive woman in a sexy devil costume emerged arm-in-arm with a guy who was either her boyfriend or someone she was hooking up with from the bar. The guy had a surprisingly grungy look. He had a scraggly beard and dirty hair. His clothes looked grimy, too. This was puzzling until Elliot took note of the plastic crossbow slung over his shoulder. At that point he realized the guy was trying to look like the redneck from the popular zombie show seemingly everyone watched these days. The girl's devil costume brought back vivid memories from that long ago convenience store confrontation. The sight of it almost stopped Elliot in his tracks and sent him scurrying back toward his car. This being the night before Halloween, there would likely be numerous other people in costume inside the bar. The thought of it brought a fresh surge of anxiety, but Elliot ducked his head down to avoid eye contact and continued on toward the bar's entrance, catching the door just before it could click shut again.

Before he could step on through the door, he heard the guy behind him snicker and mutter, "Hatchet-face."

The girl giggled. "You're bad, Trent."

Elliot's hand tightened around the edge of the door. So much for passing for normal. For one beautiful, fleeting moment there,

142

he'd been sure the initial lack of reaction from this couple proved he could mix among regular people without being singled out for derision. Now that belief suffered an abrupt, deflating demise. He knew he should go on in and get away from them, but some self-defeating impulse kept him where he was a few moments longer. He again considered abandoning this almost certainly doomed quest to somehow pique the interest of the woman he'd obsessed over from afar for so long. He doubted Susan's reaction upon seeing him would be significantly better than this. If anything, her disgust might be worse. She was a good-looking woman with an active social life. He was a social pariah who gave off a nearly radioactive "stay away" vibe.

He stayed right where he was until someone else pushed against the door from inside the bar, seeking exit. Elliot let go of the door and stepped aside as another young couple emerged. These two wore no costumes. The woman glanced at him, but her smiling expression didn't slip, nor did it morph into the usual look of revulsion. She and her companion walked on by without a word and without giving him a second look. Bracing himself for a full-on look at the contemptuous expressions of the costumed couple, he turned to watch this second couple go.

The sexy devil girl and her boyfriend were already gone. At some point they'd taken off while he'd stood here, mired in indecision and wallowing in his latest humiliation. For another moment, Elliot hovered on the brink of leaving anyway, but he decided to take the second couple's non-reaction to his presence as an encouraging sign. He reminded himself that he hadn't come this far not to see this through, regardless of outcome.

He opened the door and went on into the establishment. The music was loud and the lighting was dim. A long rail separated the bar area from a spacious dining room. A blues-rock trio was playing on a slightly elevated small stage on the opposite side of the dining room. A waitress in a tight, sleeveless top and a microscopic skirt approached him, smiling broadly.

"Just one tonight, sir? Or do you have others joining you?"

Instead of immediately answering, Elliot craned his head around, searching for Susan. There was no sign of her at any of the booths or tables in the dining area. He finally spotted her sitting at a small, high table in the bar area. There were several lined up along that side of the rail. A redheaded woman sat opposite Susan. Both women were sipping colorful cocktails.

"Sir? Are you looking for anyone in particular?"

Elliot glanced at the hostess. She was clutching a menu in her hands, her long red fingernails tapping against it in a telltale sign of impatience. Her big, face-splitting grin was still in place. An urge to punch her in the face and make it go away came and went.

"I'll just sit at the bar."

He moved away from her before she could say anything else, climbing the two steps up to the bar area. This part of the establishment was crowded and initially he feared he wouldn't find an open place to sit. Just as he was coming abreast of the table where Susan and her companion were sitting, a big man directly opposite them at the bar got off his stool, slapped some bills down on the bar, and walked away. Elliot wasted no time swooping in to claim the stool for himself.

Soon a bearded bartender approached and said, "What can I get you?"

Elliot wasn't a big drinker. He'd rarely partaken of alcohol at all, in fact. Partly because drinking was a social thing and he wasn't a sociable person, to understate, but also because of bad childhood memories associated with his alcoholic parents. But he was trying to seem normal. Normal people who bellied up to a crowded bar were there to drink.

"Um…get me a Budweiser."

The bartender nodded and went away. A moment later, he returned with an open bottle of Bud. He set it on a napkin in front of Elliot and said, "Start a tab?"

"Um…okay."

"I'll need a credit card."

Elliot had no idea if that was normal, but he had to assume so. He dug out his wallet, took out his card, and handed it over.

He'd taken exactly one sip of the beer when he felt a tap on his shoulder. This was no incidental touch. Someone was deliberately trying to get his attention. This was so unexpected that it triggered a sense of panic. His heart pounding, he swiveled slowly around on the stool, his eyes widening in shock when he saw the redheaded woman Susan had been sitting with leaning close to him.

"Hey there."

Elliot's mouth moved, but no words came out.

The redhead laughed. "My friend wants to talk to you." She turned away from him and swept a hand in Susan's direction. Susan was looking right at him. She smiled and waggled her fingers. Elliot wondered if he might be dreaming. No way could this be happening. Not like this, not this fast. The redhead tugged at his shirt sleeve. "Go on. Sit with her a bit. I'll keep your stool warm."

After another moment's hesitation, Elliot slid off the stool and allowed the redhead to hop up on it in his place. Swallowing a seemingly softball-sized lump in his throat, Elliot shuffled over to Susan's table on legs that felt ready to buckle beneath him at any moment. But he managed to get there and climb up on the redhead's vacated stool without falling over. As he did, he realized he'd left his beer at the bar, but he didn't really care. He was too stunned at having been called over to Susan's table. It still didn't feel like anything that could really be happening. Could it be that she'd spotted him on his way into the bar and had actually found him attractive? Things like that happened to people who weren't hopeless social misfits all the time.

Maybe it was finally happening to him.

Susan's arms were folded over the edge of the table. Her breasts pushed against them as she leaned forward, which had the effect of making them swell and strain against the scooped neckline of her black top. "What do you want with me, weirdo?"

Elliot's face reddened. "Um..."

All at once, his mind was empty. He hadn't the first clue how to reply.

She smirked. "You want something, don't you? I mean, you've been following me around all this time. Yeah, I noticed. You think I'm stupid? Or blind?" She shook her head. "So what do you want?"

Sweat dripped from Elliot's armpits. He still couldn't make himself speak.

Susan tilted her head. "Do you want to fuck me?"

Elliot gasped.

Susan laughed. "Jesus. You're a nervous wreck. Calm down. It's a simple question. Do you want to fuck me? Because I'll be honest. You're not really my type. Hell, I doubt you're anybody's type. But maybe we could work something out."

Elliot frowned. "Work something out?"

Susan nodded, stirring the little red straw in her nearly empty cocktail glass. "You must want me. You wouldn't follow me around like you do otherwise. Anybody who wants something that badly would probably be willing to pay for it. Am I right?"

Elliot gaped at her.

Susan rolled her eyes. "Don't look so shocked. I bust my ass at the factory and barely make ends meet. You're a stalker creep. Now, I could do what most girls do in this situation and report your ass to the cops, maybe get a restraining order. But I like to think outside the box, you know? What I see here is an opportunity for both of us. We can both get something we want. I'll fuck you. I will. I'll fuck you *so* good." She laughed. "But you'll need to make it worth my while. A thousand dollars. That's my non-negotiable price."

Elliot stared at her and said nothing. But this time his silence had nothing to do with nerves.

His expression hardened as he glared at her. A corner of his mouth twitched.

Frowning, Susan leaned forward again. "What the fuck? Do you not have anything at all to say?"

Elliot just kept staring at her. His hands curled into fists on the table.

Susan's frown twisted, becoming a scowl. "Jesus, dude. If you're trying to creep me out, you're doing a fucking great job of it." She tilted her head again, a hint of appraisal in her expression now. "Hold on. Are you…are you a *virgin*?"

Elliot got up from the table. "The next time you see me, you won't talk to me like this." Now he was the one scowling. "*Whore*."

Shaking with fury, he retrieved his credit card from the bartender and hurried out of the bar.

21

Four days until Halloween
Willow Springs, TN

The burned-out cruiser last used by Deputy Lucas was discovered by a man named George Turner just before dawn. Turner had been on his way to visit his old friends Harlan and Carol McAfee, who were still despondent in the wake of their son Lloyd's senseless murder. He was still several miles from their farm when he spotted the cruiser by the side of the state road. Though the vehicle had been reduced to a mostly blackened husk, a section of door on the passenger side was unscathed. This included the insignia identifying it as the property of the Willow Springs Sheriff's Department. The door had been left standing wide open, which likely accounted for its mostly unmarred condition. A fire department representative theorized a match had been tossed through the open door, igniting the gasoline that had been liberally splashed all over its interior.

Once the discovery was reported, a number of official vehicles converged on the scene, sirens wailing and blue lights flashing in the still-receding gloom of the dawn hour. Sheriff Lee was a late arrival on the scene, having been roused from sleep by a frantic Deputy Acker, who'd come out to his house to break the news. Deputy Lucas hadn't returned to the department at the end of his shift the previous evening, which had caused considerable concern.

Once Lee had been apprised of this new development, concern gave way to dread. He dressed hurriedly and rode out to the scene with Acker, who drive like a madman all the way back across town and out down that long and winding stretch of state road. Lee held on for dear life the whole way out there, but never once raised his voice in complaint, such was his fear of what might have happened to his deputy.

Crime techs in their white suits were already poring over the scene by the time they arrived. Fearing scene contamination, the man in charge of the unit tried waving him off, but Lee pushed past him and took a look inside the smoldering vehicle. It was a charred hunk of melted plastic and blackened metal, but he saw enough to recognize that no human remains were inside. Seeing this allowed him a moment of profound relief, but the feeling was short-lived. While Jason Lucas had escaped incineration in the cruiser, he was still missing and it seemed likely he'd met with some form of foul play.

A couple hours later, Lee sat behind the desk in his office with his third cup of coffee in front of him. He'd be needing a fourth cup before long. It was going to be a long day. There was a massive search to coordinate. A lawman had vanished under suspicious circumstances. Lee thought the man was probably dead, but the absence of a body meant an all-out effort to find him was required. So long as even the slightest chance of finding the man alive existed, nothing short of the full utilization of every tool and every able body at his disposal was acceptable.

He had Pete Acker and Vic Bailey, without question his best men, looking into the missing deputy's activities prior to when he'd gone missing. Thus far their inquiries had turned up no obvious red flags. The people Lucas had talked to at various stops along his usual patrol route had reported nothing out of the ordinary. But it was early yet. *Something* had gone wrong somewhere along the way during the deputy's patrol yesterday. And somewhere out there was a clue as to what that might have been. Sheriff Lee had total faith in the ability of his men to ferret out whatever that thing was.

In the meantime, he had a ton of other related headaches facing him. A meeting with the enraged mayor of Willow Springs had just concluded. A murderer was loose in the mayor's community and he was demanding answers. Just before storming out of Lee's office, the man issued an ultimatum—have a suspect in custody by sundown or else. The mayor was a little vague on the "or else" part, but the implications were clear.

Get results and get them soon, or get ready to step down.

It was probably all a lot of hot air. The man was a politician. He'd be up for reelection soon, which meant the need to keep his anxious constituency happy was greater than ever. As an elected official himself, Lee knew he couldn't be forced out quite that easily. There was no evidence of misconduct on his part sufficient enough to warrant his removal from the post. In truth, though, Lee wouldn't mind taking an early retirement. After all, that very thing had been on his mind a lot of late. But he remained reluctant to go away before finding Lloyd McAfee's murderer and solving the mystery of what had happened to his missing deputy.

The outer offices of the department were crowded with people interested in helping him do that very thing. These included representatives from the Tennessee Bureau of Investigation, detectives from the Hooperville police force, and various other investigators. On top of all that, there was the blinking light on his desk phone. A detective from Nashville was waiting on hold for him. Lee was in no hurry to resume talking to the man, who had taken a deeply condescending tone with him.

Reports of a brutal triple homicide had dominated the news out of that city today. The dick from Nashville was looking into any possible connections between the strange murders in Willow Springs and Hooperville. Lee couldn't see it. The thing with the pumpkins obviously linked Lloyd McAfee's murder with the double homicide in Hooperville. But there'd been no pumpkins left at the scene in Nashville. Nashville was a big city by Tennessee's standards. Shocking murders were a semi-regular occurrence there. And there was the fact that the city was more than an hour west of Willow Springs to consider. Hooperville was much closer. If the killer had taken the trouble to travel all that way out there, surely he would have left his unusual calling card at that scene, as well.

No, the Nashville dick could stew in his bad attitude a while longer. He was obviously barking up the wrong damn tree.

Lee took another sip from the nearly empty coffee mug as the door to his office came open and Cynthia Ashford poked her head in. "Bob, those TBI men are getting kind of irate. Do you think you could see them now?"

Lee sighed after draining the last dregs from the mug. "Not just yet. Oh, don't give me that look. I'll talk to them shortly." He held out the empty mug with one hand and, with the index finger of his other hand, punched the blinking line one light on his phone twice, cutting off the call from the Nashville dick. "Be a dear and get me another refill, please."

Cynthia came into the office and took the mug away from him. "Your heart's gonna explode from all this caffeine if you keep going at this rate."

Lee smiled and leaned back in his chair again. "There are worse ways to go."

22

When the lunchtime buzzer sounded, Susan Rochon stripped off her gloves and safety goggles, grabbed her purse and keys from the bottom shelf of her work station, and joined the fast-moving stream of workers leaving the building. Outside, in a large grassy area adjacent to the back door, were several picnic tables. Many of Susan's coworkers seated themselves at the tables and unpacked bland meals from various types of containers. The sun was out and the sky was clear. Chillier, gloomier days were coming and the instinct to sit outside in the sun was only natural. When daytime temperatures started dropping precipitously next week, all these same people would shift their lunchtime routines to the cafeteria.

But Susan wouldn't be joining them then either. She hated her job at the factory. It paid the bills—barely—but the work was far from rewarding. She'd been doing it for years and had long ago come to feel like a soulless automaton. She was just a cog in a big machine, and an easily replaceable one, at that. No special skill was required to do what she did, nor was any advanced schooling. Anyone could do it with just a little on-the-job training. It was mindless, soul-killing grunt work and not at all what she'd imagined for herself when she was younger. She'd had big dreams back then, higher aspirations, but it had all come to nothing. Now she was stuck in a rut of interminable shifts rendered even more numbing by a seemingly permanent state of mandatory overtime. Thus she relished any opportunity, regardless of how fleeting, to flee the premises.

She hurried out to her Dodge Dart and sped away from the factory, tires squealing on asphalt as the old car rocketed out of the parking lot and out into traffic, heedless as always of oncoming cars. Horns blared. Tires screeched. Fists were shaken. Susan paid it all no mind whatsoever. The Dart was old and on its last legs. She'd welcome a collision. It'd give her a legitimate excuse for a delayed return to the factory and, if the damage on her side of things was severe enough, she might even manage to coax a replacement car out of her insurance company. Sure, it was a long shot, but a sufficiently fortuitous accident might be her only viable means of swinging a vehicle upgrade.

The Pilot truck stop was a quarter mile down the road from the factory. Sometimes she spent her half-hour lunch breaks at the Krytal's on the other side of the street, but most days she stopped in at Pilot instead. At Krystal's, you sometimes had to wait in line an annoying amount of time to place your order, and when you finally got your food, you were lucky if you got a full ten minutes to wolf your lunch down. She could get in and out of Pilot in just a few minutes, long enough to grab a beer or soda and a couple bags of shitty junk food. Her workday diet would horrify a nutritionist, but all the empty calories never seemed to hurt her. She had a fast metabolism and stayed slender no matter what. It was one of the few ways in which she was truly lucky.

Today Susan grabbed a 40-ounce bottle of malt liquor, a bag of corn chips, a stick of beef jerky, and a two-pack of Hostess Ding Dongs. The big bottle of malt liquor was a minor risk. Usually if she opted for a quick drink at lunch, she grabbed a 16-ounce tall can. As far as she'd ever been able to tell, the junk food did a fine job of covering any smell produced by a malt liquor container that size. But a 40 was a different beast altogether. Downing this thing would be the equivalent of knocking back half a regular six-pack inside of about twenty minutes. She would have a mild buzz on when she got back to work, no question. This was mildly worrisome, but she'd done it a couple times before without getting in trouble. With only a little luck, today should be no different.

Besides, she really felt like she needed every one of those extra ounces today. The toll the job was taking on her psyche was feeling more burdensome than ever. There were times lately where she felt like she was near a breaking point. She needed a change, a big one, but she had no clue how to make that happen. A better job would require going back to school and completing her degree, but she couldn't afford to do that. She was stuck. It made her want to scream.

Outside, as she stalked across the lot to the far corner space where she'd parked the Dart, she twisted the cap off the 40 bottle and let the little piece of aluminum slip from her fingers. It hit the dirty asphalt and rolled until a pebble stopped it cold. Susan took her first swig from the paper sack-covered bottle as she neared her car. The sack obscured the nature of the beverage she was imbibing, of course, but it had to be obvious to all but the most clueless observer what she was actually doing. It was another of those little risks. One, obviously, she was willing to take.

But there were no cops in the vicinity and she made it back to the Dart without incident. As she reached the car, she fished her keys out of her purse while raising the bottle to her mouth to take another deep pull from it. She sensed the presence rushing up behind her at the last possible moment. Dropping the bottle and her keys, she reached into her purse again, frantically fumbling for the can of mace she always carried with her. The 40 bottle shattered on the asphalt as her fingers brushed the slim canister. Before she could grasp it, however, a gloved hand slapped a wet cloth over her mouth.

When consciousness returned an indefinite time later, her wrists were bound behind her back and a dirty rag was lodged in her mouth. A strip of duct tape had been slapped across her mouth to keep her from spitting out the rag. She was flat on her back on an uneven metal surface. There was a pattern of shallow grooves in the metal. Something heavy had been laid across her midsection to help keep her motionless. It felt like an extra-large sandbag. More than one, maybe. She hadn't been blindfolded, but a heavy tarp had been draped over her body, which blinded her almost as effectively. After a few moments, however, her basic situation became clear. Her abductor had loaded her into the bed of a pickup truck. Probably an old one, based on the irregular rumble of the engine and the severe jouncing motion caused by worn out shock absorbers.

The abduction had been executed with ruthless speed and precision. It'd also been a shockingly brazen act, occurring as it had in broad daylight in a public place. Despite the act's brutal efficiency, the brazenness suggested an unbalanced mind. Once this realization came to her, a creeping terror began to displace the analytical thinking that had been keeping her relatively calm. Some strange man, probably one with a fair amount of experience at this sort of thing, had taken her against her will and was now transporting her to some unknown location to do who-knew-what to her. That she'd been taken by a man seemed obvious. In general, women didn't do things like this. Unless she managed to get free of her bonds and pull off a miraculous escape, some form of sexual violation would likely be perpetrated upon her person.

And then, almost certainly, a violent death would follow.

Tears leaked from the corners of her eyes and trickled down into her ears. She whimpered behind the gag, frustrated by her inability to call out for help. The feeling was made worse by the certainty that there were people around who *could* help her if only they knew of her predicament. She heard engine sounds and tinny music emanating from car radios, as well as the occasional blare of a horn. The truck's frequent stops and starts also seemed to confirm that the driver was still making his way through city traffic. Whenever the truck rolled to a temporary stop, she imagined oblivious people sitting behind the wheels of their vehicles, never guessing that a woman in dire peril was only a few feet away. It made her want to scream. And she tried. But the combination of the gag and the myriad traffic noises rendered the sound imperceptible to anyone other than herself.

After a while, the traffic noises began to recede, taking any faint hopes of rescue with them. The truck had been puttering along at a slower speed for a couple minutes by the time it rolled to a stop again. Susan strained her ears but detected no sounds of other engines idling in the vicinity. They were no longer in the thick of midday city traffic. She flinched when a loud metal ratcheting sound penetrated the silence. Finally, the ratcheting sound stopped and the truck rolled forward again a short distance before again coming to a stop.

The ratcheting sound restarted. Then it stopped again.

The engine cut off. In a moment, Susan heard a squeak of hinges as the driver got out of the truck. This was followed by an echoing sound of footsteps as he approached the rear of the vehicle and let down the tailgate. Somewhere nearby someone was weeping quietly. Susan took an odd kind of comfort in knowing some other unfortunate soul was also imprisoned in this place. It wasn't right, but she couldn't help it. The thought of facing whatever miseries awaited her here with only the man who'd taken her for company was too horrible to bear. Her heart pounded as her abductor climbed up into the truck bed, grabbed hold of the tarp, and hauled it away from her.

A flickering overhead light provided dim illumination.

Susan stared up into the sneering face of her abductor, her heart sinking as she thought, *Oh, no. Not him.*

23

A sheriff's department cruiser was parked at the curb outside the Everly house on Broadbent Lane and a black SUV was parked in the wide concrete driveway. No family members were hanging around outside, but Ricky Bennet figured they were definitely home. The bored-looking deputy behind the wheel of the cruiser was proof of that. No way would Sheriff Fatso have one of his men stationed outside an empty house while a homicidal maniac was on the loose somewhere in Willow Springs. He was a borderline incompetent hayseed, but he wasn't completely stupid.

Ricky wanted to discuss that very subject with his old buddy's wife, but the presence of the cruiser almost prompted him to drive on by and save the idea for another time. There was just one problem with that. He wasn't sure there'd *be* time for a discussion later. After giving the matter considerable thought, he thought he knew who'd killed Lloyd McAfee. He was also pretty sure he knew *why* it had happened. The clues were there, though they would only be obvious to a select few. Of those few, one was dead and two were now missing.

For Ricky, the clincher had come earlier today, when he'd driven out to Jimmy Martin's trailer. He'd wanted to talk the matter over with him and see if he could get a sense for whether his old friend's thinking on the subject had developed along the same lines. Nothing had seemed amiss as he drove up to the trailer. The old pickup he'd occasionally seen Jimmy riding around town in was parked outside, suggesting he was probably home. When no one answered his repeated strident knocks on the trailer's door, however, he turned around on the little porch and scanned the area for signs of anything that didn't look right. It didn't take long for something to catch his eye. He stepped off the porch and knelt in the scraggly, dying grass in front of the pickup, dipping his fingers in a patch of something dark that turned out to be a pool of coagulated blood.

After making this ominous discovery, he kicked in the trailer's door and did a quick inspection of its interior. It was unoccupied. Despite the lack of a body, it seemed clear to Ricky that Lloyd's killer had come after Jimmy. He'd either been killed or abducted, though the blood staining the ground outside suggested he'd been seriously wounded at the very least. Coming on the heels of Lloyd's death and Chuck's disappearance, it was hard not to find this disturbing. Not because he genuinely cared about any of his old friends—he'd only been on speaking terms with Lloyd—but rather for what it implied for him.

I'm next, he'd thought, standing there in Jimmy's cramped little kitchen. *I'm the only one left, so the fucking psycho's definitely coming after me soon.*

His first impulse was to call Bob Lee and spill everything he knew. Once the law knew who they were looking for, tracking the man down would become a much simpler matter. But Ricky despised the sheriff, who'd given him a hard time in the old days. On more than one occasion, he'd been treated in a way that could without question be characterized as police brutality. His complaints about it had been laughed off by local officials. A lot of years had passed, but the experiences were at the root of a deeply ingrained hatred and distrust of authority figures. There was also the matter of how he would be perceived once the story of what he and his friends had done all those years ago came to light. Not just by the law, but by all the other people in his life. Friends, neighbors, coworkers. His status as a town hall agitator and loony conspiracy theorist had already reduced his social circle considerably. Ricky had a healthy disdain for his fellow man in general, but he had no wish to become completely ostracized from the community.

So the hell with telling the sheriff. Something had to be done, of course. Somewhere out there was a man who wanted him dead. He just wasn't sure what to do about it yet. In the short term, he decided he would deal with the situation by becoming a moving target. If the killer didn't know where he was, he wouldn't be able to get to him. This obviously meant he would have to avoid returning home for a while. As a lifelong bachelor, he lived alone, so this wasn't too big a deal. Someone would have to look in on his dog, but that was a problem with a relatively easy solution. He'd just call the old lady who lived next door and tell her about the rock-shaped hide-a-key stashed under his back porch.

Halloween was only a few days away. Ricky was certain the killer's quest for vengeance was tied to that event. And he had a feeling the man he'd bullied so mercilessly long ago meant to go out in a blaze of bloody glory. One way or another, then, the whole thing would be over soon. In the meantime, he would determine whether there might be some chance of profitably exploiting his secret knowledge of the situation.

From what he understood after querying mutual acquaintances, Karen believed her husband had taken off with some neighbor lady who'd confessed to an affair with him. Both had disappeared shortly afterward, which gave the idea extra credence. But Chuck's wife didn't know what Ricky knew. Maybe he could share just enough information to make her believe there was a more sinister explanation behind her husband's disappearance. And if he could do that, maybe he could shake some money out of her for a carefully edited version of the rest of it, along with a promise not to let the law know where she'd gotten the story.

He knew it was kind of a crazy idea. Withholding information regarding an active felony investigation was a serious offense in its own right. There was a chance Karen Everly would ignore his request for secrecy and blab to the sheriff about his visit. But Ricky thought it was a risk worth taking. Chuck had done well for himself over the years, better than he'd done by a factor of at least ten. There was money to be had here, potentially. Good money. And if Chuck's wife didn't bite, well, he could always phone in an anonymous tip. However, while that would certainly put the law on Elliot Parker's trail, it wouldn't put any cash in Ricky's pocket. If reward money was being offered, he hadn't heard about it yet. It had to be forthcoming, of course, but perhaps not soon enough, if Ricky's theory about the killer's Halloween-focused end game was correct.

Ricky eased to a stop at the curb outside the Everly house. He'd parked on the opposite side of the driveway from the cruiser, facing it. The deputy stared at him from behind mirrored sunglasses, distrust evident in his stolid expression. He got out of his cruiser when Ricky climbed out of his Hyundai.

"Stop right there, sir."

Ricky immediately complied with this directive, knowing from too much past experience how easily anything else could turn into a huge mistake.

The deputy came a few steps closer, his right hand dropping to the handle of his holstered handgun. "State your business here."

"I need to see Karen Everly."

"Why?"

Ricky arranged his features in an expression of bland, non-threatening friendliness. "I'm an old friend of her husband's. I wanted to check in and see how she's doing."

The deputy's unchanging expression betrayed neither belief nor disbelief, but his fingers did come away from the grip of his gun. "What's your name?"

An impulse to lie came and went. Giving this man an alias could backfire in too many ways. He kept the bland smile in place as he said, "Ricky Bennet."

The deputy nodded and jabbed an index finger at him. "Stay right there. I'll ask the lady of the house if she wants to see you."

"Tell her I knew her man when we were kids."

"Just stay right there and keep your mouth shut while I'm talking to her."

Ricky's smile froze on his face.

Fuck you, pig.

The deputy turned away from him and approached the house. After climbing the steps to the porch, he knocked twice on the door and moved back a step, turning sideways to keep an eye on Ricky. In a moment, the door opened and an attractive blonde woman appeared in the doorway. She and the deputy spoke in hushed tones, the deputy leaning closer as they conversed. The woman—Karen Everly, presumably—glanced Ricky's way a couple times during the exchange.

At last, the deputy stepped back again and waved Ricky over.

Ricky smiled in a warmer way as he approached the house. "Afternoon, Ms. Everly."

She stared at him evenly and gave only a terse nod in response. Her frosty expression did not instill confidence. Right away he perceived a distinct lack of fragility. This was a strong woman. Being spurned in so callous a way had not reduced her to an emotional wreck, which meant he'd have a much tougher time exploiting any concerns she might have for her husband. His instinct upon recognizing this was to ditch his plan and take his leave of this place after exchanging a few meaningless platitudes.

But maybe the tough exterior was an act, one she was maintaining for the sake of her kids. That was just as possible, he supposed. One way or the other, he should be able to tell within a few moments of talking to her. A lot would depend on whether they could have their chat privately. If not, the plan would definitely have to be abandoned.

Karen Everly finally addressed him when he reached the porch. "Deputy Ellis told me who you are. Ricky Bennet, right?"

"Yes, ma'am."

Karen nodded. "Chuck used to tell me stories about you. He said you bullied him terribly when you were boys. He was in therapy for years because of you."

Ricky shrugged. "I don't know about all that. We were rambunctious young men. Maybe I was more aggressive than I should've been at times, but I never meant Chuck any harm. We were pals for years before drifting apart."

"What do you want with me, Mr. Bennet?"

Ricky's initial impression of Karen Everly's emotional toughness was seeming more accurate all the time. Still, he'd come this far and felt compelled to take one last crack at this thing before being on his way. "I was hoping I could have a word with you in private, Ms. Everly. It'll only take a few minutes of your time, I promise."

Karen grunted. "A word in private about *what*?"

Jesus, this broad is one tough nut to crack.

Struggling to keep his smile in place, Ricky glanced at the deputy. The man's demeanor hadn't been friendly to start with, but a subtle shift in his posture suggested he could transition to outright hostility at any second. Ricky's gaze shifted back to Karen Everly. "I think I might have a good idea about where Chuck's gone off to, that's all." Another quick glance at the deputy. "Just trying to respect your husband's privacy by keeping it between you and me. It's not anything the law needs to know about, trust me."

A bald-faced lie, of course, but he told it with conviction.

Karen sighed. "Fine, but just for a minute." She moved back a step and waved him into the house. "Come on in. We'll talk out back. No one will bother us there. Let him in, deputy."

The deputy's expression remained distrustful as Ricky brushed past him and entered the house. Once he was inside, Karen closed the door and led him out of the foyer and down a long hallway to the kitchen. Along the way, Ricky couldn't help taking note of the tasteful decorations and expensive-looking fixtures and furnishings. Everything about the place reinforced his image of the family's prosperity. It also strengthened his resolve to push this thing with Karen as far as he could in exchange for a possible small taste of that prosperity.

He temporarily forgot all about his greed as they entered the kitchen. A tall, well-built man with blond hair was standing at the kitchen island, where he was making a sandwich. The man wore black warmup pants and a tight black T-shirt, the fabric of which adhered to his muscular build in a way that brought a flush to Ricky's face.

The blond man saw him staring and smirked. "Who's your friend?"

"He's not my friend. He says he has information about Chuck."

The man arched an eyebrow. "Oh, yeah? Shouldn't you be talking to the cops, dude?"

Ricky opened his mouth to say something, but no words would come out. He cleared his throat and averted his gaze, staring at the floor as he said, "Not a matter for the cops."

The words squeaked out.

The blond man grunted. "Whatever, man."

He went back to working on his sandwich.

It required a considerable effort of will, but Ricky made himself not look back at the man as Karen led him down into a den and then out to the patio. Though he hoped not to see him again on the way back through the house, Ricky knew he'd be thinking of him plenty later. In bed, probably, wherever he spent the night. He let out a breath once they were outside and wiped sweat from his face. Karen waved him into one of the wicker chairs on the patio and seated herself in one near it.

She leaned back in her chair and crossed her legs. "Okay, it's just us now. What is it you need to tell me? Do you really know where my asshole husband is?"

A fresh sheen of sweat appeared on Ricky's face. He felt off-balance now, more ill at ease even than he'd anticipated. For a few silent moments, he weighed how to tell some of what he knew without divulging the full truth, but that unbalanced feeling kept the right words from surfacing.

Just as the silence was reaching the point of becoming uncomfortable, he surprised himself by spitting out the truth. "I'm afraid that was a lie, Ms. Everly. We did something a long time ago. Me and Chuck and our friends. Something really bad."

Ricky's heart was pounding. He couldn't believe he'd just uttered those words. And yet, strangely, he felt no desire to take them back.

Karen looked troubled. "What did you do?"

Ricky held her gaze for a long moment. And then he took a deep breath and launched into the rest of it. The full story. The whole unvarnished, ugly truth. Tears filled his eyes as he talked. Before long, he realized he'd spent his life desperately needing to rid himself of this great burden on his conscience.

The look on Karen's face shifted many times as he talked, alternately conveying sympathy, disgust, outrage, and sadness. Ricky was most of the way through the story when the patio door creaked open. Neither of them glanced that way at first. Karen was too enthralled and Ricky was too focused on getting the rest of the tale out.

The door opened wider.

Ricky caught a glimpse of a man dressed all in black in his peripheral vision. He finally stopped talking as the man tossed something through the open doorway. Two somethings, actually. Karen screamed as the severed heads of Deputy Ellis and the blond man from the kitchen struck patio concrete and rolled. The shock of what he was seeing was initially too much for Ricky. It didn't seem real. Then the man in black—who was wearing a ski mask—was rushing toward him. Clutched in his right hand now was an object Ricky needed a moment to recognize as a stun gun.

Survival instinct belatedly kicked in, causing him to fall out of his chair as he tried to scramble away from the masked man. He landed face-to-face with the severed head of the blond man, mere inches away from a visage that had once inspired lust but was now frozen in contortions of gruesome agony. Screeching in revulsion, he swatted the head away.

Karen screamed again.

Then Ricky felt the prongs of the stun gun on his neck.

There was a click and then came the jolt.

By the time he stopped convulsing, the masked man had the situation under control.

24

Four days until Halloween,
Willow Springs, TN

Prior to returning home from a long and wearying day of listening to other people talk at length about the many ways in which their fragile psyches were damaged, Lillian Rosewater had nothing on her mind but unwinding with a glass or two of fine wine and perhaps taking a soothing hot bath. That changed seconds after she unlocked her condo's front door and stepped into the darkened foyer. She sensed the presence of the lurking intruder as she began to push the door shut. Her hand tightened on the doorknob and pulled on it, causing the door to briefly swing wide open again. For an instant, she glimpsed her parked car and the safety of the brightly-lit street beyond.

But the intruder moved faster than she could. He seized her from behind as he spun about and kicked the door hard, causing it to slam into its frame. Lillian's purse slid off her shoulder and dropped to the floor as she thrashed against her assailant. She screamed and her legs kicked in the air as he lifted her off the floor. She still hadn't seen him, but she could tell he was tall and quite thin. His gloved hand slapped over her mouth, muffling her cries. He had one of her arms pinned, but the other was free. She reached behind her in an attempt to claw at his face. Her long fingernails encountered thick fabric rather than flesh. He was wearing some kind of mask. This was unfortunate. The fabric effectively negated her one opportunity to harm him and possibly get free. But she didn't cease struggling in the wake of this failure. Instead she thrashed harder than ever. She thought she knew who this person was, and if she couldn't get free of him, she would almost certainly die.

The intruder grunted in frustration as he struggled to control her. He yelped in pain when the heel of one of her expensive shoes gouged his shin. The pain inflamed his rage and he drove her to the floor, slamming her into the marble tiles with a force that blasted the air from her lungs and caused eruptions of agony throughout her body. Even in the midst of great pain, she continued to struggle, albeit more weakly than before. A part of her knew it was hopeless now, but Lillian had never been one to give up a fight easily, as both her ex-husbands could attest. But the intruder was on top of her now. She could do nothing to stop him as he placed a cloth soaked in a pungent chemical over her face. Soon her struggles ceased altogether and the world drifted away for a time.

When she regained consciousness, she was tied to a chair in some other location. She couldn't see because of the bag over her head, but she knew she was somewhere else. There was something different in the atmosphere, an underlying sense of rot and sickness. Also, someone was moving about nearby. The echoing footsteps suggested a large, open space. And then there were the other people. She heard them out there in the dark. Not voices, but whimpers and sounds of labored breathing. Others her abductor had taken, she supposed. Based on her many years of intimately revealing conversations with the likely culprit, she imagined she could even hazard a guess as to the identities of some of these other unfortunates.

"Elliot? Is that you moving around out there?"

She heard more of those echoing footsteps, but the man who'd

170

taken her did not answer her query. The silence was a deliberate thing, she believed, a form of psychological torture. He wanted her terror to grow as she imagined what he might be doing out there in the darkness. The others had likely endured similar treatment upon being brought to this dank, smelly place. He was deriving pleasure from their fear. It was a power thing. Another manifestation of this was her shorn scalp. Elliot had shaved her bald while she was unconscious. She had only just become aware of it, with the way the rough fabric of the bag was making her scalp itch.

This was disheartening, which was the whole point. She was an attractive woman and had taken pride in her long, lustrous hair, maintaining a stylish, chic look with frequent visits to her favorite salon. Now she had been robbed of one of the hallmarks of her beauty, stripped of an element of her personal power. He had also removed her clothes. Elliot Parker was a socially inept and emotionally crippled man who had spent his life feeling the opposite of confident and powerful. Now, however, he did feel powerful. He had several terrified human beings under his absolute control. And he had them in a location where he obviously felt secure. Wherever this place was, he believed he could do anything he wanted with his captives without fear of interruption.

Lillian knew it was imperative that she continue trying to engage Elliot. Her years of access to the man's inner thoughts put her in a unique position. Among her fellow captives, she might be the only one with any chance of reasoning with him. Perhaps this was part of why he'd taken her. On some level, maybe he wanted her to talk him down from whatever he had in mind for herself and the rest of these poor people. She was frightened, but she needed to set that aside and attempt to utilize her skills as a psychotherapist.

Another thing she needed to compartmentalize was her regret. She had heard all about the strange and brutal crimes occurring across the mid-state over the last few days, and it had briefly crossed her mind to wonder whether Elliot might be behind some of it, largely due to his enduring negative Halloween fixation. In the end, she'd dismissed the idea, thinking her patient too weak and ineffectual to carry out so gruesome a campaign of carnage over so wide an area. Now, of course, she wished she hadn't been so short-sighted. She should have contacted the authorities. Doctor-patient confidentiality was a non-factor where mass murder was involved. But she hadn't done so and now there was no time for guilt.

"You don't really want to do any of this, Elliot," she said, raising her voice higher. "I know you better than anyone and I am certain of that. You're not a bad person, not really, not in your heart. Your demons have pushed you to do bad things, but it's not too late to turn back from this dark path."

Again, no reply came from the darkness.

Just more sounds of quiet suffering.

"Did you stop taking your meds, Elliot? You did, didn't you? We've talked before about that, what a bad idea it is. It took many years before you arrived at a combination that kept you nicely in balance. Disrupting that--"

She flinched when something heavy slammed against a hard surface.

"*Shut up!*"

A breathless period of near total silence stretched out in the wake of her abductor's thunderous exclamation. Until that moment, the faint sounds of suffering being made by the other captives had been almost constant, but now they ceased. Lillian sensed they were all holding their breath and cringing in anticipation of another, perhaps even worse outburst. They were afraid he might decide to vent his rage on them. She imagined they were all wishing she would keep her mouth shut. Probably they thought she was making things worse for them with her every utterance. This was an easy fear to understand. It was simple human nature. But she remained steadfast in her belief that persisting in her attempt to engage Elliot was the only hope of survival any of them had. She wasn't naïve. It was a slim hope. She knew that. But she would cling to it as long as she could.

The tense silence ended with a heavy exhalation of breath from somewhere in the darkness. Lillian let out a breath of her own when she heard it. The other captives reacted similarly, resuming their quiet whimpers and sobs. She suspected the deep sigh had come from Elliot. The sound seemed to have issued from a direction corresponding with where he'd been when he'd screamed at her. She estimated he was at least twenty feet away. The distance provided no comfort. She remained physically powerless, strapped to a heavy, sturdy chair with a thick frame. Multiple thick strands of rope and overlapping layers of tape bound her extremities to the arms and legs of the chair to the point of nearly complete immobility. The only parts of her body she could move were her head and the tips of her fingers.

In another moment, the man she assumed was Elliot began moving around again. Her heart stuttered when she realized he was coming her way. Another sound accompanied his echoing footsteps, a strange whirring from somewhere overhead. The sound ceased when her captor came to a stop at a point just behind her. She gasped when, without warning, he snatched the bag off her head and let it fall to the concrete floor.

Lillian squinted against the glare of a single overhead bulb. The bulb wasn't very bright, but the sight deprivation had rendered her overly sensitive to its glow, a condition that didn't last long. Soon she was able to open her eyes wider and take in more of her surroundings. She craned her head around as far as she could in an attempt to catch a glimpse of her abductor, but he was still effectively hidden from view. He was still playing his power games, drawing out the uncertainty, trying to make her doubt all the things her intuition was telling her.

Aside from herself and the kidnapper, there were at least four other live human beings in the big room. Two were off to her right, about twenty feet away. A woman and, probably, a man. They sat bound to chairs, facing each other. The woman was an attractive blonde in early middle age. She had been stripped of her clothes and had a ball-gag affixed to her face. She was trembling nonstop and her face was streaked with tears. The man had a pumpkin over his head, yet another indicator that Elliot's was the diseased mind behind all this madness.

There were wire cages against the wall behind her, but they were far enough to her right that she'd been able to glimpse the men confined in them. Both men had their hands bound behind their backs. Studded leather dog collars encircled their necks. Strips of duct tape covered their mouths. A heavy length of chain dangled from some type of ceiling fixture in front of each cage.

All this was bad enough, but it was the pile of corpses over by the vehicles lined up to her left that really got to her. She started trembling as she counted at least four bodies. The last of her composure began to drain away. "Elliot, this is madness. You must stop before it's too late."

A soft chuckle emanated from directly behind her. "I don't *have* to do anything, Lillian. This is my domain, my kingdom of pain. In here, I can do whatever I want." She gasped when she felt his hands settle on her bare shoulders. Her bottom lip quivered as they slid down to her breasts and groped them. "Mmm, I've always wanted to do that. All those years of sitting across from you in your office, half the time all I could think about was how much I wanted to touch your tits. The reality of it is better than I ever imagined." He pinched her nipples, hard, making her wince. "They're nice."

Lillian tried hard to keep her voice steady as she said, "Stop doing that, Elliot. It's inappropriate."

He laughed, a harsher sound than the previous chuckle. "This isn't a therapy session, you stupid bitch. You don't get to tell me what's appropriate here. In fact, you'll never again be able to lecture me about anything at all." His hands came away from her breasts. "Alas, I don't have as much time to play with you as I'd like. I'm on a mission, you see, and I only have a short while left to accomplish my goals. You're a distraction. I'll dispense with you now and get on with it."

This pronouncement was ominous enough to obliterate what little remained of her composure. "Elliot, don't hurt me. Please. I'll do anything you want."

His only reply to that was a laugh. He moved away from her for a moment, but remained out of sight. When he returned, she sensed him looming behind her, arms outstretched above her head. She turned her gaze upward, her eyes widening as she recognized the device gripped in his hands. Though she had no clue what he had in mind, she cried out in alarm as he lowered the halo brace down over her head. He applied a painful amount of pressure to the back of her head, enough to allow him to shove the rear part of the brace down behind her back. Once he'd done this, he moved into view for the first time, leaning down in front of her to secure the straps to the front portion of the attached vest.

"Elliot. Please."

He laughed.

A halo brace was typically used for stabilizing the heads of people who had suffered severe spinal injuries during their recoveries. A metal ring encircling her forehead and the back of her skull was attached to the vest by four metal bars. Additionally, Elliot wound a length of cord around the bars and tied the cord to the back of the chair to immobilize her head.

Elliot stepped back and appraised his work. "Good," he said, nodding. "Now I just need to secure the head clamp."

Tears rushed from Lillian's eyes as her terror intensified. "Don't. You can't do this. Please."

Elliot turned away from her and stalked off into the darkness. His black-clad form melted into the shadows at the far side of the large room. She heard a clank of metal objects being moved around. In a moment, the sounds ceased and he reemerged from the shadows, a power drill clutched in his right hand. Some smaller objects were clasped loosely in his left hand. She didn't have to see them to know what they were.

There were little holes spaced at regular intervals around the head ring. They were used to affix the ring to the skull with pins. Normally this was a surgical procedure performed in a sterile environment with the patient under anesthesia. Lillian started screaming an instant before Elliot drilled the first screw into her skull. The screams continued as he inserted three more screws, nausea overwhelming her with each high-pitched mechanical whir of the drill. Blood leaked from the holes and trickled down the sides of her head and her face. By the time he finished, her heart was pounding so hard she feared it would detonate like a bomb. At this point, though, that might be a mercy.

Elliot moved away again, carrying the drill back over to the table on the shadow-cloaked opposite side of the room. When he came back, he leered at Lillian and said, "I bet I know what you're thinking. That must be the end of it, right? But that's where you're wrong. Let me show you something."

He disappeared behind her again, but only for a moment. Before he reappeared, that overhead whirring sound she'd heard prior to the removal of the bag from her head came again. She rolled her eyes upward as he came back into view and saw a thick cable attached to a pulley track on the ceiling. Attached to the end of the cable was another device she recognized.

Elliot grinned. "I'm sure you know what this is, but if you don't, allow me to enlighten you. What I have in my hand here is an oscillating autopsy bone saw."

He pressed a switch and the circular metal blade at the end of the little cylinder whirred to life for a moment before he clicked it off again.

Lillian screamed.

The whimpers and moans of her fellow captives grew louder.

Elliot stepped closer, pulling the cable along with him. "Here's the deal, Lillian. The way I see it, you've failed me. I spent the better part of two decades seeing you off and on and what did it get me? That's a rhetorical question. You carry right on screaming. I'll tell you what it got me. It got me jack fucking shit. Twenty years later and you never even came close to solving my problems, all while never showing even one ounce of real humility or empathy. Oh, I know you'd say otherwise, but fuck you. You always thought you were above me, all those years of sitting across from me in those sexy designer clothes, always looking so goddamned smug and superior while you listened to me pour my fucking heart out. Well, now I'm turning the tables. Now it's time for *me* to get inside *your* head, bitch."

He pressed the button on the cylinder.

The blade began to whir.

Lillian's loudest scream yet ripped out of her lungs, filling the big room with peals of high-pitched sound that bounced off the walls, reverberating endlessly as Elliot leaned over her and applied the edge of the whirring blade to her forehead. The screams continued as the blade bit through her flesh and cut through her skull with disconcerting ease. A steady spray of blood was spit out by the blade as Elliot kept guiding it along the top edge of the metal ring encircling her head.

Lillian managed a few more screams, remaining alive and conscious far longer than Elliot imagined she would. But she did finally expire moments before he cut off the autopsy saw and removed the top of her skull, exposing her brain.

Using another tool, he scooped the brain out and set it on a plate.

Then he carried the organ up to his second floor living quarters, sliced it into several portions, and dumped those in a stovetop skillet, turning the heat up to medium.

25

The horrific, bloodcurdling screams of Elliot Parker's latest victim sickened and saddened Chuck, but they did allow him a temporary respite from his wife's accusatory, hateful glare. Elliot had affixed the ball-gag to her face before she regained consciousness, a development Chuck couldn't help seeing as a mixed blessing. On the one hand, he didn't have to listen to her berate him for his many failings or demand answers to the many uncomfortable questions she undoubtedly had for him. He deserved any abuse she wished to hurl his way, of course, but Chuck had been through a lot and didn't mind being spared this additional level of grief.

The drawback to Karen being gagged was it meant no answers to his own several burning questions, by far the most important one being the matter of whether Elliot had harmed any of their children. She had been brought to Elliot's lair along with Ricky Bennet, but he had to assume they had been taken separately. Nothing else made sense. Karen and Ricky didn't know each other, after all. Chuck figured Elliot was merely trying to take care of as much business as possible in as short a time as possible. He had an agenda, one that involved redressing grievances with a wide array of people, some for reasons known to Chuck and others that were mysteries. If he could grab two people on his list of targets during one excursion, it obviously made things simpler for him.

As with Fawn Hightower, Elliot had wasted little time dispatching the woman named Lillian. Based on what he could infer from their conversation, Chuck guessed she had been his psychiatrist or therapist. He couldn't decide whether the grotesque demise Elliot had engineered for her meant he'd hated the woman even more than the men who'd been his childhood bullies. Fawn's death by bolt-gun had been almost merciful by comparison. Judging by the way he'd ranted at her prior to cutting off the top of her head with the bone saw, it was clear he'd harbored a tremendous amount of resentment where Lillian was concerned. And maybe the depth of that feeling had been such that he simply hadn't been able to bear putting off that particular piece of vengeance.

Or maybe, as he'd told the woman, killing her now had been nothing more than a simple matter of expediency. And pragmatism, possibly. As his therapist, she would have known a lot about Elliot's personal demons, knowledge that made her a liability for a man in the midst of an epic meltdown of violence and murder. The more he thought about it, the more this made sense to Chuck. She was dead and no longer a concern.

Now the lunatic could focus his attention on the people he truly despised the most.

Me, Chuck thought. *And Ricky and Jimmy. He'll drag out our suffering as long as he can and savor every precious second of it.*

After Elliot clomped up a set of metal stairs to the building's second floor, Chuck was again forced to focus on Karen. She was back to glaring at him in that accusatory way. In all their years together, he'd never seen her look at him like that, not even close. Her wide-eyed, contorted visage radiated nothing but raw, seething hatred. It made Chuck feel like the lowest form of life on the planet, like something loathsome and repulsive dredged up from the rotten depths of the earth. Knowing he deserved nothing less was no comfort. His recently exposed transgressions aside, theirs had been a happy, fulfilling marriage. Together with their beautiful children, they'd had the perfect family.

The perfect *life*.

And now, maybe, this was all that was left of it, he and Karen imprisoned here in this vault of horrors. Chuck whimpered as his mind reluctantly returned to the question of whether his children might be dead. The possibility made him feel an aching hollowness. They were everything to him. He understood that better than ever now. If they were gone, he had nothing left to live for.

I've been a fool, he thought, not for the first time. *I had it all and took it for granted. I deserve this. But not Karen. And not my kids. Please, God, please let them be okay. Please.*

A loud, muffled exclamation emerged from behind Karen's gag. This time Chuck didn't need to hear her words clearly to know what she'd said.

You bastard!

Another high-volume, muffled exclamation followed, equally decipherable.

Fuck you!

Chuck sniffled and tried to tell her he was sorry. She seemed to get his meaning and responded with more muffled rage.

Like Lillian and Fawn, Karen had been stripped of her clothes. To Chuck's knowledge, Elliot hadn't sexually assaulted any of the women he'd brought here, but there was an undeniable element of sexual dysfunction in the removal of their garments. He might not have raped any of them yet, but Chuck feared it was only a matter of time, that he was psyching himself up to do it. He hoped he was wrong about that, but everything else about the situation suggested otherwise. Ricky Bennet, the other new arrival, was still fully clothed. This was consistent with Elliot's treatment of all his male captives. Chuck's shirt had been cut away, but that had been about something else. He was being systematically humiliated in a manner similar to what Elliot had endured in the woods so long ago. The stinking guts and viscera hanging around his neck and smeared over his chest substituted for the dog shit Chuck and his friends had smeared on Elliot back then.

Thus far Susan Rochon was alone among Elliot's female captives in having been spared the humiliation of being undressed. She had been brought here some time ago, hours before Elliot went back out and returned with Karen and Ricky. But Susan wasn't being kept down here with the rest of them. Elliot had dragged the semi-conscious woman up to the second floor shortly after bringing her here. She was still up there, as far as Chuck knew. Maybe Elliot *had* removed her clothes by now. It was possible he was up there raping her right now. Chuck hated the thought of it, but better her than Karen. Just thinking that, though, made him feel like an asshole.

He didn't know Susan very well, but they'd shared a fleeting moment together some years back, at one of their high school reunions. Karen hadn't been with him that night, having, in her opinion, attended one drunken reunion too many. As so often happened on the rare occasions when he was flying solo, he drank a little too much. Susan saw this and took advantage, cornering him in a hallway of their old school after he came out of the bathroom. They made out in the hallway for several minutes before she dragged him out to her car, where she got his pants open and went down on him. Later on, Chuck told himself this didn't count as cheating. He was drunk and in an unusual circumstance. There'd been no vaginal penetration and he hadn't returned the oral favor. So it didn't count. Not really. And nothing remotely like it had happened again, until the affair with Fawn.

Looking back, Chuck saw now how wrong-headed this view had been. He'd cheated for the first time back then. No point in continuing to rationalize it. And now he saw the incident for what it truly was—a harbinger of the darker things to come.

The squawk of a metal door opening made Chuck flinch. It

was followed seconds later by the sound of Elliot's echoing footsteps clomping down the stairs. Chuck prayed he was heading out on another of his excursions and not solely because it removed the immediate threat of physical harm to himself and the others present. Every time the man went out and engaged in more insanely risky behavior, the chances of him being interrupted in the act and apprehended went up exponentially. No one doing the crazy things he was doing could reasonably expect to get away with them forever. Sooner or later his luck would run out.

The sound the tread of Elliot's heavy boots made changed as he reached the concrete floor at the bottom of the metal steps, the resonant clang giving way to duller thumps. He did not immediately approach Chuck and the others. As he moved around in the darkness somewhere behind Chuck, a faint odor of something that might have been cooked meat wafted his way.

In a few moments, a loud rattling sound preceded Elliot's reappearance. When he came into view, the source of the rattling sound was apparent. He'd been pushing a metal cart on wheels. Atop the cart was a food tray and on the tray was a bowl. A faint wisp of steam rose up from whatever was inside the bowl. Chuck's stomach growled. He had a feeling he didn't want to know what was in the bowl, but he couldn't help the physical reaction. He hadn't eaten since being forced to ingest pieces of Fawn's viscera.

This development was disconcerting, but at least as alarming was the change in Elliot's attire. He'd changed out of his usual all-black outfit and now only wore a long yellow apron with the words "Kiss the cook" embroidered on the front in large, cartoonish red letters.

The madman smiled and rubbed his hands together. "Never let it be said that Elliot Parker doesn't have a humane side. I know you two must be famished, so I've prepared a special dish for you both. I've used a heap of special spices and seasonings to make it extra tasty." He moved the cart a little closer, until it was in the

183

center of the space directly between Chuck and Karen. His grin broadened as his gaze shifted back and forth between them. "So who wants the first taste of brain soup?"

Karen groaned in disgust and despair. She wept as her head drooped forward.

Elliot laughed. "Now here's the thing. Obviously I'll have to remove your gags in order for you to eat. Before I do that, I must set some very firm ground rules. Number one, no screaming. Number two, no talking. I mean it, don't say a word. Not to me and not to each other. Any violation of these rules will result in a rather severe punishment. I understand that the temptation to ask each other things will be strong, but for your own sake, you must resist. Unless, you know, you think you'd enjoy having appendages removed and your flesh scalded with a welding torch. But, hey, that's up to you."

Karen's sobbing grew louder.

Elliot glanced at Chuck and winked. "I'll start with your wife. Let's see how much inner strength she has. I wonder if she possesses the fortitude you so clearly lack."

He moved into position behind Karen and undid the straps of her ball-gag. After removing it from her face, he dropped the gag on the cart next to the tray and approached Chuck, who watched Karen warily through the slanted eye-holes of the jack-o'-lantern. With the constricting gag removed, she was inhaling and exhaling deeply several times, all while continuing to glare murderously at him.

But she said nothing.

Elliot lifted the pumpkin off Chuck's head and set it on the cart. The ball-gag came off next. As soon as the thick wedge of rubber was gone from his mouth, Chuck decided he would risk violating Elliot's rules. If he had to pay for it in agony, so be it.

There was something he had to know, consequences be damned.

"Karen, are the kids all right? Did he—"

Elliot's fist slammed into his jaw, silencing him.

"Now what did I tell you about breaking my rules?" Elliot waggled an admonishing finger at him and shook his head. Despite the outburst of violence, his big grin was still in place. "But here's a little something I probably should have clarified. I'm sure you thought you'd be on the receiving end of any punishment incurred for violating the rules."

Elliot moved away from Chuck and again took up a position behind Karen. He leaned over her and cupped her breasts in his hands, leering at Chuck as he did it. Karen trembled and tears spilled from her eyes as her bottom lip quivered, but she still said nothing.

"But I'm not going to torture you, Chuck. At least not yet." Another wink. "Instead I'm going to torture your wife."

"You fucking sick bastard!" Chuck hadn't been able to help it. The words had exploded out of him. But he regretted them the instant they were uttered. His eyes misted as he met Karen's gaze. "Oh, baby, I'm sorry. I'm so fucking sorry for everything."

Elliot's eyes widened in mock surprise. "Wow, you must really hate this woman. She's really gonna get it now. I wonder how I should start, hmm? Maybe I should surgically remove a breast. You saw what I did to Lillian, so you know I can do that kind of thing. I do have the equipment necessary. Of course, this would be much messier, with so many severed blood vessels and so much exposed tissue." Karen whimpered as he squeezed her breasts. She whimpered again when he pinched her nipples. "So maybe I should start by cutting off her nipples instead. But I really think I should just save the fun parts of her body for later. Wouldn't you agree that that's a good idea, Chuck?"

Shaking with rage and terror, Chuck said nothing.

Elliot's hands came away from Karen's breasts. When he stepped out from behind the chair, an erection was tenting the front of the apron. A shudder of disgust rippled through Chuck at the sight of it. Given the chance, he felt like he could tear the man apart with his bare hands. Never in his life had he felt as impotent as he did in that moment.

Elliot returned to the cart and picked up a large serving spoon, smiling as he dipped it into the steaming bowl. "You know what, Chuck? On second thought, I'm in a forgiving mood." He chuckled. "Relatively speaking, I mean. So I'll tell you what. If you can choke down the entire contents of this bowl, I'll refrain from marring your beautiful wife's body. This time, anyway."

He moved the cart closer to Chuck.

Then he lifted the serving spoon out of the bowl and held it close to Chuck's face, showing him the lump of pink tissue floating in a creamy white broth. "Time to man up, Chuck. Can you do that for your wife? Are you willing to make that sacrifice?"

Chuck's gorge rose.

He swallowed with difficulty, heaved a breath, and nodded.

Elliot looked delighted, his grin bigger than ever and his eyes showing a maniacal gleam. "Open wide."

Chuck did as instructed.

Elliot pushed the serving spoon into his mouth.

Chuck spluttered as the first slimy bit of Lillian Rosewater's brain slid down his gullet. He retched and spat it back up, causing it to fall into the mess of viscera on his chest. Elliot's smile disappeared. He swatted Chuck across the face with the serving spoon several times, opening gashes in his skin.

Then he dipped the serving spoon back in the bowl. "Let's try that again. But I'm warning you, Chuck. Throw up again and I may have to perform an intimate surgery on you, if you know what I mean. I'll cut off your dick, is what I'm saying. Now fucking open wide, asshole."

Chuck whimpered.

He opened his mouth and somehow managed to keep his gorge down as Elliot rapidly shoveled the rest of Lillian's brain down his throat.

26

The late night emergency meeting at the mayor's city hall office concluded at right around one in the morning. Bob Lee, now officially set to become the ex-sheriff of Willow Springs upon tendering his written resignation later that morning, managed to keep his composure until the very end. At that point, he cursed the mayor for his craven willingness to throw a good, dedicated official under the bus for no reason other than appeasing a panicked populace. The move would not move the investigation forward. To the contrary, it might even hamper the process, given that there was bound to be a significant amount of organizational disarray with the transition.

Nothing he said swayed the mayor in any way. The man was resolute in his belief that he had to be seen as taking decisive action in the midst of a crisis. Early on in the meeting, Lee reminded him he technically had no authority to remove an elected official from office, not without due process. But the mayor had that angle covered, too. Lee was dumbfounded as the man summoned assistants who brought in box after box of old files, all of them relating to arrests he'd made and cases he'd investigated going back to the very beginning of his career as a deputy. According to the mayor, the files were rife with evidence of gross misconduct. Some even contained photos of suspects who'd been roughed up, presumably after being taken into custody.

Lee was given the opportunity to examine a select few of the files. They were the worst of the worst, mostly from decades ago, and had obviously all been cherry-picked by the mayor's staff. Of course, the age of the files made them no less damning. They contained clear evidence of crimes committed by a hotheaded young man new at his job and still learning how to properly wield authority. Some of the pictures made him sick to his stomach and brought back memories of things he'd rather forget. For many years, he'd been under the impression that this had all been safely swept under the rug. He assumed the files had all been destroyed and could never possibly see the light of day.

How naïve he'd been.

The mayor's play was simple. Lee would voluntarily step down, formally resigning in the morning. Once he did that, the files would again disappear, sparing him the career and life-shattering repercussions that would come if they'd been made public.

So it was done.

Lee was out of a job and the killer was still out there, apparently no closer to being caught than he'd been after the discovery of Lloyd McAfee's body.

Pete Acker was waiting for him in the parking lot out back when Lee stormed out of the building. He was leaning against his cruiser, which was parked near the rear entrance. When he saw Lee, he pushed away from the vehicle and hitched up his utility belt. "How'd it go in there?"

Lee snorted. "It went like shit. I ain't the sheriff of this town anymore."

Acker grimaced, nodding. "Was afraid of that. The mayor strong-arm you somehow?"

"He sure as shit did. Goddamn son of a bitch." Lee hocked up some phlegm and spat it on the asphalt. "Vic's gonna be acting sheriff after I tender my resignation. I wanted you for the job, but the mayor had other ideas."

Acker shrugged. "Vic will do a fine job."

"He'll be a yes man. Don't get me wrong. I like Vic, but one of his best attributes is he follows orders no matter what. That's why the mayor wanted him. You're more of what they call a 'free thinker'. Pretty much the opposite of what city hall wants right now."

Another shrug from Acker. "Hell, Bob, I didn't actually want the job. I've seen the toll the stress has taken on you. I'm not that far from retirement myself. No point taking on that extra burden this late in the game."

Lee nodded and turned his gaze skyward a moment. It was a clear, still night, with only a slight chill in the air. Taking in the vista of stars glittering amidst that expanse of deep darkness helped soothe his nerves, making the severe blow to his pride hurt just a little less. The moment of calmness felt strange in the wake of all that had happened over the course of that long day.

A madman was on the prowl in Willow Springs, killing and abducting people with seeming impunity. It was bad enough that one deputy had gone missing under disturbing circumstances, but now another one was dead, slain in the line of duty in the most brazen manner imaginable. Another man, Karen Everly's brother, had also been killed. So far the maniac was succeeding through a combination of sheer luck and an eerie level of utter fearlessness. A review of footage from the dashboard cam of the deceased deputy's cruiser did not show the killer's arrival on the scene. He'd apparently had some notion of the camera's range and had remained beyond it the entire time, just waiting for the right opportunity to swoop in, eliminate the deputy, and take Karen Everly—an opportunity that came in the form of Ricky Bennet's mysterious visit to the missing woman's house.

Ricky Bennet was also missing.

The only thing that had worked out in their favor today was

that the Everly children had come to no harm. They'd never even come down from their upstairs bedrooms, remaining safely oblivious while either sleeping or listening to music on headphones. Good thing, for more reasons than one. If the lunatic had killed those kids, the townsfolk would have been marching on city hall tonight with axes and pitchforks in hand, demanding someone's head on a pike. Thankfully, however, the kids and the family pets were now safe with their grandparents in another city.

Acker cleared his throat. "So…do we think Bennet might be our perp?"

The question made Lee scowl. "Bennet's a loudmouthed asshole, but that don't make him a killer. I don't think he has the balls to pull off the kind of shit our man's been doing. Once we start matching up the killer's activities against Ricky's known whereabouts, it'll become clear he's not our guy. I'd bet serious cash on that."

He laughed.

Acker frowned. "Something funny?"

Lee shook his head. "Just the way I keep saying 'we' and 'our', as if I still had a dog in this hunt." He sighed. "It's Vic's show now, for better or worse, along with those TBI bastards. He'll have his hands full dealing with them, I'll tell you that."

The furrow in Acker's brow deepened as he stared at the asphalt with a strange intensity. "Hmm."

Lee raised an eyebrow. "Got something else on your mind?"

Acker looked at him. "Well, you know Vic and me did a lot of asking around after Jason's cruiser turned up all burnt to shit. We split up after a while to cover more ground. I found out some stuff. Stuff I haven't mentioned to Vic. Maybe important. Maybe not. Maybe ties in with Bennet showing up to the Everly place."

Despite himself, Lee found his curiosity aroused. He wanted nothing more than to go home, knock back some Tylenol PM with a shot of whiskey, and get a good night's rest before going back into the office for his last few hours on the job. Or so he'd been

190

telling himself since his dismissal from the mayor's office, but now he felt a fresh stirring of unanticipated excitement. Acker hadn't said much yet, but Lee sensed he might be on to something real. He could hear it in the man's voice.

"Spill it, Pete."

There was a new fire in the deputy's eyes as he told the rest of it. "Bennet was friends with Chuck Everly when they were kids. Real good friends, from what I was told. We already knew they were linked through Lloyd McAfee. Those boys were all part of a real tight little group. I heard versions of this story from three different individuals. They all told me this group suddenly unraveled one year in middle school. Nobody knows why exactly, except that something bad happened, something that drove them apart for good. One day they were thick as thieves, the next it was all over. Truth is probably more complicated than that, but that's the basics of the situation. Here's the kicker. There was a fourth member of that group. A guy named Jimmy Martin. I got a line on where he was living and went out there to see what I could find out from him."

A silent beat elapsed.

Lee's heart was racing. Acker was eyeing him in an expectant way, as if daring him to guess the next part. Lee had a vague inkling what it might be, but he wanted to hear Acker say it in his own words. "Go on, man. Was he there or not?"

Acker shook his head.

"Man lived in a trailer way out on that same state road where McAfee had his pumpkin stand, about seven miles down the way from there. And less than a mile from where we found Jason's cruiser. A truck was parked outside the trailer. I ran the plates. It belonged to Martin. The door to his place was open. Looked like it'd been kicked in."

Lee nodded. "Let me guess. No sign of the man."

"You guessed it, boss." A hint of a tired smile touched the corners of the deputy's mouth. "Now let me ask you this. Is it just a coincidence every member of this old group of buddies is suddenly either missing or dead?"

"Not a chance in hell." Until just these last few moments, Lee had felt weary and on the brink of total emotional and physical collapse. Now his mind was going a million miles per hour and he felt wide awake. Connections were clicking into place in his head. "Here's what I think. What's happening now is linked to that 'something bad' that drove those guys apart when they were kids."

Acker scratched his chin. "Makes sense, but there's a larger picture here, a part of the puzzle we don't have yet. Somehow all this mess has something to do with the time of year. With Halloween."

Lee nodded. That much had already been surmised by all parties involved in the investigation. It was why the mayor would be issuing a decree prohibiting all Halloween-related activities in Willow Springs until the killer was apprehended. He would also be declaring a city-wide curfew through at least the first of November. In general, the mayor would be making as big a show as possible about how he was doing all he could to protect his constituents.

It'd be a wonderful thing indeed to show the bastard up.

"These people you talked to today, you'll need to interview them again come daylight, see if you can find out anything else about the bad thing that happened. Figuring out what that was is the key to solving these murders, I'm sure of it. I'll do some asking around of my own once I've turned in my resignation. Between the two of us, we should be able to shake loose something."

Acker's expression turned shrewd. "Should I keep anyone else in the loop on this, or should it just be between us for now?"

Lee smiled. "That's up to you, my friend. Far be it from me to tell you how to do your job. I'm just another unemployed citizen now."

"Mum's the word then. For now."

Lee nodded, still smiling. "For now."

27

Three days until Halloween
Slayton, TN

The cabin in the woods was on the outskirts of Slayton, a sleepy little border town about ten miles south of the Kentucky state line. It sat on a hill above the shore of a picturesque lake. Though the main drag of Slayton was a short distance away, the terrain surrounding the cabin was dominated by a thick expanse of tall trees, which created a false sense of remote isolation. Enhancing this impression was a lack of neighbors in the immediate vicinity. From the rear of the property, one other cabin was visible and it was on the opposite shore of the lake.

The cabin belonged to Ramona Kimmell's grandfather. Her family had been using it as a convenient weekend getaway spot for as long as she could remember. A mere thirty miles north of Nashville, getting there took hardly any time at all, at least compared to heading down to somewhere like Tybee Island or Hilton Head. Ramona had many wonderful childhood memories of the times she'd spent there, things like splashing around in the lake or fishing off the boat dock during the daytime and playing board games with the family at night. But now, having recently turned nineteen, she was older and the time had come for a naughtier kind of fun.

Ensconced behind the wheel of her Jeep Cherokee, the wind

whipped her golden-blonde hair about as she sped down the interstate. It was another unusually beautiful day for late October. The sun was out and the temperature was in the mid-70s. She was glad she'd put the jeep's top down for the ride out to the lake. Bobbing her head to the EDM music currently making the vehicle's speakers thump, she glanced at her front seat passenger, Candice Steel. Candice was Ramona's best friend. They'd known each other since grammar school. Like Ramona, she was dressed only in very short blue jean cutoffs and a bikini top. The only difference was her top was a bright red, while Ramona's was a very dark shade of blue.

Often mistaken for sisters, both girls had lean, leggy builds and striking looks. They had been considered the prettiest girls at their high school, a place they had ruled for four glorious years. But now graduation was several months behind them and, like many of their friends, they were at loose ends, unsure yet how to proceed into adulthood. They were enrolled at the same college, but neither girl was faring particularly well in the world of higher education.

In high school, they could easily manipulate teachers and other people with their looks. Some geek kid could always be counted on to write important papers for them. Teachers doled out heaps of unearned extra credit simply because the girls were so enormously popular. Unfortunately, being allowed to skate through those four years so easily left the girls ill-prepared for the more academically rigorous world of college. Both were in real danger of failing all their classes. In defiance of reality, both had persisted in painting a much sunnier picture of the situation for their parents, who now believed their little darlings were becoming true scholars. Perpetuating that fiction was becoming quite stressful. And with the specter of a semester on academic probation looming in their near future, the girls had felt a burning need to get away from it all for a while.

The trip up to the cabin had been Candice's idea. She had

accompanied Ramona's family up there many times over the years. Her idea was that they should invite a bunch of their friends and hang out at the lake for a few days, possibly through Halloween. This would mean blowing off the rest of their classes for the week, but at this point, what did that matter? Besides, a big blowout party could be just what they needed to take their minds off their troubles.

After a brief initial hesitation, Ramona had agreed to pay her parents an unexpected midweek visit, ostensibly to do a few loads of laundry and help herself to some of her mother's home cooking. She would wait for an opportune moment and snag the key to the place from her father's key ring. With any luck, he'd never notice it was missing. Given the many similar-looking little slivers of metal dangling from the ring, Ramona figured that wouldn't be a problem.

As it turned out, she didn't have to bother with the cover story she'd concocted. The clean clothes she'd stuffed into a large laundry bag never left the back seat of the jeep. She entered her childhood home quietly through the back door, planning to surprise her parents, who had not been notified of the visit in advance. It hadn't seemed necessary. She'd shown up unannounced multiple other times and they'd never been up to anything too exciting, just standard old people stuff like reading the paper or watching the evening news on CBS.

But this time was different. She heard the high-pitched screams as she slipped through the back door. At first she thought her mother was being assaulted by an intruder and a stab of terror went through her. But after standing rigidly still in the kitchen for a few moments, she began to realize this wasn't the case. There was a distinctly sexual tenor to those screams. Her first instinct was to head out the door and come back for the key another time. But some strange impulse caused her to remove her shoes and creep out of the kitchen and down a carpeted hallway to her parents' room. The door was open a tiny sliver. She peeked through the crack and saw her mother bouncing up and down on a man named Boyd Dotson. Boyd was a widower who lived in the house across the street. His arms were tied to the headboard and a pair of her mother's panties had been shoved into his mouth. Ramona's father was in there, too. He sat in a chair next to the bed, facing away from the door. Ramona couldn't see much of him from that angle, but she could tell he was naked and that he was masturbating while watching his wife fuck the beer-bellied neighbor.

Ramona watched them for several minutes before carefully creeping back down the hallway to the kitchen. She found her father's keys in the usual place, on a hook by the laundry room. After taking care to remove the cabin key as soundlessly as possible, she grabbed her shoes and slipped back out of the house, praying her parents would remain oblivious until she was gone.

Hours later, she was still freaked out about the incident. The fact that her sweet mommy and daddy got up to such kinkiness came as a huge shock. In all the years she'd lived at that house, not once had she walked in on them having regular sex. The freaky shit she'd seen today never would have entered her mind as a possibility for them. Almost as disturbing was the amount of time she'd spent standing there in the hallway, spying on them. Even *more* disturbing was the inescapable fact of how horny she'd been ever since then.

There's something wrong with me, she thought. *Normal people don't have this kind of reaction to that kind of messed up shit, at least when it involves parents.*

This seemed an undeniable fact. She felt dirty. Unclean.

In need of being punished, perhaps.

She thought about Kevin, her hunky online friend, who she'd be meeting for the first time later tonight. They'd talked on the phone numerous times. His voice was incredibly sexy, low and growly. It sent a delightfully wicked shiver through her every time she heard it. And judging from the many pictures he'd shared with her, he had the body to go with it. Maybe, if things went well, he could be talked into tying her to the bed in the cabin's main bedroom. She imagined him dominating the shit out of her. Thinking about it made her squirm in her seat behind the wheel of the Cherokee.

And maybe Candice could be in the room with them, watching while they did it.

Now *that* would be hot.

Ramona glanced again at Candice as they neared the Slayton exit. She doubted her friend would be down for anything like that under normal circumstances, but who knew what she might be open to once they were at the cabin and the booze had been flowing for a few hours?

She hit the blinker switch and slowed down as she took the Slayton exit. "The guys are bringing beer, right?" she asked, after snapping off the radio. "And liquor?"

Candice nodded. "Of course."

"Lots, right?"

Candice reached over and patted Ramona's knee. "Don't worry. There'll be enough booze to float a fleet of warships. Side note, you're turning into a fucking lush, you know that?"

Ramona smirked. "I take it you'll be abstaining, then?"

"Fuck, no. I plan to get smashed out of my fucking gourd."

Ramona smiled.

Good. Perfect.

Candice leaned back in her seat and propped her feet on the dash as the Cherokee slowed to a stop at the end of the ramp. "So this Kevin person's gonna be there, huh?"

Ramona glanced both ways before turning left onto the tree-shrouded rural road. "Uh huh. That's right."

Candice frowned, adjusting the position of her dark sunglasses on the bridge of her nose. "You sure that's a good idea?"

"I don't see why it should be a problem."

"It's just…some online dude? Someone you've never met?"

She shook her head. "I just don't understand it. It's not your usual style. You're hot. Guys flock to you. Tons of them. Really good-looking ones. So why would you do this?"

Ramona shrugged and heaved an exasperated sigh. "I've told you before, I can't really explain it. I just got to talking to him and, well…he's just so interesting. Very deep. Lots of profound thoughts and shit. We've got a real connection."

Candice chortled. "Right. The beefcake pictures he sent you have nothing to do with it."

"Well…they have *something* to do with it."

"How do you know those pictures are even him? Maybe he's catfishing you."

"Not a chance."

Candice removed her sunglasses and looked at Ramona, an eyebrow lifted to indicate her skepticism. "Oh, really? How can you be so sure?"

Ramona smiled. "Because I told him I'd cut off his balls and feed them to him if he's been lying to me about anything."

"You didn't."

"I did."

Candice shook her head. "I don't believe you. That doesn't sound like you. You're not a violent person."

Ramona sniffed at this. "You'd be surprised. Anyway, if he was really some ugly loser living in his mother's basement, why would he drop everything and come out here to meet me in person? Makes no sense. No, I think he's for real."

Candice sighed. "Whatever. I just don't want you to get hurt."

Ramona turned right down a secondary road. It was significantly narrower than the road they'd been on, a winding stretch of bumpy, faded asphalt that hadn't been patched in years. The many potholes elicited several high-pitched squeals from Candice as the Cherokee's wheels bounced in and out of them. The even narrower dirt road that led to the cabin was just a few miles away. Ramona laughed at each of her friend's exaggerated squeals, her excitement level growing the closer they got to their destination. All her worries about school and how her parents might react once they found out how poorly she was doing seemed a million miles away. For a few wonderful days, she would just enjoy being a normal, carefree young girl, with nothing on her mind but partying, getting laid, and having the time of her life.

28

Three days until Halloween
Slayton, TN

The first stretch of the twisting path through the woods was an easy hike for Bill Christy and his girlfriend, Laurie Palmer. A couple hundred feet in, however, relatively level ground yielded to a steeply rising hill that required more physical exertion than they'd anticipated. By the time the ground leveled out again, both were sweating and had a rosy glow to their faces. As they continued down the path, the expanse of trees to their right thinned enough to allow glimpses of the placid-looking lake and the distant opposite shore.

Laurie clasped hands with Bill and stepped off the path, tugging at him to follow. Never a big fan of nature, Bill went along with some reluctance. He wasn't happy about it, but what could he do? She was his girlfriend. It was a good thing she was such a hot piece of ass. A girl of lesser looks might not have coaxed him into the woods in the first place. But, along with several other friends, they'd been waiting over an hour for Ramona and Candice to show up and let them into the cabin. Laurie was often restless, even out there in the civilized world, with a vast array of diversions available to her at any given time. But out here cell reception was awful and she couldn't reliably text or play on her phone. She became irritable and demanded he accompany her on a nature hike.

He gave in when the other guys started giving him nasty looks. No one liked being around Laurie when she turned shrill or fussy. Being alone in the woods with her when she was in one of her moods wasn't Bill's idea of a good time, either, but he didn't want his friends turning resentful on him. This was just one of those times in a guy's life when it was necessary to make a sacrifice for the greater good. But they'd been gone nearly a half hour. Ramona and Candice might finally have arrived by now. Bill had been on the verge of suggesting they head back to check when Laurie steered them off the path.

His mild irritation at the development faded when they emerged through the trees and stood near the edge of a small cliff overlooking the lake. At a guess, the cliff was about twenty feet above the lake's surface. Stepping closer to the edge, he raised a hand to his forehead to shield his eyes against the glare of the afternoon sun.

Laurie put a hand against the small of his back. "I could push you over right now. You wouldn't be able to stop me."

Bill tensed. She'd let go of his hand and was behind him now. She was right. He wouldn't be able to stop her. "Um. That wouldn't be a good idea."

Laurie applied a little more pressure to his back. "Yeah? Why not? Can't swim?"

"The water's dark. There might be rocks right under the surface there. It could kill me."

Laurie laughed softly and pressed herself against him. "Hmm. Maybe that's why I brought you out here. Did you think of that? Maybe I want to get rid of you and make it look like an accident."

Bill turned away from the edge of the cliff and seized her by the wrists. "You'd never do that."

She smiled. "Oh? And why is that?"

"Because you love me."

"Don't you ever watch the news? People who love each other kill each other all the time."

Bill shook his head. "You are so fucking morbid sometimes."

She giggled. "It's one off the things you love about me."

He let go of her wrists and put a hand on her chest, squeezing a breast through the flimsy fabric of her top. "Not as much as I love your boobs."

Laurie laughed. "They *are* nice boobs. You're a lucky guy."

Bill craned his head around, peering in the general direction of the cabin. It wasn't visible from this vantage point, obscured by the curvature of the land and more jutting cliff faces. And there were no boats in the vicinity at present. Laurie was right. This was a perfect spot to kill someone and make it look like an accident. If you waited for the right moment—a moment like this one, for example—you could do it completely unobserved. But Bill didn't have any real enemies. No one he knew was loathsome enough to inspire murderous thoughts.

However, the cliff's relative isolation also made it an ideal spot for activities of a more amorous nature. Sensing his thoughts, Laurie leaned into him and kissed him, thrusting her tongue into his mouth. She angled a thigh between his legs and pressed it against the bulge at his crotch. Bill grabbed her ass and pushed against her. There were gasps and sighs from both of them as the foreplay quickly became more heated. As it continued, they moved away from the edge of the cliff and closer to the line of trees. Within a few more moments, they were shedding their clothes, and then they were naked on the ground together. Bill mounted Laurie as she spread her legs wide, groaning in ecstasy as he penetrated the hot wetness at her center.

He'd only thrust into her a few times when he felt the stab of agony at the center of his back.

The dark presence looming over them belatedly registered. A

disconnected part of Laurie had sensed movement from the direction of the trees before Bill's face contorted in pain and his shrieks of agony began. But the rest of her had been too focused on the intensely pleasurable sensations lighting up seemingly every nerve-ending in her body. She had never banged anyone as well-endowed as Bill and she had orgasmed with that first deep thrust. Even without this distraction, though, she might not have sensed the danger until it was too late. If anything, she likely would have attributed the rustling of leaves to harmless forest creatures. Squirrels and rabbits or whatever. Maybe a deer.

That changed when Bill started screaming.

A jolt of terror ripped through Laurie when she looked up and saw the tall, black-clad man standing above them. He was wearing a black trench coat over a black shirt and jeans. His face was hidden by a black ski mask. His gloved hands clutched the black handle of a long silver shaft. A length of rope attached to the shaft was coiled around the man's wrist. A blade or sharp point at the opposite end of the shaft was embedded in her boyfriend's back. Laurie felt something wet trickle down her thighs and realized it was blood.

A spear, she thought. *That's what that is. Or a harpoon. Something like that.*

Bill screamed again as the masked man ripped the sharp end of the weapon from his back. A steady patter of blood dripped from the crimson-soaked tip. The assailant raised the spear—or whatever it was—high over his head, face contorting beneath the mask as he prepared to thrust it down again. This time when it came down it went most of the way through Bill's body. The thrust penetrated so deeply the tip of the spear distended his stomach. Laurie felt it press against her soft belly. Panic engulfed her as she realized that probably less than inch of flesh separated her from impalement. Bill spluttered and his eyes jittered in their sockets as blood bubbled from the corners of his mouth.

The masked man had a harder time ripping the spear free this time. He roared in frustration as he tugged hard at the handle and shaft. Laurie felt trapped. The only thing she cared about by then was escape. Bill was dead or dying. There was nothing to be done for him. But she was pinned to the ground by his body and the pressure of the spear. When the masked man was finally able to tear the spear free again, she gathered every ounce of strength she had and shoved Bill's corpse away from her. She managed to roll away just in time to avoid impalement. The killer grunted in frustration as the tip of the spear scraped against the ground instead.

Instinct brought Laurie quickly to her feet. Her flesh felt sore and her heart was pounding from the terror coursing through her, but she knew this was no time to treat herself gently. Any hope of survival hinged on pushing herself to her absolute limits. Despite knowing this, she couldn't help stumbling when the tender soles of her bare feet scraped against sharp rocks and prickly undergrowth. She fell to her knees more than once as the killer followed her into the woods, but each time she managed to quickly grab on to a low-hanging branch, haul herself upright again, and get moving. She had no choice. The trampling of the killer's booted feet through the undergrowth told her he was right behind her, maybe only a few feet away, too close to even risk a glance back. It wouldn't be long before he got within striking range with that spear. She worried he might even throw it at her, bringing her down regardless of distance.

But then she emerged from the woods and onto the path. She turned to her left and took off running in the direction of the cabin. Salvation lay in that direction. Once they understood what was happening, the guys would protect her. The killer wouldn't dare attack a larger group of people with just a spear. She felt her first real flicker of hope at this thought, which was so all-consuming that she neglected to account for the steep hill she and Bill had climbed on the way up to this godforsaken place. She stumbled as she encountered the slope and went tumbling down the path, crying out at the various impacts her body absorbed. By the time she reached the bottom of the slope, she was momentarily incapable of movement, even though her mind kept urging her to get up and start running again.

At least a full minute elapsed before she was able to lift herself up off the ground and cast a glance back up the hill. The killer, apparently more sure-footed than she, was making his way down at an alarmingly fast rate. He'd discarded the spear. In its place was a machete with a long, curved blade, which was covered in a dark substance Laurie guessed was probably dried blood.

She screamed and resumed running, moving faster now along the twisting path. That flicker of hope flared within her again when she heard music emanating from somewhere just ahead. After rushing past another curve in the path, she glimpsed the cabin through the trees. She couldn't see her friends yet, but they were there. She heard voices singing along with the music.

Before she could call out to them, the sole of her right foot landed on a particularly sharp rock, penetrating the flesh and drawing forth a thick flow of blood. She was unable to avoid falling to her knees again. It was one stumble too many.

The killer was right behind her.

Laurie opened her mouth to scream.

The killer grabbed a handful of her hair and pulled her head sharply back. Then he dragged the sharp edge of the blade across her throat. Blood gushed from the gash in her carotid, spattering the leaf-covered path. She spluttered and gagged as the blood continued to pump, and the killer held her by her hair, waiting for her to bleed out.

29

Three days until Halloween
Slayton, TN

As the jeep neared the end of the dirt road, Ramona glimpsed two vehicles already parked in front of the cabin, a green minivan and a vintage red Camaro. The Camaro's windows were open and music was pumping from its stereo. As she'd hoped, her friends had gotten there ahead of her. Whenever possible, she liked to keep people waiting, preferably for what would, for anyone else, constitute an egregious amount of time. She'd been doing this going back to middle school, back when she first started coming into her own as a real beauty, which of course caused her popularity to soar. One thing she learned early on was that practically everyone was willing to cut the most popular girl around a seemingly endless amount of slack. Truthfully, she got off on it. It was a power thing.

In the months since the end of her high school career, however, opportunities to indulge her diva side had been infrequent. Teachers at the college didn't fret over her absenteeism. Indeed, they seemed not to care at all. This had been a rude awakening for someone accustomed to being the center of everyone else's world, teachers included. Even worse, her new social acquaintances at the college were far less inclined to cut her slack than their high school counterparts had been. They simply stopped inviting her on social outings after a few incidents of extreme tardiness.

This was why only high school friends had been invited to the cabin. Ramona longed for a prolonged period of fawning indulgence and total adoration and thus had only contacted those she deemed most likely to accommodate this desire. She was unsurprised, however, to learn that Laurie Palmer and Bill Christy had gone off into the woods after Laurie had tired of waiting for Ramona.

In Ramona's mind, Laurie had been the only question mark among the invitees. Alone among their peers, she'd previously demonstrated a relative lack of willingness to put up with her shit. Ideally, Laurie would have been left behind, but she and Bill Christy were a package deal, and having Bill around was a must. Ramona had dated him briefly in freshman year. Even after unceremoniously dumping him, he'd never stopped worshipping her. If anyone idolized her more than Bill, Ramona couldn't imagine who that person might be.

She was a little put out at not seeing his dumb puppy dog face among those of her friends hanging around outside the cabin. The feeling dissipated when Tom Glover, a former top jock at the high school, filled her in on the situation. By then Ramona had her first beer in hand and was more interested in getting the party started than worrying about Laurie's attitude issues.

The remainder of the welcoming party was comprised of Jake Feldman, Adrienne Bartram, Kirsten Charno, Paul Gillette, and Amy Miner. Jake and Adrienne were a couple. Kirsten was Tom Glover's girlfriend. Paul and Amy were single, though there was little chance of sparks flying between those two. Paul was a small, kind of funny-looking guy who'd avoided ostracism in school through sheer force of personality. He was always cracking jokes and making people laugh. The cool kids adopted him as one of their own early on, but Amy Miner was out of his league. In terms of looks, Amy was only the slightest, almost imperceptible level below Ramona and Candice. Even if she'd been willing to overlook Paul's relative deficiency in the looks department, Ramona suspected it wouldn't have mattered. She had a strong feeling Amy was a closet lesbian. Despite being gorgeous, the girl had shunned all suitors after breaking up with her sophomore year boyfriend. She'd never said why this was, but what other explanation could there be?

Once the booze had been loaded into the cabin and everyone had stowed their stuff in their designated rooms, the festivities began in earnest. Because Halloween was just a few days away, Amy Miner had crafted a playlist of seasonally appropriate music using a streaming app on her phone. She insisted on connecting her phone to the stereo receiver in the living room. No one had any objections to this and throughout that afternoon the cabin's interior reverberated with songs by the likes of Rob Zombie, Marilyn Manson, Type O Negative, the Bile Lords, Bauhaus, and more. The girls bounced around to the more energetic tracks while the guys chugged beers and watched them. At one point, Amy veered away from the other girls and ran up to her second floor room, the pounding of her bare feet on the steps audible even over the music.

She came back down some five minutes later bearing Halloween masks. They were the flimsy plastic kind sold cheaply in drugstores every year in October. There were three of them. One was a crude knockoff of the Ghostface mask from the *Scream* movies. Amy kept that one for herself. The other two she gave to Ramona and Candice. Ramona frowned for a moment at the mask Amy had pushed into her hands. She wasn't sure what it was supposed to be, though the pale countenance and trickles of blood trailing down from the corners of the mouth vaguely suggested a vampire. She shrugged and pulled the mask on despite its lameness. Once she had it fitted over her face properly, she scanned the room until she spotted Candice. Her best friend's mask was cooler-looking, a more detailed depiction of a rotting zombie, with an eye hanging out of its socket. The mask was almost gruesome enough to distract attention from her amazing body.

Almost.

Adrienne Bartram wanted to know where her mask was. So did Kirsten.

"You don't get one," Candice told them. "They're only for the *really* cool kids."

Adrienne rolled her eyes, but she was smiling as she did it. She probably thought Candice was just playing with her. But Candice meant what she'd said. Ramona knew it, too, and so did Amy. Everyone here was special in some way, but the three of them were on a higher level. The coolest of the cool, the most special of all.

As a Bauhaus song gave way to a pulsating industrial track, the masked girls started capering around the room in a faux-ghoulish way, making claws with their hands and attempting to hiss like hideous beasts. The guys pretended to be scared and retreated from them. Beer sloshed out of the bottle clutched in Jake's right hand as he hurriedly circled the sofa in the middle of the room in an effort to keep away from Ramona.

"Stay back, foul beast!" he cried.

Ramona let out a louder hiss as she climbed up on the sofa and vaulted over its back, intercepting Jake before he could circle around again. She grabbed handfuls of his tank top and went up on her tiptoes to put her masked face close to his. "I've got you now, puny human! Prepare to meet your fate."

Jake waved his arms around in mock helplessness. "Someone help me! Please!"

For a moment, Ramona was intensely aware of how close Jake's powerfully muscled body was to hers. She yearned to tear her mask off and kiss him. But then Adrienne was there, pulling him away from her. She thumped Ramona's chest with the base of a fist. Hard. "There. I've driven a stake through your heart, bloodsucker. You're dead."

Ramona just stared at her, smiling behind the mask.

You know exactly what's on my mind, don't you? she thought. *But I'll fuck him if I want, and there's nothing you can do about it.*

Adrienne clasped hands with Jake and tugged him in the direction of the staircase. "This way, baby. I just saved your life. Time for my reward."

There was a lascivious tinge to Jake's smile as he followed his girlfriend up to the second floor.

Behind the mask, Ramona's smile wilted, yielding to a frown. After staring at the empty staircase for a moment, she removed the mask and gave it to Kirsten. Kirsten accepted it gleefully and started capering around the room in imitation of the other girls. Ramona went into the kitchen and examined the selection of booze bottles crammed onto the counter by the sink. There was lots of beer in the fridge, but she was in need of something stronger.

After spying a bottle of Smirnoff vanilla vodka, she grabbed it, twisted off the cap, and drank deeply straight from the bottle. She took the bottle away from her mouth long enough to take a deep breath, then she took several more big gulps.

There, she thought. *I should be feeling just fine as soon as that hits my system.*

She set the significantly depleted vodka bottle back on the counter, grabbed a beer from the fridge, and went back out to the living room, where she plopped down on the sofa and stared at the blank screen of the TV mounted on the opposite wall. The early exuberance of the gathering began to fade shortly thereafter. Amy turned the music down to an unobtrusive background noise level. Some of the others settled into chairs and recliners. Candice curled up next to her on the sofa. They talked about inconsequential things and laughed at Paul's intermittent jokes.

The rest of them laughed, that is. Ramona just stared at the TV.

Audible sex noises drifted down from upstairs, eliciting chuckles. Ramona knew Adrienne was being purposely loud, wanting Ramona to hear.

After a while, most of Ramona's friends went outside to hang out on the porch and watch the sun set, while Amy disappeared to her room. Candice put her head in Ramona's lap and dozed off. Ramona absently stroked her friend's hair for a few minutes before taking out her phone. It'd been a while since she'd checked her messages. She anticipated numerous texts from Kevin, who'd never been up here before and might have gotten lost on the way.

There were numerous texts from several people, as usual.

But none from Kevin.

Ramona's mood spiraled downward. Until now, her other friends and the booze had distracted her from the pending meeting with her online boyfriend. She'd almost forgotten how much she'd been looking forward to seeing him for the first time. But now it all came rushing back, stirring anew that feeling of queasy yearning that often came over her when she thought about him. In the relative quiet, her mind went to places it normally avoided and she realized, not for the first time, that Kevin represented something her supposedly perfect life was lacking. An anchor. A new, more focused direction. Maybe even the possibility of real love.

She sent him a text: *Where are you?*

Several minutes passed. No reply came.

Ramona's eyes misted and her bottom lip trembled.

Perhaps sensing her friend's distress, Candice stirred and shifted position on the sofa, turning her head so she was staring straight up at Ramona. "Oh," she said, her features crinkling in concern. She reached up and gently touched Ramona's face. "Tell me what's wrong."

Ramona swiped at her eyes and shook her head.

Candice sighed. "It's him, isn't it? The online faker. He's not coming, is he?"

Instead of answering, Ramona shifted sideways, disengaging herself from Candice. She got to her feet and headed in the direction of the kitchen. The back door was through there.

Candice sat up. "Hey. Where are you going?"

Ramona didn't glance back. "Down to the boat dock. Don't follow me. I need some time alone. To think."

Candice sighed. "Okay. Hurry back."

Ramona didn't reply.

She went on into the kitchen and out through the back door.

30

Three days until Halloween
Slayton, TN

Lurking just inside the tree line at the edge of the clearing, Elliot watched Ramona leave the cabin through the back door and walk down the sloping back yard to the boat dock. She passed close enough to allow him a good glimpse of her face. Her mood wasn't difficult to decipher. She was upset about something and he had a pretty good idea what it was.

Ramona was one of several girls he'd talked to online utilizing a variety of fake personas. He'd started doing this years ago with no nefarious purpose in mind. Instead, it was a way of dealing with his crushing loneliness, though he'd never had any intention of meeting the women in real life. After all, none of them would want anything to do with him after getting a look at his real face. Out of necessity, then, the relationships were primarily cerebral and emotional. They filled a space in his otherwise dark and empty heart for a brief time. His steadfast refusal to meet in person meant most of these relationships fizzled after a few months. A couple lasted as long as a year. Ramona was his latest and only current online girlfriend. He'd been chatting with her for three months. Lately he'd been thinking it was time to start distancing himself from her because she'd started making noises about wanting to meet.

But then early today she'd told him about her plan for a multi-day getaway with her friends. They'd be staying at her grandfather's cabin. There'd be lots of booze and no old people around to put a damper on things. Elliot, who was lagging behind in his goal to reach thirty-one kills by All Hallow's Eve, realized this might be an excellent opportunity to pad his body count significantly in a short period of time. So he asked for directions to the cabin, made sure everything was locked down tight at his lair, and drove up here as fast as he could, intent on getting to the cabin ahead of everyone else. He succeeded at that goal, arriving ahead of Ramona's friends by just under a half hour. This gave him just enough time to stash his Civic in an out of the way spot and hightail it through the woods to the cabin. And then that couple had gone on their little hike, giving him the perfect chance to score his first kills of the day. Hours passed. Weirdly, no one ever came looking for the dead ones. He assumed the rest of them were all too busy partying and getting drunk to care much.

Elliot continued watching Ramona until she'd walked all the way down to the far end of the boat dock. She sat at the dock's edge, dangling her feet above the calm water. His gaze shifted back to the cabin. He heard voices emanating from the front porch. There was a pronounced slur in some of those voices. Elliot was happy to hear it. The high level of booze circulating in their systems would make them easier to kill.

After checking the windows to make sure no one was watching, he slipped out of the tree line and hurried across the patch of open ground to the side of the cabin. When he got there, he moved quickly to the rear corner and peeked around it. His hope was that Ramona had left the back door unlocked. The less noise he'd have to make getting in, the better. No one else was loitering around out back. Elliot glanced in the direction of the boat dock again. Ramona was still sitting at its edge, facing the lake. He let out a breath and approached the back door. The wooden steps to the little back porch creaked as he climbed them. His hand shook a little as it closed around the knob. He'd done a lot of daring things lately, but this was perhaps the brashest of them all. There were a lot of people gathered here, which meant there were lots of ways things could go wrong. But extreme risk was inherent in accomplishing the things he wished to accomplish. He was already resigned to being dead before Halloween was over. If the end came a little sooner than he'd hoped—and in the course of trying to achieve greatness—so be it.

His hand tightened on the knob.

He turned it and it yielded to the pressure.

Smiling, Elliot Parker pushed the door open and stepped inside the cabin.

With Ramona gone for the time being, Candice stretched out on the sofa and stared up at the lazily spinning ceiling fans. There were two of them. The blades of each fan were coated with a fine layer of dust. This wasn't surprising. The cabin was often unoccupied for months at a time. Candice had last been up here on a day trip with Ramona's father. That was two months ago.

The man had offered her $5,000 to have sex with him. This was after he'd confessed to having lusted after her for years. Obviously he was a pervert—not to mention old and gross—but the money had been too much to turn down. So she'd done it. And she'd regretted it ever since. The man was constantly trying to get her to agree to another rendezvous. He was almost sort of stalking her, which creeped her out. Once she'd threatened to report him to the police, but he reminded her she was eighteen now and therefore legal.

It'd changed a lot about her relationship with Ramona's family. Until recently, she'd thought of her friend's parents as secondary father and mother figures. That's how close they'd been. But now she couldn't stand the thought of being around Ramona's dad and always begged off any time Ramona asked her to go over there with her. Being in school, she had loads of legitimate excuses. She needed to study for a test, research a paper, or some other load of bullshit like that.

Sooner or later, though, the secret would be forced out of her. She dreaded having to tell Ramona about it. It made her feel dirty and cheap. But, also, she worried about her friend. There was no one in the world she was closer to than Ramona. With a creep like that for a father, she had to wonder if there were any darker secrets lurking behind closed doors at the Kimmell household. Ramona might even have been molested as a child. She'd never hinted at anything like that, but maybe it'd happened and she'd repressed the memories. Such things happened. Candice knew it from watching talk shows. Hell, it happened a *lot*.

Candice loved Ramona more than anyone else in the world. The possibility of having to one day hurt her with this information was a terrible mental burden. Sometimes it was all she could think about. Right now, for instance. She was obsessing over it again when she should be having fun. That's what this trip was all about, after all. A chance to leave all their worries behind.

She sighed.

What I need is a drink, she thought. *Lots of drinks*.

A faint buzz of laughter and voices was audible from the porch. Everyone out there seemed to be having a good time. Thinking she would grab a beer and join them, Candice got up from the sofa and went into the kitchen. She was through the archway and halfway to the refrigerator when the presence of the black-clad man she'd swooped past belatedly registered. Wheeling about, she saw a tall, lanky individual in a black trench coat. A ski mask hid most of his face, but there was no hiding the wild look in his eyes. The machete in his right hand was smeared with dark, coagulating blood.

Rather than immediately fleeing in terror, Candice stood her ground. She simply couldn't accept the idea of a masked, machete-wielding killer invading a cabin in the woods to wreak bloody havoc on a group of partying young people. It was too absurd. This had to be some kind of prank.

She struck a defiant pose, smirking as she folded her arms beneath her breasts. "Nice costume, but it's not Halloween yet. Is that a rubber machete? I bet it is. Good job with the fake blood."

The masked man tilted his head, squinting at her. He seemed almost comically confused.

Candice laughed and took a tentative step toward him, unfolding her arms and holding out a hand. "Can I touch your little prop?"

The man gasped and backed away in apparent surprise.

Candice shook her head, her brow furrowing. "What is your deal, man? Who are you, anyway? Oh, wait." Her expression hardened. "You're that Kevin guy, aren't you? You fucking asshole. What were you thinking with that silent treatment bullshit? Do you have any idea how upset Ramona is?" She sniffed, her mouth curling in an expression of withering disdain. "And you did it for, what, some stupid Halloween trick? *Idiot.*"

The man who was probably "Kevin", if that was even his real name, retreated another step, even though she had moved no closer. He seemed rattled. She noticed the hand clutching the machete was shaking visibly. The furrow in her brow deepened. This was really odd behavior for a supposedly hot stud like Ramona's online boyfriend. She was getting a vibe from him she'd encountered many times from guys with low self-esteem. They always got very nervous around her. They often stuttered and sometimes were unable to speak at all. His eyes kept jittering crazily in their sockets. There was an audible click in his throat as he swallowed with some difficulty. She had the distinct feeling the face hidden beneath the ski mask was flushed red with embarrassment.

"Take off the mask."

The masked man shook his head.

Candice moved a step closer. "Take it off."

Another shake of the head was his only reply.

"You are fucking pathetic," Candice said, making a sound of disgust. "Look at you. You're skinny as a rail. Not exactly the buff hunk in your pictures, are you? I bet you photoshopped those. Or maybe the guy in the pictures wasn't you at all." Her tone was growing steadily more heated as she talked. She felt like she was on the verge of losing control and flying into a real rage, but she didn't care. No one got to treat her best friend the way this asshole had and get away with it. "Take the goddamned mask off, you fucking loser."

The masked man's timid demeanor abruptly changed. He stopped shaking and his hand tightened around the handle of the machete. Some instinct told Candice he was about to come at her an instant before it happened. As she spun away from him and dashed toward the back door, a grim awareness gripped her. She hadn't been wrong about this man's identity. She still felt that as strongly as she had just seconds ago. But now she knew she'd been wrong in thinking he wasn't actually dangerous. And he wasn't decked out like he was as part of some stupid prank. That machete in his hand was real, as was the still-wet blood smeared along the edge of its blade.

Candice had her hand on the doorknob when she felt the first slice of the blade as it cleaved through her bikini top string and opened a deep gash between her shoulder blades. The first sting of agony hit her as she cried out and fell against the door. Her hand was still on the doorknob. She tried to turn it as blood flowed down her back in a thick stream, but her grip on the knob was too weak. The masked man grabbed a handful of her hair and yanked her away from the door. She cried out again as he twirled her about and flung her across the room. Candice lost her footing and took a tumble on the floor, landing hard on her ass. Blood from the gash on her back pattered on the cheap linoleum. She scooted rapidly backward as the masked man came at her again, then attempted to get to her feet when she reached the archway leading to the living room. But the hand she braced on the floor with the intent of propelling herself upward slid in a smear of her own blood.

The masked man loomed over her, raising the machete for a killing blow. Candice rolled out of the way just in time to avoid having her head split down the middle. Instead, the blade chopped deep into the linoleum. Managing to get to her hands and knees, Candice decided to make another try for the back door. The cut strings of the bikini top slipped down from her shoulders as it fell away from her, leaving her breasts bare. This time the masked man caught up to her before she reached the door. He seized her by the hair again and hauled her to her feet. Turning her around, he drove the machete blade into her abdomen as hard as he could. She felt the hard steel push through her flesh and whimpered, knowing the fight was over.

I don't want to die, she thought. *It isn't fair. Oh, please God, don't let this happen.*

It happened anyway.

The killer held on to her throat and drove the blade in deeper, staring intently into her eyes as various vital organs were perforated. When she was dead, he dragged her over to the pantry, shoved her inside, and closed the door. After a moment's hesitation, he opened the door again, stared briefly at the beautiful corpse, and then took a bag of flour down from a shelf. He again closed the door and ripped open the bag of flour, dumping its contents over the various blood spatters on the floor. The cursory attempt to cover up what had happened wouldn't hold up to close examination, but the killer was sure it wouldn't matter in the end.

He dumped the empty bag in the trash and went into the living room.

Adrienne Bartram sat in a rocking chair by the window in the second floor room she was sharing with Jake Feldman for the duration of their stay at the cabin. As she listened to the faint sound of voices drifting up from the porch, she swiped at her phone's screen and reviewed the new pictures she'd taken of Jake, who was still tied to the bed behind her.

"How long do you plan to make me wait?"

Adrienne swiped at her phone again. She enjoyed taking pictures of her boyfriend in various bondage poses. There were hundreds of them on her phone by now. Ignoring his question, she closed the photo app and leaned forward in the chair, straining again to hear whether Ramona had joined the rest of them on the porch. After listening intently for a couple more minutes, she decided she still wasn't out there. And the last time Adrienne left her room to peek into the living room, she hadn't been there, either. Only Candice was down there, stretched out on the sofa and apparently oblivious to Adrienne's presence at the second floor railing. She looked lost in thought and, judging from her expression, possibly troubled about something. About what, Adrienne didn't care.

Right now all Adrienne gave a shit about was the less than subtle way Ramona had tried to get intimate with her boyfriend. Right in front of her, no less. Obviously some form of payback was necessary. For the rest of the trip, Adrienne planned to flaunt the firm grip she had on Jake's affections,, rubbing it in Ramona's face whenever possible. But the girl's disappearing act was putting a crimp in those plans.

Sighing, she got up from the rocking chair and approached the bed, circling it as she raised her phone and snapped a few more pictures.

"Those are gonna come back to haunt me someday, aren't they?"

Adrienne laughed. "Probably."

At last, satisfied that she'd taken enough pictures of her tied-up boyfriend for one night, she put the phone on the nightstand and climbed up on the bed. After straddling Jake and guiding his erect cock into her pussy, she shifted around a little, getting comfortable.

224

A look of intense pleasure twisted Jake's face. "Mmm. That's nice."

Adrienne leaned forward a little, lightly clasping his throat with both hands. "I'm sorry I made you wait so long. Do you want me to do the choking thing again? I know it's your favorite."

He grinned. "Yes, please."

Adrienne increased the pressure of her grip on his throat as she continued to slowly ride his cock, which was already very stiff. She knew, though, that it was about to get even bigger. It always did when she choked him. According to Jake, the temporary air deprivation intensified his pleasure to an insane degree. She usually did this crazy thing for him at least a couple times a week. It made her nervous, though. Jake always liked her to really bear down while she was doing it. Sometimes she worried she might wind up accidentally choking him to death, but he never failed to complain afterward if he thought she was doing a wimpy, half-assed job of it.

And more than ever before, she wanted him thoroughly satisfied with her sexual attentions. So now she further tightened her grip, bearing down harder than ever. In a few moments, his eyes widened in panic. He turned his head to the left and started spluttering, desperately trying to communicate something. Adrienne frowned. Jake usually lasted much longer than this before they went into the begging for mercy routine.

Then she heard a booted foot clomp on the floor behind her. Before she could turn her head to investigate, someone slapped a gloved hand over her mouth. She squealed and tried to twist away from the unseen assailant, her hands finally coming away from Jake's throat in the process. A reedy sound issued from his throat as his depleted lungs worked hard to pull in air. At least for the moment, he sounded incapable of raising the alarm. Realizing this meant help wouldn't arrive soon enough to save her, Adrienne intensified her efforts to thrash free of the man's grip. Though she still hadn't seen him, she sensed clearly that, whoever this was, he wasn't one of her other friends pulling some kind of sick prank. He was an unknown intruder, a malicious predator with only one goal in mind.

To kill.

On the verge of losing his grip on her, the intruder climbed up on the bed, pinned her down atop the still spluttering Jake, and pressed the tip of a sharpened screwdriver against her temple. She squirmed and squealed behind the glove as he began to push it into her head. Blood dripped from the newly created hole and pattered on her boyfriend's chest. Adrienne experienced a few more moments of increasing desperation as the slender length of cold metal continued to push through her temple. And then it entered her brain and the killer took his hand away from Adrienne's mouth as her body began to convulse.

When she stopped moving, the killer retracted the screwdriver, shifted position slightly on the bed, and plunged it into Jake Feldman's throat, silencing him just as he was on the cusp of having recovered sufficiently to start screaming for help.

The killer jerked the screwdriver from Jake's throat.

Then he plunged it in again. And again and again, several more times, needlessly perforating the flesh of a man who'd already expired.

The killer left the screwdriver embedded in Jake's throat as he walked on down the hall to the next occupied room.

Still wearing her Halloween mask, Amy Miner stared up at the ceiling from the bed in her room. It was a vaulted ceiling, with a thick central beam dividing opposing rows of wood planks. A small ceiling fan hung from the center beam above the bed. As she watched the fan slowly rotate, her thoughts again returned to the question she had spent so much of the last few years contemplating. In many ways, her contemplation of it defined her life. This fact would likely have saddened a normal person, but

Amy felt nothing. That was the crux of the problem, actually. She felt empty inside, devoid of any strong emotion. It was why she'd shied away from intimate relationships since breaking up with her sophomore year boyfriend. There was no point. She had nothing to offer anyone. No compassion. No empathy. Nothing like true love.

The closest she ever came to feeling normal was when she was around her best friends from high school. She felt a degree of affection for them, particularly for Ramona and Candice, but she didn't actually love them. Over their years of friendship, she had learned how to convincingly fake such feelings, which was an easier thing to do than faking amorous feelings for boys. Or girls, for that matter. Her entire life, she'd felt no genuine sexual attraction to anyone, regardless of gender. She never stopped being aware of how strange this made her. In truth, no one was stranger than her. No one came close, not even the most pathetic misfits from back in high school. They were normal compared to her. And no one knew it. No one had any inkling.

As a result, Amy always felt alone, even when surrounded by people. If she'd ever opened up about this to anyone, she might also have gone on to reveal that she spent hours every day imagining how she might kill herself. This wasn't an idle exercise. From slightly after the onset of puberty, she had known she would do it one day. Method aside, the only real question was when it would happen. As she lay there and stared at the ceiling, she realized she was edging ever closer to believing she should do it sometime over the next few days. At least that way she could die surrounded by the only people who mattered at all to her. They would be upset, of course, but Amy wasn't much concerned about that. She wouldn't be around to bear witness to their pain, after all.

When the door creaked open, she lifted her head off the pillow and watched as the man in the ski mask entered her room. She felt no fear. She didn't tremble and her heart didn't start pounding. The man's black trench coat was streaked with blood spatters.

Some of the blood was dry and flaking away. Some of it looked wet. He opened his trench coat and took a hunting knife with a long, thick blade from an inner pocket.

Amy propped herself up on her elbows. "Are you here to kill me?"

The man in the mask nodded.

"How will you do it?"

The masked man shrugged. Then he made a jabbing motion with the knife.

Amy nodded. "Okay. That works. Your knife looks very sharp. You should cut my throat." She tilted her head back, exposing her neck as she drew an index finger across it. "Like that. I'll bleed out fast."

The masked man was at the side of her bed now.

He hesitated.

Amy sensed he was frowning behind the mask. "I was thinking about killing myself before you entered the room. No, seriously. I always think about killing myself. It's my thing. My *only* thing. But it'd probably be easier if I had someone else do it, so I guess I'm glad you're here. Will you kill my friends, too?"

He cleared his throat and, in a low, growly voice, said, "Yes."

Amy grunted. "Probably for the best. They won't have to be sad that I'm gone." She tilted her head back, exposing her neck again. "Do it. Do it now."

Sighing, the killer leaned over her.

He did as she asked.

Later, while driving back to his lair, the killer would think about Amy Miner and sob uncontrollably for several minutes, nearly making himself drive off the road.

When Elliot came out of Amy Miner's room, he edged carefully to the second floor railing and scanned the living room below. Seeing that it remained unoccupied, he proceeded quickly to the

228

staircase and hurried down the stairs. A peek through a window verified that most of the others were still out on the porch. The only one missing was Ramona. He assumed she was still down at the boat dock.

Treading as lightly as he could, he moved to the front door and paused there, listening to the voices of those on the porch to gauge level of intoxication. They had seemed significantly impaired before he'd entered the house, but they were worse now. Their voices sounded thick and strange. They struggled to enunciate, not just words, but individual syllables. This rapid progression of impairment puzzled Elliot, but then his nostrils flared, detecting a sharp odor he recognized as weed. At some point between his dash from the cover of the tree line and now, the kids had decided to get high. Evidently, the stuff they were smoking was extremely potent.

Elliot reached inside his trench coat, tugged the handle of his machete free from the Velcro strap that held it there, and gripped the doorknob with his free hand. A spike of adrenaline set his heart to racing. There were three of them out there. Under ordinary circumstances, that would be too many to handle at one time. His original intent had been to retreat to a hiding place and wait for a chance to pick them off one at a time, but now he thought that might not be necessary. Logic dictated that people too fucked up to enunciate mere syllables were likely incapable of defending themselves.

Just do it, he thought. *The sooner you get back, the better. You know that, so do this fucking thing.*

Psyching himself up for what he was about to do, Elliot inhaled and exhaled sharply several times.

Then he opened the door and stepped out onto the porch.

Three faces turned his way as the porch planks creaked beneath his tread. Two young men and a girl. At first their slack features registered only confusion. Then their mouths stretched wide in amusement. They pointed and laughed. A guy who looked like a typical jock had a lit joint pinched between thumb and forefinger. He toked from it even as he laughed. The other guy, the one who reminded Elliot of a diminutive and more gregarious version of himself, tried to say something, but, predictably, the words came out garbled. Elliot raised the machete and swung it around, cleaving the little one's face at a diagonal angle.

The girl shrieked and tumbled out of her chair. An unintelligible utterance that might have been some kind of threat came from the jock as he rose from his chair, took a wobbling step in Elliot's direction, and then fell against the porch railing.

Elliot ripped the machete blade from the little one's face, gave the body a kick that sent it tumbling off the porch, and grabbed the girl by an arm, jerking her to her feet. The jock made another vaguely threatening noise as he tried and failed to propel himself away from the railing. The girl squealed and made a weak attempt to pull away from Elliot. He pushed the tip of the machete blade into her stomach, allowed her a moment to feel the pain as it cut through her buzz, and then pushed it in another few inches. When he withdrew the blade, he let go of her arm and she dropped to her knees. Elliot swung the machete and the blade hacked into the side of her neck. Blood sprayed from the gash when he yanked it away.

The jock made another attempt to throw himself at Elliot. This time he succeeded at propelling himself away from the railing, but he wasn't able to maintain his footing and fell onto his side on the porch. Elliot positioned himself above the doomed young man, pausing a moment to observe how strongly he resembled guys who'd tormented him when he was in school. An echo of an old bitterness stirred inside him. After allowing the bitterness a moment to fully reawaken and consume him, he snarled in rage and started hacking away at the last of the stoned trio. The blows came in a rapid, bloody frenzy, spatters of gore flying from the blade each time he tore it away from the body and brought it down again.

When he finally stopped hacking away at the boy, who was now very dead, Elliot knelt on the porch and took a few moments to catch his breath. Once he felt a little more in control of himself, he got up and went around to the back of the cabin. The sun was a bright orange ball hanging right at the edge of the horizon, making the lake light up in hues of scarlet. Darkness was encroaching, but he saw Ramona. She was still sitting down there at the edge of the boat dock.

Elliot watched her for a moment.

Then he turned away from her and went to retrieve his Civic from its hiding spot.

Ramona sat at the edge of the dock until several minutes after the sun had finally disappeared beneath the horizon. With the arrival of full dark, the loud screech of cicadas in the trees had become almost deafening. The mosquitos were out in full force, too. When she felt them sucking blood from her legs and arms, she decided it was finally time to stop sulking and go back inside.

As she got to her feet and headed back down the boat ramp, she mentally rebuked herself for all the hours she'd wasted moping alone out here. Her alcohol buzz had dissipated long ago, which meant she would likely find her friends extra annoying when she arrived back at the cabin. She was sure they were all good and fucked up now. It was a problem with only one solution. Well, technically, more than one. She could go to her room and go to sleep, she supposed, but fuck that. She'd come out here to party and have fun and, damn it, she meant to do just that if it killed her. A concentrated burst of power-drinking was the one acceptable solution. She would catch up to the rest of them and party until the break of fucking dawn. Tomorrow she would tell Kevin to go to hell and never talk to her again, but tonight was for fun.

Shortly after entering the cabin through the back door, her feet slid on something on the floor. She grabbed an edge of countertop to keep from falling over. Frowning, she took a look around the kitchen. Someone had dumped flour out in various places in a half-assed attempt to cover up some kind of horrible mess. Rather than freaking out about it, Ramona couldn't help laughing. It was exactly the way a severely stoned person would think to deal with a problem overwhelming their dulled senses. Treading more carefully, she headed for the archway that led to the living room.

That was when she heard the thump from the pantry.

Halfway across the kitchen, Ramona froze in her tracks and turned toward the pantry. Its folding door bulged outward. She had glanced that way after coming into the kitchen and was sure the door had been properly closed. Now, as she stared at it, it bulged outward a little more.

Frowning, she approached the door, gripped the little knob at its center, and pulled it open.

Then she screamed when the hacked and bloodied body of her best friend fell out onto the floor. Her heart hammering, she stared at Candice's dead face, trying to convince herself that what she was seeing wasn't real. She couldn't do it and screamed again. Not knowing what else to do, she ran out to the living room, her mind barely noting the carved jack-o'-lanterns arranged on the coffee table in front of the sofa as she headed for the front door.

After yanking the door open, she froze at the threshold, paralyzed by the spectacularly gruesome tableau of blood and carnage. When the temporary paralysis passed, she threw the door shut and backed into the center of the living room. That was when the presence of the jack-o'-lanterns finally registered. One of the pumpkins was open at the top. Trembling and crying, she edged closer to it and peered inside, saw Tom Glover's face peering up at her.

She screamed again and backed away from the coffee table.

The front door opened and a tall man in a black ski mask and trench coat entered. His right hand gripped the handle of a machete dripping with the blood of Ramona's dead friends.

Ramona unleashed yet another scream and took a few shaky backward steps away from him. She knew she should be running from the killer, but something about him—something subtle she couldn't quite understand—held her there, compelled her attention.

"Wh-who are you?"

The killer peeled off his ski mask, revealing the sharply angular, hawkish face of a guy she didn't recognize. He looked ancient, maybe as old as forty.

"Hello, Ramona."

Her heart almost stopped at the sound of that voice.

She shook her head. "Oh, no. No, no, no. It can't be."

The killer smiled. "But it is. It's me, Kevin, your beloved. Only that's not my real name, as I'm sure you're finally realizing."

Ramona sniffled. "You bastard. You fucking *bastard*. What have you done to my friends?"

"Well, Ramona, I've pretty much fucking slaughtered them. I thought that was kind of self-evident. And guess what? You're next."

His face changed then, becoming ugly as it twisted in a snarl of hatred.

The killer raised the machete and charged at her.

Ramona screamed, whirled about, and took off running. She got to the kitchen ahead of him and kept moving, taking care to avoid the splashes of flour and whatever they were covering. The killer neglected to do this and slid in a puddle of flour-caked blood. His feet slipped out from under him and he crashed to the floor. By the time he regained his feet, Ramona was out the back door and was running for the woods. The killer followed her, but he wasn't able to catch up to her. She knew the terrain far better than he did, having grown up here. Before long, he gave up the chase as lost and opted to flee while he still could.

Later that night, many hours after she'd finally made it over to the local sheriff's office to report the massacre at the cabin, she was taken to a hospital and treated for shock. She wasn't able to talk to the authorities in anything like a coherent, calm fashion until much later the following day, at which point she provided a sketch artist a detailed description of the murderer.

But by then it was too late to matter for just about anyone.

31

Three days until Halloween
Willow Springs, TN

Eating the therapist's brain gave Chuck one of the worst cases of the shits he'd ever experienced, exceeded in his memory only by the unfortunate aftermath of a visit to a cheap Mexican restaurant on the occasion of his sixteenth birthday. In that case, at least, he'd been able to sit on a toilet and evacuate his bowels in a sanitary, albeit painful, way. This time, of course, he had no choice but to stew miserably in an odiferous, squishy puddle of his own waste. His underwear and the seat of his pants were filled with runny excrement. Some of it had been forced outward, away from his groin and pelvic region. A thick layer of filth coated his thighs. Still more had trickled down his legs and pooled inside his shoes.

The severe episode of gastrointestinal disturbance didn't begin until hours after he'd ingested the last morsel of the dead woman's gray matter, enough time to lull him into a false sense of security. Onset of the disturbance was signaled by a sudden awareness of a queasy pressure in his stomach. The pressure increased dramatically within seconds, discomfort yielding quickly to agony. Tears rushed from his eyes as he screamed behind the gag in his mouth and squirmed uselessly against his tight bonds. The pressure continued to build and build, until it felt as if his stomach lining was on the verge of ripping apart. His puckered asshole strained and strained as he sought desperately to void himself. When the evacuation of his bowels began at last, the initial burst of relief he felt triggered another rush of tears. The smell that arose from the center of his bound body was immediate and intense, eliciting a sound of disgust from Karen.

Hearing her sickened reaction made Chuck feel ashamed, but he hadn't been able to help himself. It wasn't the first time he'd relieved himself in his pants since being taken prisoner by Elliot Parker, but somehow this particular episode felt worse than all the others combined. Part of it was the simple knowledge that there were partially digested bits of a dead woman's brain floating around in all that mess. Also, it seemed to him the stink really was significantly worse than all those other times, worse even than the sharp stench of urine emanating from the immediate vicinity of each remaining prisoner in Elliot's lair. Even if by some miracle he survived this nightmare and escaped this hellish place, he suspected it'd be a very long time before he ever felt truly clean again.

Their captor had been gone for a much longer time today than he had at any point the previous day. Or what felt like a previous day, anyway. After multiple days of captivity, time had taken on a strange malleability. He'd begun to lose any real sense of how long he'd been tied to the chair. It might have been only a few days, but it could have been a week or longer. He just didn't know. All he did know was Elliot had been gone a really long time. Most of a day, at least, long enough to renew Chuck's hope the crazy son of a bitch had finally run up against someone he couldn't handle.

That hope intensified briefly when, at long last, the loud ratcheting sound signaling the raising of the rollup door commenced again. Chuck turned his head in that direction and peered through the slanted eyes of the starting-to-rot jack-o'-

lantern as the door lifted, revealing a pair of bright headlights piercing a vista of black. He prayed the vehicle was a police cruiser and that soon this den of horrors would be swarming with cops.

But then the car rolled slowly into the building and the ratcheting sound started again as the door began to close. As the front of the vehicle neared the faint circle of light at the center of the large room, Chuck saw that it was the same Honda Civic Elliot had left in earlier. Soon the car's engine cut off and then the door opened as the driver emerged. A fresh wave of crushing despair assailed Chuck as Elliot stepped into the circle of light. The madman was back and soon a new round of torture and horrors would commence.

Karen yelled something incoherent at Elliot from behind her gag. There was a ferocious level of defiance in the sound. Hearing it added yet another layer to Chuck's ever-deepening shame. His wife still had some fight left in her. But Chuck did not. Elliot's belated return confirmed all his worst fears about their situation. They were caught in the depraved clutches of a man who could not be stopped, a diabolical genius who'd planned his campaign of terror with meticulous care. A plan that accounted for virtually everything that might conceivably prevent him from accomplishing his demented goals.

Salvation wasn't a real possibility, not even remotely. Hope was pointless.

We're doomed, Chuck thought. *I wish he'd just kill us all now and be done with it.*

Elliot paused between the bound husband and wife and peered at each of them in turn for a few moments. Chuck immediately perceived that something in his demeanor was different now. There was still no hint of anything like mercy or empathy in the man's expression, but he was more haggard-looking than Chuck had ever seen him. The smudges under his eyes were darker than before, the rest of his face even paler than it had been. These things and the way the overhead light played off the angular planes of his face combined to make him resemble a walking cadaver. He looked beleaguered, like a man pushed nearly to the point of total collapse. Chuck puzzled over this a moment before noting what looked like many new splashes of blood on Elliot's dirty trench coat. He'd evidently been very busy while he was away.

At last, Elliot sighed and moved away from them, approaching the wire cages where Ricky Bennet and Jimmy Martin sat quivering in puddles of their own waste. Digging a key out of his hip pocket, he opened the padlock securing Ricky's cage and pulled the door open, motioning for Ricky to come out of the cage. Instead of doing as commanded, Ricky squealed in fright and cowered against the back of the cage.

"Come out, Ricky. You've got no choice."

Bennet stayed where he was and squealed again.

"There's something you don't know," Elliot told him, his weariness evident in every syllable he uttered. "The bottom of that cage is electrified. Here, I'll demonstrate."

A box approximately the size of a pack of cigarettes dangled from a cord between the cages. Embedded in the center of the box was a metal switch. Elliot flipped the switch. A silent second elapsed and then Chuck heard the low buzz of a building current. Ricky yelped as the buzz quickly intensified into a loud crackling. He squealed continuously as he wriggled his way across the metal bottom of the cage. His bound wrists made rapid progress impossible and Elliot laughed at the way he slithered and twitched his way to the front of the cage. When he finally made it to the opening, Elliot flipped the switch again, cutting the current.

Elliot reached through the opening, grabbed hold of the studded dog collar encircling Bennet's neck, and dragged him out of the cage. After hauling the trembling, sobbing man to his feet, Elliot clipped the length of heavy chain dangling from the ceiling above the cage to Bennet's collar. He then gave Bennet a hard shove and sent him staggering in the direction of Chuck and Karen.

The overhead whirring sound came as the other end of the chain moved along the ceiling track.

"Stop right there!" Elliot commanded.

Apparently having learned his lesson about disobedience, Bennet came to an immediate halt.

Heaving a tired breath, Elliot again moved into the space between Chuck and Karen. "You two are probably wondering why I've dragged this miscreant out of his cage. The thing is, I've had a long and exhausting day. I accomplished a lot and now I'm much closer to my desired kill total. Unfortunately, I fell short of total success and as a result there's a strong chance I won't have as much time as I'd hoped to finish the job here. I'd planned to deal with Ricky the day before Halloween, but I'm pretty sure I'll be dead by then, so my schedule needs adjusting. Chuck, you'll be happy to know I'm saving you and your lovely wife for last. You guys get to live just a little bit longer than everyone else. Don't you feel special?"

Karen yelled at him again.

Fuck you, it sounded like.

Elliot nodded. "Yes, fuck me. Except that I'm already fucked. In fact, Mrs. Everly, I was fucked for life by your husband and his friends a long, long time ago. They did something terrible to me when I was a boy and now you're paying the price for it. How do you feel about that?"

Karen's head swiveled slowly back toward Chuck.

She was silent, but her eyes told him exactly how she felt about it.

Once again, Chuck wished Elliot would just hurry up and put him out of his misery. And, yet again, his wish was not granted.

Elliot smiled. "It's true what they say, isn't it? Eyes are the window to the soul. A time of judgment is at hand, Mrs. Everly. A time of retribution. Your husband has a short while remaining before he answers for his sins, but for Ricky Bennet that time is *now.*"

Ricky Bennet squealed and tried to retreat when Elliot approached him, but he moved in the wrong direction, backward rather than left or right, which would have caused the ball attached to the other end of the chain to move along the track. Elliot clapped a hand on his shoulder and kicked his feet out from under him, causing him to drop to his knees. He kept the hand firmly in place on Bennet's trembling shoulder, preventing him from getting back up.

Elliot looked at Chuck. "Hey, Chuck. Did you know your old friend is a homosexual?" Bennet's head drooped as he began to sob. "It's true. It's one of the most fascinating of the many revelations I uncovered while tracking you assholes over the last several months. Ricky spent a lot of time in the gay bars of a neighboring town, I guess to avoid being spotted by people he knew. Now, I'm not homophobic and wouldn't care at all if not for the rich, rich irony. I'm sure you remember how Ricky used to love calling other people faggots. I mean, Jesus fucking Christ, it used to seem like every other word out of this cretin's mouth was a homophobic slur. In retrospect, a classic case of overcompensation. Like I said, I wouldn't care, but I figured his old friends should know the truth before he dies." His brow furrowed as he glanced briefly at the cages. "Well, Jimmy's pretty out of it, from the look of things, the pitiful fat slob. But it's enough that you know, Chuck. You're the one who really matters here. You and Ricky, that is."

He reached into his trench coat and took out a hunting knife.

"Originally I'd hoped to deal with Ricky in a more creative way, something symbolic of his particular hypocrisy. You know, like what I did to my therapist." When he sighed, there was a tinge of wistfulness in the sound. "Again, though, there's no time for that. Goodbye, Ricky. You goddamned piece of shit."

His face twisting in a snarl, Elliot rammed the thick blade of the hunting knife into Bennet's right temple up to the hilt. Bennet's body spasmed for a few moments, then went still, stretching the chain taut as he sagged toward the floor.

Elliot moved away from him, leaving the knife embedded in his temple. "And now, if you two will excuse me, I believe I'll head upstairs for the night. I've left my bride-to-be waiting alone up there all day. I'm sure she's lonely. I'll see you crazy kids in the morning. Try not to have too much fun while I'm away."

His booted feet echoed on the concrete as he headed for the staircase.

Chuck frowned beneath the pumpkin.

Bride-to-be?

But then it came to him. The lunatic could only be referring to Susan Rochon. The reference to her as his bride was bizarre, but then so was everything else about this fucked-up situation.

Chuck looked at Karen.

The eyes are the window to the soul.

Chuck shivered as Elliot's words came back to him. If that was true, then Karen's soul had been usurped by that of a hate-filled demon consumed with a burning desire to skin him alive and revel in the beautiful music of his endless screams.

32

Three days until Halloween
Willow Springs, TN

In those first hours after being brought to her abductor's lair, Susan Rochon nearly returned to full consciousness a few times. Each time, though, the man who'd snatched her from the truck stop parking lot was there to administer another dose of sedative. During these brief periods of semi-wakefulness, she'd been just cognizant enough to take in a few details of her surroundings. She was being kept in a space roughly the size of a standard studio apartment, with a kitchen nook and a smallish main room. Closed doors obscured the probable locations of a bathroom and closet. The main room was sparsely furnished. The bed was a queen-sized mattress atop a box-spring. Its rumpled, dirty-looking sheets suggested a distinct lack of interest in proper housekeeping. There was no frame. A boxy old TV sat atop a stack of plastic crates opposite the bed. A ratty-looking recliner that looked like it'd been rescued from someone's curb was situated near the TV. Someone, almost certainly her kidnapper, had defaced the white walls with red spray-paint, inscribing it with slogans that were a testament to his insanity.

RIGHT THE WRONGS.
KILL THE WHORES.

KILL KILL KILL.

And similar cheery things.

Susan saw none of these things during her first prolonged period of full consciousness. She awoke in a much smaller space that looked as if it had once functioned as a supply closet for a now defunct business. Against the back wall was a rack of metal shelves. All but two were bare. Various types of car repair manuals were stacked in haphazard piles along the bottom shelf. Piles of pre-printed forms and stationary pads bearing the name ZEKE'S AUTO BODY were on the shelf above it.

The only other item of interest in the closet was a copy of a Willow Springs middle school yearbook from 1990. It'd been left on the floor near the closed door. After trying the door and finding it locked and unyielding to her attempts to break it open, Susan gave up and sat cross-legged in the middle of the dusty floor with the old yearbook open in front of her. It'd obviously been left in the closet for her to find and peruse. Her initial instinct had been to ignore the thing and not play along with whatever demented game her abductor was playing, but she dismissed the defiant impulse after a mere moment's consideration. She was helpless here. A prisoner. She wasn't tied up or confined to a little cage like the people she'd groggily glimpsed downstairs earlier, but she was a prisoner nonetheless. There was no such thing as blissful ignorance in this situation. If the yearbook held any potential clues about the man who'd taken her and his motives, she needed to give it a thorough examination.

Her first impression after opening the book and leafing slowly through the first few pages was that it was an original copy from 1990 rather than a reproduction. She had a friend who'd bought reproductions of all her old yearbooks. You could easily get them online from various sites. But this one had a lot of edge wear and its binding was loose. The person who owned this copy had looked through it often over the years. It was, however, the strangest old yearbook she'd ever examined. There was no name inscribed along the top of the pasted-down end paper in front, as was commonly done to indicate ownership. More curious, however, was the absolute lack of classmate inscriptions and signatures. Either this was an extra copy from the original printer or its owner hadn't found even one person willing to sign his yearbook.

She was still puzzling over this when she came upon an image that nearly made her heart stop cold. It was on a page filled with rows of black-and-white student photos. In the middle of the second row from the bottom was a picture of a boy named Elliot Parker. She recognized that face. Long-forgotten memories of a meek boy who kept to himself and moved cautiously through the hallways of their school came back to her. She remembered occasionally feeling vaguely sorry for him back then, though not enough to extend an offer of friendship. Despite being perceived as rebellious as a kid, she'd wanted to fit in as much as anyone else. And fitting in didn't involve befriending obvious pariahs like this boy.

His face was leaner and harder now. But she saw the bitter, broken man the child would one day become in that younger version. That hollow-eyed look was exactly the same. His was the only unsmiling face on the page. Despite her fears about what Elliot Parker possibly had in store for her, seeing this triggered a faint pang of empathy. For the first time in a lot of years, she regretted not reaching out to him when they were young. Something like that, a basic gesture of kindness, might have made all the difference in the world at a crucial time in Elliot's life. The feeling passed quickly, though. Whatever the guy had gone through in the past was no excuse for the horrible things he was doing now. He was sick in the head. And extremely dangerous. She needed to remember that above all else.

She resumed leafing through the yearbook, but stopped again when she arrived at the page with her picture. A heart had been drawn around it in faded ink. Susan started trembling when she saw this. His outcast status aside, Elliot had been like a lot of his male peers back in middle school in one crucial way. He'd harbored a crush on her. Unlike the rest of them, however, he'd never let go of it. He'd stalked her and kept track of her ever since those days. It was a haunting, horrifying revelation. Shaking her head, Susan groaned in memory of the callous way she'd attempted to deal with him at the bar last Halloween. She saw now it'd been the biggest mistake of her life.

Kill the whores.

On reflection, that slogan really didn't bode well for her.

After completing her thorough examination of the book, she again tried the door, alternately kicking at it and ramming her shoulder into it. She risked this because the total silence from the outer room suggested it was empty, an assumption seemingly confirmed by a lack of reprisal from Elliot. Again, however, the door did not budge. It felt like it'd been reinforced in some way.

Hours passed. A lot of them.

Eventually, she gave up the intermittent efforts at escape as obviously useless and stretched out on the floor. After a while, her eyes fluttered shut and she slept for a long time.

On the verge of collapse when he reached his second floor rooms, Elliot went into the kitchen nook and took a tall can of Red Bull from the refrigerator, popped the tab, and chugged it down fast. He crushed the empty can in his hand and tossed it at an overflowing wastebasket in a corner. The can missed the basket. Elliot didn't bother retrieving it from the floor. He had a building full of ripe-smelling corpses downstairs. Cleanliness wasn't exactly one of his priorities these days.

He walked out of the nook and stared for a moment at the closet door. The girl he'd spent most of his life yearning after was on the other side of that door. His heart sped up a little at the thought. This amazed him. Even now, after the awful way she'd treated him a year ago, the mere idea of her proximity was enough to stir strong echoes of the anxious, fluttery feelings she'd first provoked in him during their school days. He supposed the allure of her would remain with him until he'd drawn his last breath, persisting despite her obvious loathing of him.

The door was reinforced with an iron bar across its center. He'd installed it after stashing her in the closet. It was secured with the sturdiest, most expensive padlock the local hardware store sold. Though he had taken care to ensure she was securely locked away, he was committed to treating Susan more humanely than his other captives. This was largely because, in spite of her hatred of him, the feelings she'd inspired in him through the years were the closest he'd ever come to feeling normal. Despite everything, he loved her. She had to pay for her sins, just like the rest of them, but she wouldn't suffer like them.

Elliot took a key from his hip pocket and inserted it in the padlock, giving it a twist. He removed the padlock from the clasp when it clicked open and tossed it over his shoulder. It landed with a heavy thump on the floor behind him. He wouldn't be needing it again. Pulling the bar away from the clasp, he opened the door a crack and peeked inside the closet.

Susan was asleep on the floor.

Watching her, he thought back to the day before and his initial rough treatment of her. That had been a product of adrenaline and residual anger over what she'd done. He felt no anger now, not where she was concerned. It was over and done with, her transgression against him, just like everything else in the past. Soon it would all be less than meaningless.

But for now...

He pulled the door open wider and she stirred at the sound of the creaking hinges.

Her eyes opened and she stared up at him in silence for a moment before she said, "You're back."

The strange thing was how calm she seemed. She spoke in the

placid tone of a housewife greeting her husband upon his return home from a long day at work. He pulled the door fully open and retreated from the doorway. "Come on out of there."

She yawned and got to her feet. After rubbing her eyes, she squinted at him and said, "Are you going to kill me now?"

"I have plans for you," he said, his tone noncommittal.

Her expression turned wary. "What sort of plans?"

"Come on out and I'll explain."

Shaking her head, she sighed in resignation. "I don't trust you. Obviously. But I guess it makes no difference whether you kill me in here or out there."

Elliot didn't reply to that.

Susan came out of the closet, pausing just outside the doorway to take a longer look around at the room. Elliot felt a pang of self-consciousness as she did this. Her gaze flicked briefly to the huge pile of dirty clothes by the bed. He glanced that way and knew she likely had spied the multiple pairs of hole-riddled underwear, the seats of which were stained brown.

He looked at her. "I apologize for the mess. Take off your clothes."

She frowned. "What?"

"You heard me."

She stared at him evenly for a long moment before shrugging. Then she pulled off her top and tossed it aside. "So you're gonna rape me now, is that it?" she said, unclasping her bra. "How does that make sense? You've spent your whole life pining away for me. You shouldn't want to hurt me."

She let go of the bra, crossing her arms over her breasts as the scrap of black fabric fell to the floor.

Elliot drew in a deep, shuddery breath and slowly expelled it. The sight of Susan's partially nude body was as breathtaking as he'd ever imagined. Now that he'd taken things this far, he needed to see the rest of it. There was no other choice. "I never wanted to hurt you, Susan. Not before you hurt me last year, anyway."

"I'm sorry about that, Elliot. I should have been more sensitive. It was a mistake."

He nodded. "Yes, it was. Take off the rest of your clothes."

She sighed and took her arms away from her breasts. She undid the snap of her jeans and began to wriggle out of them, but she paused when she finally took note of the dark-gray garment bag on the bed. He'd taken it from the closet and put it there prior to stowing Susan away. "What's that?"

Elliot smiled. "My mother's wedding dress. I had it cleaned for the occasion."

She frowned again as she finished wriggling out of the jeans. "What occasion?"

His smile broadened. "Our wedding." He held out his arms, beckoning her forward. The gesture caused multiple metal objects inside his trench coat to clank against each other. "Come to me, my bride. I'd like you to try on the dress, but I desperately want to hold you in my arms first. I've wanted that for so long, Susan. Come to me. Come now."

Susan's expression was warier than ever, but it was clear she knew she had no choice. She kicked the jeans aside and went to him, shuddering as he wrapped her up in his arms and crushed her against him. Her trembling intensified and he made soothing noises in her ear as he stroked her hair. They stood together like that for several minutes, Elliot sighing as he felt her tears on his neck. Despite her obvious deep fear of him, his gentle treatment of her began to work. Her trembling had nearly ceased completely by the time he took her neck in his hands and snapped it.

Elliot sobbed as her body sagged in his embrace.

He held her limp form for a time.

Then he carried her over to the bed and laid her down next to the garment bag. After spending a few moments brushing her hair away from her face and adjusting the angle of her head, he took off his trench coat and draped it over the back of the recliner. It would only get in the way of the delicate work he needed to do now.

249

He allowed himself several minutes to admire Susan's beautiful body.

Then he went to the bed and unzipped the garment bag.

33

Two days until Halloween
Willow Springs, TN

Bob Lee's last morning as sheriff of Willow Springs began on a
sour note when he walked into his office and found the mayor
already there waiting for him. Vic Bailey, formerly one of Lee's
most trusted and dependable men, was at the mayor's side. Vic's
flat expression betrayed no emotion, but the way he refused to look
him in the eye was telling.

But Lee found it hard to hold a grudge against the man. Vic
was only doing what anyone with an ounce of real ambition would
do. He was smart enough to know his boss was on the way out
regardless of any stance he might take on the matter, rendering any
gestures of defiance or solidarity pointless. If nothing else, Lee
figured he could rest easy in the knowledge that, at least until the
next election, the department would be in steady, competent hands.

Lee's feelings regarding the mayor and his underhanded
tactics weren't nearly so magnanimous. He wanted to knock the
smirking, hair gel-abusing bastard on his ass. Instead, he
maintained his composure long enough to power on his office
computer one last time and type out a brief note announcing his
resignation. After printing it out on official department letterhead,
he handed it over to the mayor, turned his department-issued

handgun and badge over to Vic Bailey, and walked out of the building carrying a box of the few personal effects he cared to take with him. He left by the back exit to avoid the awkwardness of exchanging goodbyes with his former underlings.

He returned home long enough to stow the box of personal effects in a closet, change into civvies, and retrieve his personal handgun—a .357 snub-nosed revolver—from his office safe. Less than a half hour later, he drove away from his house in his Toyota Celica and began a long day of tracking down and interviewing known associates of Ricky Bennet and the other missing men. Coordinating with Pete Acker by phone, they methodically worked their way through a list of likely possible confidantes.

Lee began the process with a high level of enthusiasm. He was certain one of the missing men must have spilled something about their shared secret—whatever that was—to someone at some point over the past twenty-some years. But that enthusiasm waned as the day wore on, morning yielding to afternoon with no new information garnered. Lee knew the passage of time was the single biggest complicating factor. Most of the people he talked to that day had only vague recollections regarding their former acquaintances. Those who admitted to remembering the splintering of that group of friends insisted they had no idea why it happened, saying that none of the boys had ever been willing to talk about it. After so many years in law enforcement, Lee had a good sense for when someone was telling him a pack of lies. As best he could tell, no one he talked to that day was lying to him or attempting to conceal information.

By the time he emerged from the double-wide trailer home of a man named Leon Jenkins at half past two that afternoon, Lee was on the verge of admitting defeat. Jenkins had been an associate of Ricky Bennet's during their early post-high school years. The two had been arrested together multiple times for various kinds of troublemaking. Lee had once caught the men in what could be described as a compromising position in the back of Bennet's car late one night in an otherwise empty K-Mart parking lot. Though he could have busted them for public indecency that night, he'd given them a break, much to the tearful Bennet's relief. As per usual in such cases, Lee had figured an arrest would be a pointless exercise in embarrassment for everyone involved. Instead he admonished them against indulging in amorous activities in public places and sent them on their way. It was this memory that made Lee believe Jenkins might represent his best shot at uncovering a possible former confidante.

But Jenkins, a devout born again Christian, was a dead end. He spoke of his former friend with obvious disdain, calling him a sinner and saying he was doomed to burn in hell. The man was full of opinions on the subject of eternal damnation and was eager to share them with Lee, but he knew nothing about the bad thing that had driven apart Ricky and his old friends.

As Lee walked away from the trailer, a text came in from Pete Acker. Lee glanced at his phone's screen as he reached his car. Acker had sent him an address, along with a message to drop everything and meet him there as soon as possible. He'd explain when Lee got there. Lee recognized the address, as would anyone in local law enforcement. It was at a rundown apartment complex clear on the other side of town, a place that was a known center of criminal activity.

His enthusiasm suddenly on the rebound, Lee got in his Celica and sped away from Jenkins' trailer, making it to the complex local jokesters had long ago dubbed Mos Eisley—in reference to the "wretched hive of scum and villainy" from *Star Wars*—in under fifteen minutes. As he drove through the complex, Lee noted numerous shady-looking young men loitering in breezeways, some of them clutching 40-ounce bottles of malt liquor wrapped in paper bags. He knew if he'd been in his cruiser they would have gone scurrying away. Instead they tracked his progress through the complex with dead-eyed stares. One especially young man, who looked like he should be in school rather than in this breeding ground for future felons, flashed him a middle finger. Lee knew this was just a taste of what the future held in store for him, now that he no longer wore the uniform.

He arrived at the address Acker had sent him moments ahead of the deputy. When Acker pulled up in his cruiser outside building K of the complex, the young men loitering in the breezeway there abruptly decided there were other places they needed to be and vanished within seconds. Seeing this made Lee laugh. It was like a magic trick. One he was no longer capable of performing.

The men got out of their vehicles and approached each other.

"Who we seeing here, Pete?"

The deputy's head swiveled in the direction of building K, his gaze tilting upward a moment. "Guy named Scott Logan. Unit 8, second floor."

Lee arched an eyebrow. "Dangerous, you think?"

"Nah. He's in a pretty bad way, from what I hear. Has a real bad case of emphysema."

Acker told him the rest of it as they started heading toward building K. Prior to calling Lee, the deputy spent more than an hour interviewing a woman named Kate Hartley, who'd once been briefly engaged to Jimmy Martin, before, as she put it, he "turned into a fat piece of drunken shit". From the beginning, Acker sensed she knew a little more than she'd wanted to let on. Though there was no paraphernalia in plain view, a strong odor of marijuana had permeated her apartment. Making her believe she might wind up in jail for possession once he took a closer look around the place—this despite his lack of a search warrant—he intimidated her into telling what she knew.

As it turned out, that wasn't much. She knew Jimmy had some deep, dark secret he was carrying around with him, something that weighed on him horribly and made him want to be drunk all the time. He alluded to it frequently throughout their relationship, but without ever spilling any of the details. But she thought he *might* have told Scott Logan everything.

"What makes her think Logan knows anything?" Lee asked as they climbed stairs to the second floor.

Acker answered as they reached the landing. "She says Jimmy made one serious attempt at getting sober when they were together. This was when he was in his early twenties. He was off the booze for almost a year, went to AA all the time. Scott Logan was his sponsor. According to Hartley, the two used to talk for hours in private, and he'd never tell her what they talked about. But she said he cried a lot after those talks with Logan. The crying was another reason she gave for leaving Jimmy. She called him a pussy."

"Sounds like a lovely lady."

Acker chuckled. "Lovely isn't the word I'd use."

They arrived at the door to unit 8.

Acker knocked loudly. "Sheriff's department," he called out in an authoritative voice. "Open up, Mr. Logan."

A moment elapsed.

Then a faint, wheezing voice replied from inside. "Just a minute."

More than a minute passed, enough time for the men on the landing to get fidgety. At last, they heard a series of clacking sounds as multiple locks were unlatched from inside. The door came open and a frail-looking elderly man ushered them into the dimly-lit apartment. He wore a white tank top and a ratty pair of gray sweatpants that looked like they hadn't been washed in months, if ever.

Lee and Acker followed him into his living room, where he wheezily settled himself into a recliner and regarded them warily as he asked them why the law was bothering a sick old man like himself.

Acker said, "We believe you may be able to help us with an ongoing investigation. You've heard about the murders that have happened around town the last few days, I imagine."

Logan pulled a hand down over his tired-looking, emaciated face and scratched at his whiskery chin. "Sure. Can't see how I could help you with that, though."

"I wouldn't be so sure about that," Lee told him. "Though you may have to dig deep into your memory for the information we need." He glanced at Acker. "Tell him what you told me, Pete."

Acker told the story again.

Logan listened in stony-faced silence, staring at the old movie playing on the muted TV screen opposite the recliner. He remained silent for a long moment after Acker finished talking.

Then he sighed and looked at his visitors. "The things a man tells his AA sponsor are meant to be kept between just the two of them. Like a doctor-patient confidentiality kind of deal, you know? Only I've been out of AA for a long time, and I reckon finding your man is more important anyway. You're gonna want to look into some kid named Elliot something-or-other. He's the one Jimmy and those other boys tortured."

Lee's breath caught in his throat, his pulse quickening.

Logan had just tentatively identified the killer, he was sure of it.

Acker said, "Tortured? Was this Elliot a classmate of theirs?"

Logan leaned back in his recliner, face twisting at some internal pain. "That's right."

He told them the rest of what he knew.

34

Another long stretch of time passed in the darkness. As before, it possessed a nightmarish malleability. Another full day might have passed, but it was possible it had only been a few hours. Chuck had no way of knowing. All he knew for certain was he'd pissed himself a couple more times and that he wasn't feeling well. Some kind of sickness had come over him during his latest period of fuzzy unconsciousness. He had a chill and his back and joints were aching in a way that couldn't solely be attributed to being tied to the chair for so long. His mouth felt thick and dry and his head was throbbing.

His discomfort was so pronounced it caused him to strain against his bonds with something resembling determination for the first time in a while. He knew there was only so much abuse the human body could take. Unless he was rescued soon or somehow managed to escape, odds were he'd die in this chair before much longer. The way he was feeling, he might well expire from illness long before Elliot got around to executing him.

But his bonds remained as unyielding as ever. Nor could he rock over the chair. Its legs were secured to metal brackets on the floor, which had been drilled into the concrete with thick bolts.

The same had been done to Karen's chair. This made them virtually impossible to move. After a few minutes of straining as hard as he could manage, Chuck gave up the effort and resumed sobbing. His wife was unimpressed by this display of emotional distress. More noises of hateful contempt emanated from behind her gag.

Chuck was glad most of them were indecipherable. He no longer desired her forgiveness or confirmation regarding the fate of their children. His misery had become too great. Whatever happened from this point forward, it was clear his marriage to Karen was damaged beyond repair. Of course, a part of him was still concerned for his kids, but his suffering had caused him to become disconnected from those feelings. And then there was the fact that Elliot had repeatedly shown he was a monster capable of perpetrating the most heinous acts imaginable, so the kids were probably dead. It was better not to know for sure. That way he could go to his inevitable grim fate in this place with at least the hope that they were somehow okay.

Maybe he would see them again someday, up in heaven.

The thought elicited a soft grunt of amused laughter. Chuck didn't know whether he believed in an afterlife or the religious concept of some kind of eternal reward for good behavior, nor was he sure about the idea of a fiery netherworld where sinners were consigned to suffer forever. In the event such places *did* exist, however, it was likely he'd wind up in the warmer place.

He deserved nothing less, after all.

The sound of a heavy door opening somewhere beyond his range of vision came right on the heels of this thought. It was followed by the clang of heavy footsteps descending metal stairs. Elliot was emerging from his room upstairs again at long last, apparently. But another, stranger sound accompanied these noises. Elliot was humming something as he descended the stairs. The tune was immediately recognizable as "Here Comes the Bride."

Chuck flashed back to his last clear memory of Elliot before his latest retreat to his chambers. As usual, he'd said a lot of crazy things. Among them had been an apparent reference to Susan Rochon as his bride. That Susan would willingly marry someone like Elliot seemed unlikely. No, more than that. It was absurd. Susan was sexy, outgoing, and well-liked. Elliot was the opposite of all those things. Then there was the fact that she'd been brought here under obvious duress. Anyway, Chuck figured it was wrong to interpret Elliot's remarks or behavior on anything like a literal level. Whatever this wedding stuff was about, it was certain to be deranged in some way.

Elliot reached the bottom of the stairs. His booted feet clomped on the concrete in the usual loud, echoing way as he approached the circle of faint light illuminating the area where Chuck and Karen were being held. When he entered the illuminated area, Chuck saw right away that his guess had been correct.

Oh, Jesus, he thought. *That poor woman.*

The baser part of Chuck couldn't help recalling how Susan's mouth had felt wrapped around his cock that night at the high school reunion. She'd demonstrated an oral skill he wouldn't encounter again until commencing his affair with Fawn Hightower years later. But Susan wouldn't ever again be giving anyone a drunken, thoroughly pleasurable backseat blowjob.

She was dead.

Elliot held her body cradled in his arms. The garish angle of her broken neck was hard to miss. At some point she'd been forced to change into an old wedding dress that had seen better days. It was frayed-looking and faintly yellow along the seams. After setting the corpse gently on the floor, Elliot turned his attention to Ricky Bennet, whose body was still dangling from a chain a few feet away. He unclipped the chain from the dog collar around Bennet's neck and pushed his corpse out of the way. After that, he retrieved Susan Rochon's body, hoisting it up high enough to wrap the chain around her midsection and then around her neck.

Once this was done, he moved back a step to inspect his work, tilting his head and frowning at the way her limp form lolled inside its makeshift harness. But then he shrugged, evidently deciding this was the best he could do under the circumstances. He continued humming "Here Comes the Bride" throughout all of this.

The humming ceased as he let out a breath and shifted his focus to Chuck and Karen. "Thank you for being here on this special day," Elliot said, smiling broadly. "Susan and I really appreciate it." He glanced at the dead woman. "Isn't my bride lovely?"

The building's interior was silent for a moment, save for a nearly imperceptible low moan issuing from Jimmy Martin's cage.

"I think she's beautiful," Elliot said, still smiling. He glanced at his chained "bride" again. "Though she's been more radiant than this, I'll admit. Has Chuck ever told you about Susan, Karen? He remembers her, I'm sure. She's the girl all the guys lusted after back in the day. She developed early. We were all kind of hypnotized by her breasts. To be fair, they were *really* nice breasts. Still are, as you can see." His smile began to slip as his voice took on a wistful tone. "From the time I first saw her, I knew there could never be anyone else for me. She was special. We were meant for each other. And now we're finally man and wife. I always dreamed this day would come and now it's finally here." He dabbed at his eyes with the ball of a thumb. "Sorry, guys, I'm getting a little emotional, I guess. Alas, even the best moments of my life are always tainted in some way. She's dead. I know that. I'm not completely crazy, believe it or not. I know we're not gonna have a life together here on earth. But it's okay, because I know she's waiting for me on the other side, and I'll be joining her shortly."

A little spark of hope ignited inside Chuck.

Kill yourself, he thought. *Do it now, you psychotic piece of shit.*

Of course, it was a futile hope. Chuck knew full well Elliot had no intention of going anywhere without first taking care of his other unfinished business.

Elliot sighed. "Right, well, I'm sure you've both had your fill of my sentimentality. Under better circumstances, I'd put off what I'm about to do a while longer yet, but I can sense the clock running out on me. Maybe I'm wrong and it'll yet be a little while before the cops get here, but that's not a chance I'm willing to take. I accept that I didn't kill thirty-one people this week, as I'd hoped. It doesn't surprise me. It was perhaps an overly ambitious goal. And falling short in the things I attempt is pretty much the story of my life, after all. More often than not, everything I've ever tried has ended in tears and heartache, if not outright disaster. But I should still be able to do the last part of what I had in mind, if I hurry."

He moved away from them then, disappearing into the darkness somewhere behind Chuck. His rapid gait suggested an urgency that normally wasn't there. A new sense of dread stirred within Chuck as he mentally reviewed Elliot's words. It was hard not to read a note of finality in them. This whole horror show scenario he'd constructed for them was coming to an end, which meant Chuck and his wife were likely in the last moments of their lives.

Chuck's breath wheezed in and out rapidly around the thick rubber gag. His chest heaved as his heart began to thud heavily. On one level, he'd known this was coming all along, but now that it was actually imminent, he was not at all prepared for it. All the times he'd prayed for his death in order to escape the horror were now exposed for the exercises in delusion they really were. He didn't want that. Not at all. Not ever. He wanted to go on living, no matter what. Tears flowed from his eyes in ceaseless streams until he heard a metallic clatter coming his way. He opened his eyes and blinked away the tears when he sensed Elliot moving into his field of vision again.

The clattering sound he'd heard had been produced by a metal

261

cart on wheels, probably the same cart Elliot had used when serving Chuck the bowl of "brain soup". On the bottom shelf of the cart were several clear jugs of water. Piled on its surface were some neatly-folded clean clothes and a pair of shoes. There was also an extra-large container of liquid soap.

Leaving the cart parked alongside Chuck's chair, Elliot moved away from him and bent to the floor to pry loose the big hunting knife he'd left embedded in Ricky Bennet's head. It came loose with a wet sucking sound. Standing up, he wiped the blade on his pants leg and glanced at Chuck before taking up a position behind Karen. Chuck's wife stared at him, her eyes going wide with fear. Elliot wound her long blonde hair in his left hand and pulled her head sharply backward, exposing her neck.

He placed the sharp edge of the knife against her throat.

Chuck screamed behind his gag.

Elliot was no longer smiling. His expression had turned hard and unforgiving. "Spare me your theatrics, Chuck. If you really cared about this woman, you wouldn't have been fucking that whore all this time."

Chuck screamed again.

Karen sobbed quietly. The visible tick of her pulse made the tender flesh of her throat quiver against the sharp blade. Seeing this reinforced her essential vulnerability like nothing else had. Chuck screamed and strained against his bonds harder than ever.

Elliot pressed the blade deep into Karen's flesh and dragged it slowly across her throat. Blood poured out of the slit in a thick red sheet as Karen gagged and spluttered. Elliot pulled her head farther back, opening the gash wider. He held on to her until the blood flow slowed to a trickle. Then he relinquished his grip on her hair, moved out from behind the chair, and approached Chuck.

Chuck sobbed.

A fresh void opened within him, the sudden, violent loss of his wife hitting him with devastating force. He sobbed and screamed until he ran out of breath. It wasn't right that she was gone. She'd been a beautiful, vibrant, wonderful, loving wife and mother, a quality human being in virtually every way. And now she was no more. The wrongness of it was overwhelming.

All my fault, he thought. *All my fucking fault.*

He sensed Elliot looming over him and realized he was probably about to die. But then he felt Elliot tugging at the rotting pumpkin. He lifted it from Chuck's head and tossed it aside.

"Better?"

Chuck screamed at him, a shrill wail of grief and outrage.

Elliot nodded. "Right, well, I want you to know your kids are alive, Chuck. I know that's been weighing on you. It has, hasn't it? Well, I never touched them. Not because I'm not capable of doing something that horrendous. We both know better than that by now, don't we?" He grunted, his face twisting in a sneer riven with deep bitterness. "No, I didn't spare them out of the goodness of my heart. Any goodness in me died along with my brother. The cancer that had been eating away at him for years took him that same night you assholes left me tied to that tree. I didn't even get to say goodbye. Well, it took me all my life to get around to it, but I'm finally paying you back in a fitting way. I didn't kill your kids because I want them to live with the knowledge of what you did to me, and that *you're* the reason their mother is dead." His sneer shifted, gave way to a smile again. "And I want you to live with it, too."

He leaned over Chuck and started slicing through the thick lengths of rope binding him to the chair. As he watched the sharp blade of the hunting knife fray and part rope strands, a profound confusion supplanted Chuck's terror. He couldn't imagine why Elliot would bother to cut him free from the chair before killing him. Surely if he was enacting his end game, that wouldn't be necessary.

But then the man's last words echoed in his mind.

And I want you to live with it, too.

The madman continued to work at his bonds for several

minutes. Completing the job required a fair amount of exertion. The rope lengths were the thickest Chuck had ever seen, perhaps a full inch in diameter. At last, though, he finished and moved back a few steps, holding on to the knife as he peered curiously at Chuck.

"I'm setting you free, Chuck," Elliot told him, still smiling. He waved a hand toward the metal cart and the items on it. "You can clean yourself with the water and soap. These clothes should fit you, I think. This is what you did for me, remember? So the way I look at it, we're all even-steven now. This little gesture totally makes up for everything else I've done. Doesn't it, Chuck?"

Chuck stared at him in absolute horror for a long moment.

Then the rage began to rise up inside him.

He reached behind his head and fumbled with the snaps of the ball-gag, pulling at them with increasing frustration until he was finally able to get them unsnapped. That accomplished at last, he pried the rubber gag from his mouth, coughed, and tossed the device aside. Every muscle in his body shook as he tried hard to rise from the chair. There was nothing in his mind but the need to get at Elliot and tear out the murdering bastard's throat.

But he only managed to raise himself partway out of the chair before he pitched forward and fell painfully to the concrete floor. Still shaking all over, he braced his hands on the floor and tried again to rise, but it remained an impossible task for the time being. He was too stiff and sore and weak from his days of confinement to the chair. The onset of the illness wasn't helping matters. His desire to get to Elliot and kill him was as intense as before, but at present he wasn't capable of the effort.

Elliot grunted. "Yeah, you're not gonna get to kill me, Chuck. Had a hunch you wouldn't even be able to try in your debilitated condition. Even if I'd been wrong, I couldn't let you do it. I can't allow you that satisfaction, regardless of how empty it'd ultimately be for you. I'm gonna leave you here now, asshole. Still pretty sure the cops will track me down by the end of the day, but maybe I can still get out there and finish the rest of my work before that happens. Thirty-one kills for Halloween sure would feel better than twenty-six."

Chuck raised his head and glared at him. "You...you..."

Elliot laughed.

A loud metallic bang made both of them flinch. Elliot turned toward the sound, which seemed to have come from somewhere near the row of vehicles. Consulting his memory, Chuck decided this placed it in the vicinity of the metal door he remembered from his first visit to this place. Not the big rollup door, but the standard one at the top of the short set of concrete steps.

The second bang was louder than the first.

Elliot muttered a curse before saying, "Guess I won't get to finish, after all. Figures."

After a third bang, the door under assault slammed open and afternoon sunlight poured in from a corner of the room, illuminating cars and piles of dead bodies. Turning his head in that direction, Chuck saw two men, one old and fat and the other younger and thin, come into the building with guns drawn. Upon spying Elliot, they aimed their weapons at him and ordered him to drop the knife.

Elliot shook his head. "I don't think so."

The men came closer, approaching cautiously, heads swiveling about as they took in the horror of the scene. Reacting against the stench permeating the room, the younger one covered his face with a hand and said, "Oh, lord. Look at all these bodies, sheriff."

Chuck belatedly recognized the fat one as Bob Lee, sheriff of Willow Springs.

Only he wasn't wearing his uniform for some reason.

Lee nodded grimly as he continued to come closer. "I see them. Think it's safe to say we got our man." Pitching his voice louder, he addressed the killer again. "Put the knife down, Elliot.

It's over. We're taking you in."

"No, you're not."

Elliot raised the knife and charged at the sheriff.

Lee and the other man shouted final warnings.

Elliot ignored them and continued his charge.

Both lawmen discharged their weapons multiple times, the big booms reverberating deafeningly in the huge space. Elliot's body absorbed several hits to the torso before he finally stumbled and slid to a stop on the floor. He landed facing Chuck, who stared into the madman's dead eyes while the sheriff and the deputy moved about the place, checking for survivors among the bodies.

The deputy called to the sheriff from the vicinity of the wire cages. "Got a live one over here. Think it might be Jimmy Martin."

Lee approached Chuck.

"Are you okay, Mr. Everly? Can you stand?"

Chuck didn't respond.

He was still staring into Elliot Parker's unblinking eyes.

Eyes are the window to the soul.

But Chuck saw no evidence of a soul there, not even the faintest dying flicker. He saw only a deep, deep abyss. And, no matter how hard he tried, he could not look away from it.

ABOUT THE AUTHOR

Bryan Smith is the author of numerous previous novels and novellas, including Slowly We Rot, The Reborn, Depraved, Depraved 2, Go Kill Crazy!, 68 Kill, The Killing Kind, Strange Ways, House of Blood, The Freakshow, and The Diabolical Conspiracy. Bestselling horror author Brian Keene described Slowly We Rot as, "The best zombie novel I've ever read." Bryan lives in Tennessee, where he spends the bulk of his non-writing time binge-watching things on Netflix. Visit his home on the web at www.thehorrorofbryansmith.blogspot.com.

NOTE: Yes, I know I had a prominent character named Chuck in the Killing Kind books. Obviously the Chuck in ALL HALLOW'S DEAD is a different guy entirely. There's more than one Chuck in the world, you know. Actually, I was a good ways into writing this book before I remembered the guy from the KK books. I could have changed it at that point, but then I thought, "Fuck it." As I so often do…

Usually I include a Spotify playlist specially designed for each novel. This time, however, I'm providing a link for the general Halloween playlist I've maintained since joining Spotify years ago. For a while, I changed the name each year to reflect the current year. Now I just call it Halloween Eternal, because for some of us Halloween never ends.

Check it out:

https://open.spotify.com/user/bryandsmith/playlist/4nCIF9K7H6bq NK3WJpfPUo

BRYAN SMITH'S SLASHER HALL OF FAME:

Halloween (John Carpenter version)
Halloween 2 (John Carpenter version)
Friday the 13th

Friday the 13th Part II
Friday the 13th Part 3 in 3-D
Friday the 13th Part IV: The Final Chapter
Friday the 13th Part V: A New Beginning
Friday the 13th Part VI: Jason Lives
My Bloody Valentine (original)
Prom Night (original)
The Burning
The Prowler
Terror Train
Happy Birthday To Me
Madman
Alone In The Dark
Curtains
The Texas Chainsaw Massacre
A Nightmare On Elm Street
Scream
Maniac (original)
Sleepaway Camp
The Slumber Party Massacre
Graduation Day
Final Exam
Just Before Dawn
Visiting Hours
Hatchet
Black Christmas

Printed in Great Britain
by Amazon

42520162R00166